BLACKMAIL

Heather Burnside

HEAD
of ZEUS

An Aries Book

ISBN (PB): 9781801107945
ISBN (E): 9781801107921

Typeset by Siliconchips Services Ltd UK

Printed and bound in Great Britain by
CPI Group (UK) Ltd, Croydon CR0 4YY

Head of Zeus Ltd
First Floor East
5–8 Hardwick Street
London EC1R 4RG

WWW.HEADOFZEUS.COM

For Pascoe and Kerry

Prologue

Beth didn't want to go walking in the woods that day. It was cold, and the rain that had fallen throughout the previous week had turned the ground to a sludgy mess. But Rex, her one-year-old Maltese, pawed at the front door until she finally gave in. Her fearless side reasoned that a bit of muck would do them no harm.

One look at the muddy path and she hesitated, almost turning back, but she could feel Rex straining at the leash. It was his favourite walk, and it didn't seem fair to deprive him when they had come this far. This area was normally popular among families and courting couples, but today it was quiet. Maybe the weather had kept most of them at home.

'You'll be having your feet washed when we get back,' said Beth, frowning as Rex splashed his way through puddles and the white fur of his legs became filthy.

As they passed an elderly lady walking an overenthusiastic Collie, Rex cowered behind Beth, whimpering. She tugged at his lead to try to get him to carry on walking. 'Don't be silly, Rex,' she coaxed.

'It's OK, he won't harm him,' said the lady 'It's just his way of being friendly.'

'I know,' said Beth. 'Rex is just a little softy.' She smiled. 'I think he's too used to getting his own way.'

The lady and her dog passed by, and Beth was finally able to get Rex to come out of his hiding place behind her legs and continue walking. 'Come on, you daft thing,' she said.

After a while, Rex settled down and seemed to be enjoying his walk. They'd reached a more desolate area of the woods and hadn't spotted anybody for some time. This was the part of the walk Rex enjoyed the most when it was just the two of them. Beth knew it was because he didn't feel threatened by other dogs or over ebullient children.

He began yanking at his lead just as they reached a sloping area of the muddy path. 'Steady!' said Beth, feeling her feet slip beneath her. 'You almost pulled me over.'

She released him and watched in amusement as he bounded playfully through the trees on the left. The path was narrower here, the shrubbery denser, and the branches of the mature trees spread widely, almost meeting on either side of the path and blocking out most of the light.

She heard Rex growl. That wasn't like him. Something must have upset him, maybe another dog, or a wild rabbit perhaps? She carried on walking, calling his name. But Rex didn't come to her. Instead, he began barking frantically and Beth grew concerned. What if he had hurt himself?

She increased her pace, calling his name and listening. His barking had changed to a distressed wailing, which was becoming closer. Beth felt an eerie sensation as her ears tried to pinpoint his exact whereabouts. But it was difficult with the sound of the howling wind, which caused the trees to sway so dramatically that their tentacled branches seemed to be reaching out for her.

Telling herself not to be silly, she ploughed on in search of Rex. But she couldn't help noticing how the woods now seemed abandoned and somehow threatening. She suddenly developed a strong sense of unease. If it hadn't been for her dog, she would have doubled back and gone home. But she couldn't leave her treasured Rex. He was still a puppy and he needed her.

As she squelched along the path in her haste to get to Rex, his wailing became louder. She was getting near to him. Then she sensed movement to her left and his wailing switched back to a bark. What if he was stuck in some sort of trap?

Beth left the path and fought her way through the undergrowth, feeling the sting of nettles through her jeans. The trunk of a large tree stood just to the right, surrounded by bushes. As she drew close to it, Rex's barking grew more insistent, and she knew he was aware of her presence.

She tried to reassure him. 'It's alright, Rex.' 'I'm coming.'

His barking suddenly stopped, and Beth stiffened. She could still hear movement, but it was slight. What on earth could have happened to him? Frantic now, Beth carried on battling her way towards Rex till she had almost reached the end of the clump of bushes.

'I'm nearly there, R—'

But the words got stuck in her throat when a man leapt out from behind the bushes. Then he was hauling her towards the tree. She screamed until he clamped his hand around her mouth. His other hand was clasped around her middle, but it felt weighty, as though he was holding something, which was prodding her stomach.

He dragged her out of view of the path. Then Beth looked

down, shocked to discover that he was clutching a blood-drenched knife, which was rubbing against her clothing and staining her coat.

Beth struggled to escape but the man was too strong. He tugged at her until she was behind the densest area of shrubbery, right next to the large tree trunk. And then she saw Rex. Lying in a pool of blood. His lovely white fur stained a hideous pink.

The shock diminished her defences, and the man pushed her to the ground. Beth felt the hard earth beneath her back, and the weeds and twigs snagged at her clothes. Immediately, the threatening bulk of the man was on top of her, his evil eyes staring back at her and his ragged face full of menace. His stale breath was hot on her cheeks as he tried to overpower her, and his eager hands clawed at her jeans.

A strange sensation enveloped Beth. All her emotions were flooding her at once. Fear. Sorrow. Horror. It was hard to believe this was happening. Her poor dog lay lifeless. And now this man was trying to rape her. She couldn't let him take her. She wouldn't! But what could she do to defend herself?

Beth looked around her desperately in search of a way out. Then she spotted something. And that was the moment when everything changed.

I

Three Years Later

'Ooh, this is nice,' said Beth, as they walked inside the upmarket cocktail bar called The Amber Room. She gazed around at the modern furniture, eye-catching lighting and well-stocked bar area. The décor was all in creams, golds and subtle shades of yellow, fitting with the name of the place and very tastefully done. Emeli Sandé played in the background, creating an atmosphere that was both contemporary and serene.

'I told you it was, didn't I?' replied Brady, her husband of only a few weeks. 'I take you to all the best places. They sell food as well. We could come here to eat one night, if you want? It's Mediterranean style – sharing platters and little dishes of olives and almonds, that sort of thing.' As Beth smiled at his enthusiasm, he nodded at a table for two with plush chairs covered in a fawn-coloured fabric. 'Tell you what, you grab that table there and I'll get the drinks. What would you like?'

Beth grinned impishly. 'I'll have a Sex on the Beach,

please. Oh, but I'm only having the one. We've got work tomorrow, don't forget.'

Brady soon returned from the bar, and she felt a warm glow as she watched him walk over. He was tall, slim and good looking with jet-black hair, and she thought for the umpteenth time how lucky she was to be married to him.

'How many times have you been here before?' asked Beth, staring into Brady's dark eyes.

'Oh, once or twice. It's not been open long. Me and the lads used to come into Marple a lot.'

'I know, you told me. It's a good job you were slumming it in Romiley on the night I met you then, isn't it?' she teased.

'Eh, Romiley's not so bad.'

'I know,' said Beth.

They had both been living in Romiley when they met two years ago, Beth in her own flat and Brady in a three-bed semi he owned. As their relationship progressed, they decided to pool their resources and upgrade to a three-bedroom detached home in the more affluent area of Marple. Marriage followed shortly after, and Beth felt she had never been happier.

The new home suited Brady, who was aspirational and liked the fact that he was now residing in Marple. Beth loved him to bits. He had impeccable taste, and they were fortunate enough to like most of the same things. Brady was also very attentive to her, but the one fault she found in him was his overambition. To Brady, money and status were everything.

Still, she supposed there were worse flaws to have. Brady was a senior sales executive for a beauty products company called Repertoire and was determined to go all the way to the top. He was also the man she wanted to spend the rest of her life with and have kids with eventually. She knew that his drive would ensure their family would be well provided for.

They chatted for a while about their plans for the house, their jobs and other mutual topics till their drinks ran out and Beth decided to go to the bar. It was a long bar with rounded corners and a small side area at either end housing just a couple of stools. She took her place next to one of the rounded corners and a barman rushed to serve her.

'A gin and tonic please, and a pint of lager,' she said.

The barman went to tend to her order, and as Beth waited she became aware that she was being watched. That wasn't unusual. With her long blonde hair, flawless complexion and trim figure, she often attracted male attention. But she was curious about the person whose eyes had never left her since she walked across the room. She turned her head to the side to get a better look and noticed a distinguished, good-looking man of about forty sitting on a stool at the end of the bar.

He smiled disarmingly, and Beth noticed it made him look even more handsome with his perfect white teeth. 'Is your boyfriend leaving you to buy the drinks?'

'He's my husband. And it's my turn. I always pay my way. That's what women do these days.'

She knew it was a skit at his age, but she couldn't help herself. Something about the way he was staring made her feel on edge. But if he was offended, he didn't show it.

'Sorry,' he said. 'I didn't think you looked old enough to be married.'

Beth didn't know whether it was intended as a compliment

7

or an insult, and she snapped back. 'I'm twenty-nine, actually.'

He chuckled in amusement. 'Have you tried our selection of flavoured gins? They're very good, particularly the rhubarb and ginger one.'

Suddenly it dawned on Beth that he must be the manager, and she became embarrassed by her abrasiveness. 'Erm, no, I'm alright, thanks.'

'You sure? It's definitely worth a try. Tell you what, I'll let you have this one on the house.'

Beth could feel herself blush. Something about his intense stare was unsettling. His eyes were a beautiful pale blue, and she couldn't help but be drawn to them. 'Erm, no, it's OK, thank you.' Her attention shot back to the barman as she fished for her purse.

'Go on, I insist,' said the manager. He then addressed the barman who was putting her drinks on the bar, 'Dylan, can you add a rhubarb and ginger gin to the order but put it on the house.'

Dylan did as ordered, and Beth found her eyes wandering away from Dylan and back to the charismatic man at the end of the bar. 'Thank you.'

He smiled that lovely smile again. 'That's alright. I always like to keep the customer happy.'

Dylan then gave Beth her change and she noticed there was too much. She took out a pound coin and said, 'You've given me too much.'

'Oh, thanks,' said Dylan, holding out his hand.

Out of the corner of her eye, Beth noticed the manager watching her, but before he had a chance to comment, she rushed away from the bar, feeling flustered.

'What the hell was all that about?' asked Brady, 'And why have you got three drinks?'

'One of them's on the house,' she said. 'I think the manager's trying out his new gins on his customers. It's probably to get them hooked so they'll buy the more expensive ones.'

Brady seemed to pick up on her ill feeling. 'Well, you're not complaining, are you? Make the most of it if it's a freebie. Oh, and he's not the manager, by the way. He's the owner. He's got a few bars and nightclubs all over south Manchester and the city centre.' Then he lowered his voice, 'Rumour has it that he's a bit dodgy and he's running other businesses on the side.'

'What kind of businesses?' asked Beth.

'Shush.' Then he whispered, 'Illicit ones.'

'Really, what's his name?'

'Martin something, I don't know his surname.'

'Oh,' said Beth, then she quickly changed the subject. That was all the more reason to give Martin a wide berth as far as she was concerned.

When they arrived home, Brady decided to fix them a drink. He strolled over to the hostess trolley, which stood against one wall. The piece of furniture had been carefully selected by both of them to give the place a cool retro vibe. It blended well with the rest of the room, which was modern in style.

The walls were painted in a relaxing dove grey aside from a feature wall, which was papered in a deep-blue and grey pattern with touches of silver. The sofa was also grey but darker and covered with scatter cushions in various shades of greys, blues and a mustard colour. That same colour scheme was picked up in the expensive rug, which adorned the polished wooden flooring, and in the heavy navy-blue textured curtains.

Beth's mind was still on Martin. But she couldn't understand why. He was so much older than her, not her usual type at all. His hair was going grey, and he was muscle-bound and rugged looking, whereas she preferred her men more sophisticated and slimmer like her husband.

She peered at Brady who was busy fixing them a nightcap. Yes, he was just her type: tall, slim and good-looking with a head of thick jet-black hair. When they'd first met, she had been bowled over by the fact that he was so charming and couldn't seem to do enough for her. And he was fun to be with; they often shared banter and had a good laugh together. If she was honest with herself, she'd also initially been attracted by the fact that he was so ambitious. And at twenty-eight, he was more her age too. She couldn't believe she was even making the comparison with Martin. What had got into her?

'What's the matter?' asked Brady when he caught her looking.

'Oh, nothing.' She walked over to him and took the drinks out of his hands. 'I was just admiring my handsome husband.'

Then she put the drinks down on the coffee table and leant over to kiss him. He returned her kiss with ardour, and she could feel him hard against her as his hands roamed down her body and clenched her firm buttocks. She gently pulled away.

'Shall we go upstairs?'

Without waiting for a reply, she led the way with Brady following eagerly behind. The drinks were forgotten, as were all thoughts of Martin when her husband made passionate love to her until, satiated, they both drifted off to sleep.

Beth had felt content in her husband's arms. But then the nightmares started again. The walk through the woods. Her frantic search for Rex. The man. And the blood. Rex's blood!

Beth jolted awake just at the point where the man was dragging her behind the trees. She shot up in bed, clutching her stomach and yelling Rex's name. Then she looked down to where she'd placed her hands. There was no knife, no blood and no strange man. But she was still panting, and her heart was throbbing.

'Jesus, Beth!' she heard Brady yell and she turned to look at him. 'You woke me up. What's wrong? Is it another one of those bloody nightmares?'

Beth nodded sombrely but didn't say anything.

'You know, you really should go and see someone about them,' he said tersely. Then he seemed to realise he had been a bit harsh, and he put his arm around her. 'Sorry, love. It's just that you gave me a fright. I was fast asleep.'

'Sorry,' she muttered. 'I'm just under a lot of stress at work at the moment. It's not easy being the new girl and having to learn everything.'

'I know,' he said automatically. Then he paused before adding, 'But we both know that isn't really what the nightmares are about, is it? I know it must have been a shock finding your dog like that.' He planted a soothing kiss on her lips. 'I meant what I said, love. You should go and see someone. I don't think you've ever got over what happened that day.'

'It's alright. I can deal with it.'

Beth didn't say anything more. She had already told Brady the tale of what happened that day. Or at least she told him *a* tale, a fabricated one, about Rex running off and then her finding him dead in a pool of blood. It was unexplained, she had said. She reported the incident to the police at the time, she told him, but nobody had been able to tell her what caused Rex's death.

And that was the tale she stuck to. Because she couldn't risk sharing the events of that day in the woods with anyone. Not even her beloved husband.

2

When Beth got up the next day she felt exhausted. After the nightmare, she had lain awake for hours watching the rise and fall of Brady's chest as he snored gently beside her. Unfortunately, once the memories resurfaced it was difficult to banish them from her brain, and she kept replaying it all over and over in her head.

Beth knew Brady was right. She really should get help with the nightmares. They were happening far too often and the only way to stop them would be to receive counselling for her trauma. But that would have meant reliving everything.

'You OK?' asked Brady when he came downstairs, smelling fresh from the shower.

Beth forced a smile. 'Yeah, sure. Are you ready?'

Brady nodded and they left the house to set off for work.

They both worked in the city centre, and Beth was glad Brady was driving as he weaved his way through the early morning traffic in his petrol blue Audi, singing along to Ed Sheeran. She was feeling so tired that she didn't think she could have negotiated her way through the hordes of cars, vans and pedestrians that abounded in Manchester's streets.

Brady drew up outside the offices of Vixus Insurance Ltd, stopping the traffic along busy King Street. Beth alighted from the car to the sound of tooting horns from impatient drivers and blew Brady a kiss before turning away and heading inside the building.

Beth went straight up to the top floor. It was her second week with Vixus and she was the PA to Mr Ballantyne, who held a leading role within the company as the admin manager. Beth was loving it. Although she'd held similar roles in the past, she was still learning how the Vixus systems worked, but all the staff had been so friendly and eager to offer their support, especially Nicola, who was the PA to one of the directors.

Beth shared floor space with the other PAs to the senior management team. Each of the PA's desks was located outside a glass box that housed their particular director or manager.

As she passed her colleagues, Beth said a cheery hello.

'Did you have a good weekend?' asked Nicola.

Beth smiled, noticing that Nicola was dressed immaculately as usual in a smart long-sleeved blouse with her hair in a bun, which emphasised her high cheekbones and dazzling eyes. 'Yes, I could have done with staying in last night though,' she said, yawning. 'What about you?'

'Chilled but nice, y'know?'

She then passed Anita, the managing director's PA. She was the most senior of all the secretarial staff but was due to retire soon. Anita greeted her and Beth did likewise. Anita was a pleasant lady, but Beth had far more in common with Nicola, who was in her late thirties.

Before sitting at her desk, Beth popped her head inside her boss's office and wished him good morning, then offered to get them both a drink. Mr Ballantyne was a small, stocky man in his late forties. He was good to work for most of the time, but like all people, he could have his moments, especially when work stress was getting to him.

Once she had got the drinks and settled at her desk, Beth began to work her way through Mr Ballantyne's emails so she could delete any junk and bring the important ones to his attention. 'You've got a meeting at one o'clock with some of the department heads,' she said, getting up from her desk and popping into his office again to make sure he had heard her.

He looked up. 'One o'clock? That's bloody short notice, isn't it?'

'I know, I thought the same.'

'Which department heads?'

'Mr Hall and Mr Suture.'

Mr Ballantyne nodded. 'Aah yes, I know what that'll be about.'

Beth went back to her desk and worked steadily throughout the morning, pausing occasionally to ask for guidance from one of the other secretaries because she was still learning the system. Despite feeling tired, she organised her boss's diary and dealt with correspondence until it was time to go for lunch. She went to the canteen with Nicola, returning just before one to find that Mr Ballantyne had already left for his meeting.

Fifteen minutes later, Beth was surprised to see her boss return. *That was a quick meeting*, she thought to herself.

'Beth, a word,' he said, storming into his office.

She flashed Nicola a look of concern and Nicola gave her an encouraging nod. Beth followed Mr Ballantyne, taking a seat opposite him while he perched behind his desk and began tapping at his keyboard.

'I thought you said the meeting was at one o'clock,' he said.

'Yeah, that's right. It was.'

'Well, how come I've just sat in the room alone for the past ten minutes?'

Beth felt herself flush. Oh no! Had she got it wrong? 'I–I'll go and check.'

'No need. I can do that myself,' he said, still hammering at his keyboard. 'Aah, here it is.' He scanned through the items on his calendar, his face a mask of confusion. 'Nothing down for today. How did the notification come through?'

'By email from Mr Hall, I think.'

He carried on tapping at the keyboard, switching from his diary to his email account and then studying the items on the screen. Beth watched his expression change and knew that she had cocked up.

'The meeting is *next* Monday, not today,' he snapped. 'Did you not read the email properly?'

'Well yeah, but…'

'Make sure you do in future,' he ordered. 'I've got better things to do with my time than waste it sitting alone in a bloody meeting room.'

Beth apologised, then headed back to her desk and waited for her flushed cheeks to cool down. She felt like a fool. Normally she would never make such a mistake. But she knew she was overtired after last night's bad dream. The problem was, for some reason her nightmares were becoming more frequent. She couldn't understand why, unless all the change from the past few weeks had unsettled her, having started a new job within weeks of moving house.

Still, it felt as though the past was coming back to destroy her happiness.

Worried that she might have made other errors, Beth quickly checked the tasks she had carried out that morning. Sure enough, she had booked Mr Ballantyne into the wrong hotel for a forthcoming conference. Beth had plumped for the Marton House Hotel in London as it was the first one listed on an Internet search. But he had wanted the Marton House Hotel in Edinburgh.

Beth quickly made a couple of calls, cancelling the incorrect booking and switching to the right hotel. She was shaking as she made the phone calls, hoping that Mr Ballantyne wouldn't come out of his office and twig what she was up to. Her earlier mistake had already got her into his bad books, and she didn't want to risk getting on the wrong side of him again.

Later that afternoon when he nipped out of the office, Nicola came straight over to Beth's desk.

'Are you OK? You looked a bit flushed earlier.'

Beth felt her cheeks heat up again as she admitted, 'I made a mistake and he wasn't very happy.'

'Well, I bet it's nothing that can't be put right, is it?'

'No. I've already corrected it.'

'There you go then. Don't worry about it. He can get like that sometimes, but he's OK most of the time and he doesn't hold a grudge. And it is only your second week so you're bound to make the odd mistake.'

'Thanks,' said Beth, grateful for Nicola's show of support. It was great to have somebody onside who was looking out for her.

***

Later that evening, Beth told Brady about her errors, hoping for his backing. But she was surprised by his reaction.

'Bloody hell, Beth. That's not like you. You'll need to pull your socks up if you want to go for that promotion.'

'What promotion?'

'I thought you said that older secretary was due to retire soon. What was her name? Erm...'

'You mean Anita, the MD's PA?'

'Yeah, that's the one.'

'Well yeah, she is retiring, but that doesn't mean I'll be getting a promotion.'

'Why not? Won't the job be advertised in-house before they go external?'

'Probably not. Rumour is that they'll give it to Nicola. She's the next in line for the job. It certainly won't be me. It's only my second week with the company. I'm still learning how things work. In fact, Nicola is the one who has been mentoring me so it would be wrong of me to expect the job.'

'She's not necessarily the best person for the job though, is she?' challenged Brady. 'Why don't you throw your hat in the ring, show them what you've got to offer? I mean, bloody hell, Beth, you've got a good degree, for God's sake!'

'I don't care. I'm not doing that, Brady. Nicola's been good to me and I wouldn't do that to her.'

Brady flicked his hands out, palms upwards in a display of hopelessness. 'Suit yourself, but you're missing out on a great opportunity.'

'Can we just leave it please, Brady? I've had a bad day and I'd rather not talk about it anymore.'

What she said wasn't exactly true. Beth had wanted to talk about it, but she expected a different reaction to the one she received. She had wanted Brady's support rather than him making her feel worse. Beth loved him to bits, but she wished he could be more empathetic at times and appreciate that not everybody was as much of a go-getter as him.

3

Martin Bradshaw was sitting in his usual seat at the end of the bar of The Amber Room, his large, muscular arms resting on the gleaming wooden surface. While his usual choice of chilled music played in the background, he gazed around the room. Across from him, a group of young professionals were engaged in conversation. They'd been there for a couple of hours, and he had watched them becoming progressively drunker, their political debates getting more heated.

That type don't know they're born, he thought, *living in an affluent area with their designer shirts and expensive watches*. They were obviously educated. He could tell that from overhearing their conversation. It was all world issues, university reminiscences and music festivals.

It had been so different when he was young. He grinned in amusement thinking what his old mates would have made of his bar. Their discussions usually only stretched as far as footy, birds and getting pissed. He doubted they would have gone down well with the young and upwardly mobile crowd opposite. And the feeling would have been mutual. His old friends weren't the type to listen to the likes of that lot without passing comment.

Last orders had passed a while ago and Martin had noticed how the table of youngsters doubled their round. But they were so busy in heavy discussion that the drinks were getting neglected. He told his barman to gee them up a bit and watched as a few of them made a half-hearted attempt at finishing their drinks. But Martin wasn't worried. As soon as it was time for them to go, he'd make sure they went whether they liked it or not.

Ten minutes later and very few customers remained, just a middle-aged couple who were waiting for their taxi to arrive, and the table of Hoorah Henrys. Martin decided it was time he made his presence known.

'Time please, gentlemen. Finish your drinks up now or they're going down the sink,' he shouted across from his seat at the bar.

Four heads turned to look at him. Three of them picked up their pints and began necking them as quickly as possible. But not the fourth. *There's always one*, Martin thought, grinning to himself as he heard the lad mutter something about being rudely interrupted before continuing his monologue on the failings of the Labour party while his friends downed their pints.

Martin got up from his seat and strode over to the table where his barman, Dylan, was collecting the empties. He grabbed the lad's remaining drink and handed it to Dylan. 'This one's for the drains.'

The young man stood up. 'You can't do that!' he said, turning around.

His friend shook his head. 'Leave it, Jeremy. We're ready to go now anyway.'

But Jeremy was having none of it. He spun around ready

to confront whoever had the audacity to take his half-finished pint. And then he saw Martin. All six foot two of him, with bulging biceps and a fierce expression.

'It's really out of order, you know,' he muttered.

But even as he spoke, he was moving away, and his friend let out a sigh of relief. Martin watched them dashing for the door to join their other friends who were already on their way out, and he chuckled.

'It's a good job there's not another bloody world war if we have to rely on the likes of them to save the country,' he said to Dylan, who joined in his laughter.

Martin helped Dylan clear the empty glasses, aware that his staff had been delayed by the hangers-on and would therefore finish later. He was fair in that way, and always made sure his staff got a good deal. He liked only good, reliable staff to run his bars, and the best way to keep them was to treat them well.

'Are you here again tomorrow?' asked Dylan.

'Not sure yet,' said Martin.

He usually toured all his bars and his nightclub most evenings, checking that everything was running smoothly. But lately he had been spending a lot of time in The Amber Room and he knew his staff had noticed. They didn't know why though. But he did. It was in the hopes of seeing the leggy blonde he had spotted a few nights ago. She'd only been in once, but there was a chance she might come in again.

He hated himself for thinking that way, but he couldn't help it. He'd had his share of women over the years, most of them only too eager to bed someone with his reputation. But it got boring after a while. He wanted something more.

He hadn't known what that was until he'd spotted the girl. There was something different about her. She was classy and upmarket, but not in a conceited way like those idiots who had just left. No, she was special. She had a cool reserve about her and he doubted whether she would be the type to throw herself at any man, no matter who he was. She'd certainly put him in his place when he'd tried flirting with her a few nights ago. And in a way he admired the fact that she'd refused to reciprocate when he'd flirted. It showed she was loyal to the man she was with.

She was honest too. He liked the way she had pointed out Dylan's mistake when he had given her too much change. It made a refreshing change from many of the women he had known who were all out for what they could get. But, aside from all that, she was bloody stunning.

He checked himself. What on earth was he doing mooning after a woman at his age, especially someone so much younger? And a married woman at that. To his consternation, when she'd mentioned being married, he'd eyed the wedding ring on her finger accompanied by a flash engagement ring. A ring that size was a statement in itself, letting the world know that she was taken.

He'd checked out the husband, a good-looking young professional type who oozed confidence; just the sort of guy he'd have expected an attractive woman like her to be with. They'd seemed alright as a couple, if first impressions were anything to go by. And yet he still couldn't get her out of his mind.

They'd almost finished clearing up when he was alerted by two new arrivals, male and in their early twenties by the looks of them. His doorman, Des, had nipped to the loo so that left Martin, Dylan and two barmaids inside The Amber Room. Daisy was the only one standing behind the bar with him; the other two staff were front of house, wiping tables and straightening chairs. Martin was washing glasses behind the bar when the two men dashed over and stood facing him, the one at the front brandishing a gun.

'Empty the fuckin' till!' demanded the gunman.

Martin appraised him coolly and noted that, despite his bravado, he was shaking. His accomplice cowered behind, hands in his pockets, one of them thrust forward as though he had a gun concealed there. He was looking around at the two members of staff in front of house, trying to appear menacing. But Martin wasn't daft. He knew that if there had been a second gun the lad would have been waving it around instead of keeping it hidden.

His guess was that these two were a pair of amateurs who had somehow acquired a gun and thought they would try their luck. They were certainly nobody he was familiar with. And if they had known the lie of the land, they would have realised how foolish it was to try it on with him.

He walked over to the till where Daisy was standing and opened it up. Then he grabbed a wad of cash. Daisy flashed him a look which told him she was shocked at his complicity. Unlike the two upstarts on the other side of the bar, she was aware of Martin's reputation. He indicated with a flick of his eyes that she should move from the till, and he pretended to gather the cash until she was a safe distance away.

Even with his back to the two lads he could sense them getting jittery, especially when one of them said, 'We want all of it, no fuckin' about!'

The slight tremble in the lad's voice was apparent although he was trying hard to disguise it. Martin turned around and his eyes locked with those of the gun-toting youngster, but the other lad's focus was elsewhere as he continued to stare at the two members of staff. In that moment Martin knew that they had dropped their guard slightly, expecting him to come forward with the money.

But he didn't do that. Martin ducked down quickly, concealed beneath the bar where there was a row of glasses on a shelf. Lifting his head just enough to take aim, he launched a pint glass at the two youths, swiftly followed by another. The glasses hit the ground and shattered, surrounding them with bouncing shards of glass. The lad with the gun panicked and fired a shot.

Guessing he'd probably never used a gun before, Martin took advantage of the pause while the lad recovered from the shock. He jumped up and leapt over the bar, delivering a rapid kick to the gut. The lad bent forward to grab his throbbing midriff and dropped his weapon.

His accomplice turned around and made a grab for the gun. As he bent to the floor, Martin booted him in the face, and a crimson spray burst from his nose. Martin seized the gun and aimed it at the two lads who cowered. Both began pleading for their lives.

Then there was movement from a side door and Martin watched as Des walked back inside the room. 'You took your time,' he said. 'I thought you'd never fuckin' get here.'

Des smirked. 'Looks like you're managing alright without me, boss.'

'Grab hold of the little one,' Martin replied. 'We'll take them out the back.'

Martin stuffed the gun inside his pocket; he wouldn't be needing that tonight. He preferred to deal with these two in his own way. He and Des frogmarched the two lads out of the fire exit and into the yard at the back of the pub while they whimpered and pleaded for leniency.

'That'll teach you not to take liberties in my fuckin' bar,' Martin said, looking at the injuries he had inflicted on the two lads. 'In future, you need to know who the fuck you're dealing with. Martin Bradshaw's the name. I suggest you check out my CV before you chance your luck again.'

'We won't do owt like that again, honest,' said one of the lads.

'Yeah, we didn't know who you were,' added his friend.

'Regardless of who I am, you shouldn't be fuckin' doing it. I should really ring the cops.'

'No, no, please don't,' begged the first lad.

But Martin knew he wouldn't do that. There'd be too many questions asked about the lads' injuries and he'd end up in as much bother as them. He believed the lads when they said they'd never do anything like that again. He could tell by the terrified looks on their faces,

Then, glancing at Des, he said, 'Come on, let's get rid of them.'

He grabbed one lad and dragged him across the yard, dumping him outside the back gate. Des did the same then slid the bolt.

'Fuckin' tossers!' yelled Martin, who was fired up by now.

It was always the same after a fight. He could feel the adrenaline pulsing round his body and it was hard to come back down. He'd had it since being a kid when he'd had to take on the bigger boys and had been hailed a hero by his school friends when he emerged as the victor.

Nowadays he tried not to get into too many scrapes. He was getting older and didn't feel the need to prove himself anymore. But it was still handy to know he could handle himself whenever the need arose.

He went inside the bar and poured a brandy to steady his nerves, offering Des one too. Daisy noticed the blood on his knuckles. She didn't say anything, but Martin could tell it had unsettled her. She needn't have worried. He drew the line at hitting women and children. His own dad might have been a rough arse, but he did have some values which he'd instilled in Martin. When it came to scrotes like those two out the back though, he had no qualms, and he would always do whatever it took to protect himself and those he cared about.

4

Beth and her husband had been shopping that day. They'd splashed out on a new dining set Brady had spotted the week before. He never ceased to amaze her with his design flair and, even though the set was on the pricey side, she loved it and knew it would look great inside their home. Life was good. She was married to a wonderful guy and was enjoying decorating and furnishing their new house together.

It made her think of how much her situation mirrored that of her parents who had always been so happy in their marriage. They both had successful careers but still somehow managed to raise their children well and remain happy as a couple. Beth had always aspired to be like them, and when she met successful sales executive Brady, she thought that she would eventually have the happy family life she'd always had with her parents.

'I can't wait till they deliver the dining set,' she said as they sat down with their drinks inside The Amber Room.

They'd chosen to come here again. In fact, Brady had insisted, knowing how much she had been impressed by the bar last time they had visited.

'I told you you'd like it, didn't I?'

'You know me so well,' quipped Beth.

Brady patted her on the leg. 'I think it's more a case of us both having the same great taste. I mean, you did choose me, didn't you?'

Beth laughed at his show of ego. 'I'm saying nothing. You're big-headed enough.'

He removed his hand from her thigh and took a sip of his pint. 'Eh, I didn't tell you yesterday, did I? We've got a new client at work.'

'Really?' As she spoke, Beth's gaze drifted to the bar area. The owner hadn't been there when they had arrived and, telling herself it was just curiosity, she wondered if he had entered since.

Brady carried on speaking, oblivious to where her mind was. 'Yeah, it's a new hotel, quite a big one in the centre of Manchester. They're opening a beauty and hair salon inside the hotel, and somebody recommended us. It's doing really well, and I heard through the grapevine that they're thinking of opening a second one in Liverpool. It's a great opportunity.'

On and on went Brady, and Beth smiled at his enthusiasm, but her eyes were still wandering around the bar. Then Brady paused before demanding, 'Are you listening to me?'

'What? Oh, yeah. 'Course I am.' To demonstrate that she was interested in what he was saying, she asked, 'What's the name of the hotel?'

'The Pembrook.'

'Oh, I haven't heard of that one.'

'I told you, it's new. But don't worry, everyone will soon know the name.'

'Oh, sounds like a good opportunity for you then.'

'Yeah, it is,' said Brady, who then took a swig of his pint.

Beth was used to him divulging the names of clients and suppliers that he dealt with. In fact, he discussed his business contacts so frequently that Beth almost felt as though she knew them as well as he did. She had met one or two of them at business functions she'd attended with him, which made it easier to visualise the people he often spoke about.

She was just about to congratulate him on his company's new acquisition when a crowd of youths entered The Amber Room. 'Jesus,' whispered Brady as they passed their table. 'I don't like the look of this lot.'

'Why?'

'Well, they're lowlife, aren't they? Look at them, all bloody tattoos, shaved heads and loud mouths. I don't know what they're doing, letting them inside a nice bar like this. I thought I'd brought you to an upmarket bar, not a bloody dive.'

Beth knew he was a bit of a snob, but she let his comment go. Nobody was perfect, and he was good to her in so many other ways that she didn't let his snobbery get to her. In fact, she thought it was good that he always made sure she had the best. And most of the time he treated her like a princess.

'I shouldn't be surprised really,' Brady continued. 'After all, the owner's a bit of a wide boy by all accounts, so they're probably friends of his. Mind you, he does know how to kit a place out well, I'll give him that.'

As he spoke, he gazed appraisingly around the room, taking in its stylish features. Beth was relieved that he wasn't looking directly at her because she felt her face flush at the mention of the owner. She hated herself for it. *What's wrong with me?* she thought. *I've got a perfectly*

*decent husband who treats me really well, so what the hell
am I doing mooning after some other guy, who's bad news
anyway from what I've heard?*

But Beth couldn't help but think about Martin. He had
bad boy written all over him, but he was also manly and
charismatic, and those penetrating blue eyes were enough
to make any girl feel weak at the knees.

As soon as Brady had suggested going to The Amber
Room again, she had felt a rush of excitement. But then
she'd checked herself, knowing it probably wasn't a good
idea in view of how badly she was attracted to the owner.
But she couldn't think of a good excuse to give Brady as to
why they shouldn't go, so here they were.

'Are you OK?' asked Brady, switching her mind back to
him. 'You're not worried about that gang of guys, are you?'

'No, 'course not, I'm fine.'

For the rest of the night, she tried to focus on her husband,
but she couldn't help but ask herself whether Martin would
enter the bar at some point and how she'd feel if he did. The
evening passed by uneventfully, and when it was time to
go she surprised herself by feeling intense disappointment
because the owner had kept away. No matter how much she
tried to fight her attraction, she couldn't help it.

Martin would have preferred to spend yet another evening
at The Amber Room, but he knew he was just being foolish
in the hopes of setting eyes on the mystery blonde again. So
instead, he did a tour of his other businesses.

He entered *Virtuoso* nightclub where the DJ was banging
out a series of club classics. The current offering was 'Show

Me Love' by Robin S., but Martin wasn't feeling it. To him, it was just fuelling the overexcited clamour of the pissed-up patrons and he couldn't help but compare it unfavourably with the chilled vibe of The Amber Room.

As soon as he reached the bar, the staff seemed to stand to attention. Two barmaids were sitting on stools engaged in chatter while a barman coped with the glut of customers alone, but when the two girls spotted Martin, they slid off their stools. Once they were back on the staff side of the bar, one of them rushed over to take his order. Martin asked for a scotch on the rocks and swung around on his barstool so that he could watch what was going on inside the club.

It wasn't long before an overly eager leggy blonde draped herself around him. He had to admit to himself that she was his type, well, apart from the fake boobs and eyelashes and the plumped-up lips. Just why did girls do that when most of them looked ridiculous with their trout pouts?

Her conversation was banal as she wittered on about the clubs she'd been to and the celebrities she'd met. It was obvious she already knew he was the owner of Virtuoso and she seemed intent on trying to impress. But he wasn't with her for her sparkling repartee. A man had needs and she would satisfy his for tonight.

Later, they went back to his home in Bramhall. It was a huge, four-bedroom detached house with a large, sweeping drive, an enormous lounge and a separate dining room. The modern kitchen had a central island with a granite worktop to match the other work surfaces.

Martin had bought the house several years ago, deciding that he might as well enjoy the luxury that his status in life afforded him. If he was honest with himself, though, he was rattling around inside the place. Friends and relatives occasionally stayed, but he'd never been married and didn't have any children to occupy the bedrooms.

The girl was called Marissa, and as soon as she walked inside the vast hallway, she was agog, her eyes as wide as saucers and her jaw hanging loose as she took in the opulent surroundings.

'Bloody hell, this is alright, innit?' she commented.

Martin walked through to the kitchen. She followed him, her eyes wandering around the room, checking out the smart appliances and fancy gadgets. He fixed them both a drink and led her up to the bedroom. It was obvious to him what she really wanted, but he decided that there was no way she would get her feet under the table. Although he'd made that mistake in the past with women like her, he was older and wiser now.

Once they reached the bedroom, Martin was glad to see that Marissa had finally stopped gazing around in awe and she seemed to have remembered why he had invited her there. After flinging off her clothes, she jumped on top and was soon riding him like a prize-winning jockey. It wasn't long before Martin climaxed and let out a groan of relief. He was done and the girl jumped off, her expression one of disappointment.

Martin felt a bit of a shit. He had used her, but he had done it knowingly. He had no desire to make love to a girl like her. It was just sex. And he was under no illusions as far as she was concerned. He was almost old enough to be her father and knew she wouldn't even have been there if he hadn't been the owner of Virtuoso.

Martin dropped off to sleep shortly afterwards. The

following morning was a repeat performance. This time he took a little longer, but it still wasn't what he would have termed lovemaking. He jumped out of bed and took a shower, leaving her lying there.

'Are you not getting up?' he asked when he returned to the bedroom.

Marissa pouted sulkily then tapped the bed. 'Aren't you coming back in?'

'No. I've got business to attend to.'

His reply was brusque, and he hoped she'd take the hint. She got up from the bed languorously, making her way slowly to the en suite. He tried to pretend he hadn't noticed her peek over her shoulder as she stepped inside, as though willing him to join her. He'd done what he set out to do and now he just wanted her to go.

Downstairs, he waited for an hour until she entered the kitchen. 'Do you want some breakfast?' he asked, feeling obliged to at least show some hospitality.

'No, I've called a cab. I'll be going soon so I'll be out of your hair.'

She looked at him expectantly, as though wanting him to refute her last comment, but Martin remained tight-lipped. She finally asked, 'Will I see you again, then? I'm free next weekend if you wanna do something.'

'Leave me your number. I'll see what I can do,' he replied, trying to let her down gently.

It seemed an age till her cab arrived, and he was beginning to think he'd never get rid of her. It was with relief that he swung open the front door and waved her on her way, passing her a twenty-pound note for her cab fare.

34

Once she was gone, he was left with the same feeling of disenchantment that often dogged him lately. Surely there was more to life than fast and easy sex with an equally fast and easy woman!

5

The following Friday, Brady told Beth he was working late, so she caught the train home from work as she didn't fancy waiting around for him. By the time he arrived home at seven- thirty, she had a chilli con carne cooked and keeping warm.

Beth was standing by the hob when Brady walked in and kissed her on the cheek. 'Sorry I'm late, love, but I've been celebrating.'

'Celebrating? What, when you're driving?'

'Oh, don't worry, I only had the one. My boss wanted to mark the occasion, so it was only polite. Anyway, aren't you going to ask what I've been celebrating?'

'Sorry, yes. I was just worried about you drink-driving, that's all.'

'Don't be silly. You know I'd never do that.' He paused for a moment then prompted her again, 'Well?'

She grinned. 'Go on, what is it? What are you celebrating?'

'I've only gone and got a promotion, haven't I?'

'Really, what to?'

Brady preened. 'Sales manager.'

'Wow! How come? What happened to the other one?'

'Robert? He left. I kind of knew it was in the offing. I

threw my hat in the ring as soon as I heard he was leaving, but I didn't want to tell you in case it didn't happen. Anyway, my boss made the announcement today and suggested we have a little drink to celebrate. He's probably still in the pub with the other department heads now.'

'Congratulations! You should have stayed. I wouldn't have minded. It's your promotion they're celebrating, after all.'

'No, it's a bit of a waste of time when I'm driving and can't have a drink, isn't it? Anyway,' he added, kissing her on the cheek, 'I wanted to celebrate with you, which is why I called at the supermarket on the way home and brought this.'

He held up the carrier bag he had been clutching and reached inside, pulling out a bottle of champagne.

Beth smiled. 'Aw, you're so good.'

'Only the best for you, love.' Brady placed the bottle on the granite worktop and reached inside the bag again. 'That's not all,' he said, pulling out a boxed cake.

'Is that what I think it is?' she asked.

'Yes, your favourite. Coffee and walnut.'

She beamed. 'Aw, Brady. You're so good to me. Anyone would think it was my promotion. How could I ever make it up to you for all the lovely things you do?'

He laughed. 'Well, I can think of one thing, but we've got some eating and drinking to do first. I bought some wine to go with the meal. We can have the champagne afterwards with the cake, if you like?'

'Oh, yes, that'll be lovely.'

'What, the champagne and cake or what I've got lined up for afterwards?'

Beth laughed and tapped him playfully on the arm. 'Come on, I'm starving, and I've cooked one of your favourites too. Chilli con carne.'

'Great! This is turning into one hell of a night.'

By the time they'd eaten and worked their way through the best part of two bottles of wine, Brady was becoming very talkative. His excitement was spilling over as he chatted about their future. She loved it when he was like this. It gave her a warm glow knowing that they were going to have a wonderful life together.

'This job will be the making of us, y'know. And it's only the start. Why don't you go for that promotion at work too? There's no reason why you shouldn't. With both of us getting promoted, it could set us up well by the time we have a family.'

'Brady, I thought we'd already talked about this.'

She was referring to the prospect of starting a family as much as the promotion. When they'd discussed the former, she'd let him know that it was something she wanted in the future but not quite yet.

He shrugged. 'Suit yourself, but you're a fool to let this job promotion pass you by.'

Beth didn't respond. She didn't want to go over old ground so it was Brady that filled the silence, switching back to the topic of his recent promotion.

'I'm already familiar with most of my company's customers and suppliers, but this position will really put me in the know. And it's handy information to have.'

'What do you mean?'

'Well, why stop at that? I could always set up on my

own in the future. That's why it's good to have a few major contacts.'

'But wouldn't that mean stealing customers from your boss?'

'Not really. It's a free market, and I found a lot of the bloody customers anyway.'

'Yeah, but Mr Dodds isn't going to be happy if you do that, is he?'

'Who cares! He'd do the same to me given half a chance. It's a dog-eat-dog world out there, y'know.'

Beth wasn't really keen on this side of Brady's character, and she was glad when he changed the subject.

That night, Beth found it difficult to sleep. It seemed to her that Brady had their whole lives mapped out before them and she sometimes found it unsettling. It felt as though she was being swept away in a mighty tide of Brady's enthusiasm, which was great but a bit scary at the same time. When she first met him, she'd found his ambition attractive. After all, she was ambitious too, but she was beginning to realise that Brady took it to a whole new level.

She hadn't met anyone like him before. He never let anything stand in his way. If he wanted something he would go for it wholeheartedly, whereas she was a little more cautious. And he could put up such a convincing case for what he wanted that she felt almost foolish for putting obstacles in the way. His passion was so infectious that she would begin questioning herself, unable to understand why she felt the need to pull back.

Brady's confidence was rubbing off on her to such an extent that she felt sure he would always find a way to make things work out. With those thoughts in mind, by the end of the night she had reached a decision, and she couldn't wait to share it with him.

When morning came and she felt him stir in the bed, she turned and beamed at him. Brady wiped the sleep from his eyes and gazed back at her. 'What is it? What's wrong?'

She laughed. 'Nothing's wrong. Does there have to be something wrong for me to be happy? You did give me a lot to smile about last night, after all.'

Brady returned her laughter and grabbed her around the waist. 'You ready for a repeat?'

Beth chuckled as he tickled her. Then he grabbed her again, rolled on top of her, and began running his hand up her leg and wriggling his fingers about in a tickling motion. Beth squealed in delight then succumbed to his ardour.

6

Beth was still in good spirits when she arrived at work on Monday until Mr Ballantyne asked to see her.

'Don't look so worried, Beth,' he said.

'I know you've only been with us just under a month, but apart from that little blip a couple of weeks ago, I think we can safely say that the quality of your work is excellent, and I just wanted you to know that we're very pleased with you.'

'Thank you,' she said, getting up to leave.

Mr Ballantyne held up his hand. 'Not so quick. I haven't finished yet. There's another matter I want to discuss with you.'

His words took Beth by surprise, and she became tense again until Mr Ballantyne spoke. 'You're probably aware that Anita will be leaving in a few weeks.'

'Yes.'

'Well, I'd like to put you forward for the job.'

'Oh, but...'

'Why are you so surprised, Beth?'

'Well, it's just that...I would have thought one of the other secretaries would have been in line for the job, like Nicola, for example.'

'Nicola? Oh no, I don't think Nicola could handle that level of responsibility.'

'But she's got far more experience than me.'

'In Vixus systems perhaps, but you're a quick learner, Beth, and your credentials are impeccable. We received very good references from your previous employers, and I can see why. I've spoken to Mr Worthing and he's happy with my recommendation. We both think that you would be the perfect person to take up the position as his PA.'

Beth was quiet for a while, then Mr Ballantyne spoke again. 'Are you worried about what the rest of the staff will think?'

'Well, in a way. I suppose it's just come as a bit of a surprise, that's all. And to be honest, I wasn't expecting it.'

'Don't be surprised. You're a very capable young lady. I'll be sorry to lose you. You've been a pleasure to work with in the few weeks I've known you, but that shouldn't be reason to stand in the way of your career. I think you've got a glowing future with the company, and you'd be foolish to turn down the position because of what the staff might think. It's what you think that matters. So, what do you say?'

Beth felt a surge of guilt. How could she take the job when she knew very well that everyone expected Nicola to get it? How would Nicola react to Beth's promotion?

But then she thought of what Brady had said a couple of days ago. Why shouldn't she apply for the job? Surely the fact that the management team were encouraging her, rather than Nicola, told her that they thought she was more suitable.

She smiled at Mr Ballantyne. 'OK, I'll take it.'

'Excellent,' he said, rising from his seat and shaking

her hand. 'Keep it under your hat for now though. Mr Worthing will want to formalise things before he makes an announcement, and from what he said, I think he prefers to wait until Anita retires. She's given many years of good service to the company, so I hope you understand that we don't want to make her feel pushed out.'

'Yeah, sure,' said Beth, who then left his office.

As soon as she was back at her desk, she noticed Nicola looking across at her. She had her handbag on her desk as though she was waiting to go somewhere, and Beth suddenly realised that it was lunchtime.

'Won't be a minute,' she said, gathering her own things together.

Once Beth was ready, they walked out of the office. While they were waiting for the lift, Nicola said, 'You look happy. I take it things are going well with Mr Ballantyne, then?'

'Yeah,' said Beth. 'It's going okay, thanks.'

She looked at Nicola's eager face and could tell she was waiting for Beth to furnish her with the details. Beth decided not to confide in her yet, choosing to wait until Mr Worthing was ready to make the announcement. But as she looked at Nicola, she couldn't help but feel like a Judas, and she wasn't looking forward to the day when the news was out.

7

'You sure you'll be OK while I'm away?' asked Brady as he plonked his suitcase down in the hallway.

'Yeah, 'course I will. You'll only be away for three days, and I'll speak to you every evening. Anyway, Sally will be here on Friday, so I'll only have to stay on my own for three nights.'

Brady frowned. 'OK, as long as you're sure.' He checked the time on his watch. 'Taxi should be here any minute.'

'I would have taken you to the station, y'know.'

Brady looked at her disparagingly. 'What, in your dressing gown?'

'No, silly. I would have got up earlier if you'd wanted me to.'

'It's fine. The company are paying expenses anyway.'

They were interrupted by the ringing of Brady's phone. He picked it up and checked the screen. 'Taxi's here.'

Beth flung her arms around him. 'OK, I'll see you Saturday.'

Brady gave her a quick peck on the lips. 'OK, you take care. I'll ring you once I arrive.'

She followed him to the door and waved him away as he set off to catch the train to London. Brady had been booked into a trade show by his company. It was the first time they had been apart since they had married, and Beth knew she would miss him.

Beth thought about the last few days. Ever since they had decided to try for a baby, Brady had been so attentive. And of course, the frequent lovemaking had brought them even closer together. She knew it would be difficult staying here without him, but she hadn't told him that as she didn't want to worry him.

Later that day, Brady was sitting in the bar area of a four-star London hotel with some other representatives from the trade show he was attending, and he was in his element. He always enjoyed these events and now that he had been promoted, he would have many more opportunities like this.

All in all, Brady was happy with his status in life. He'd grown up as one of two children and had always been aware of the fact that his parents doted on his older brother. At times it seemed that no matter what Brady did, in his parents' eyes he would never be able to match his sibling.

But now he felt as though he was winning. He had a good job, a nice home and a beautiful wife. He'd loved the look of admiration on his parents' faces when he'd taken her to meet the family, and the look of envy on his brother's. But Beth wasn't just good-looking, she was smart too, and with a bit of encouragement from him she would do really well in her career, unlike his brother's wife, who was a boring stay-at-home mum.

Today he was feeling particularly smug. Sales events

always gave him a chance to let his hair down and act like a single man. As much as he loved Beth to bits, everyone needed a break now and then, and this was his. And the best thing about it was, she wouldn't know a thing about what he got up to. Granted, he often learned a lot while he was there about new products on the market and other interesting snippets. It was also a chance to suss out the competition, but apart from all that, it was a good excuse for a piss-up at the company's expense.

He'd already figured out that the three guys he was sitting with were from less successful companies than the one he worked for. Two of them were from the cosmetics distributor Blessons, a sales manager and an HR manager, although Brady didn't have a clue what an HR manager was doing at a trade show. Wasn't he supposed to look after staff rather than products? The sales manager was a pompous twat, but when it came down to it he didn't really have much in the way of people skills; his over eagerness was all a front.

The third guy sitting around the table was from a company Brady hadn't heard of previously. At first, he thought he might have a bit of competition. The guy was smart and seemed professional, and he had come over well in the workshops. Intrigued, Brady had done a quick Internet search of the firm the guy worked for while he was in the gents. He was satisfied to learn that they were only a small outfit.

As he held court, the three men hung on to his every word, which was currently on the topic of wives and the home. 'The secret is,' he said, 'you've got to let the missus think she's in charge. But in reality, it's all on your say-so.

It's easy. All you have to do is butter them up, let them think you're doing everything for them, when in actual fact, if I want to decorate my home in a certain way then I'm gonna do it no matter what she fuckin' says. But I'll do it so subtly that she'll end up thinking the décor was her idea in the first place.'

The three men laughed and, warming to his subject, Brady continued. 'At the end of the day we're really pulling the strings. And let's face it, guys, most women are too foolish to even realise who's really running the show.'

As he looked around at the other delegates, checking that they were still engrossed in listening to his view of domesticity, he noticed a group of young women walk past. He'd already spotted one of them at the conference: a good-looking brunette with ample curves, and now that she was in the bar, he decided it was time he got to know her better.

'Hang on, guys, it looks like we're in business,' he said, taking his drink and going to join the girls at the table they had just taken up.

As he crossed the bar, Brady prepared his patter. 'Hi,' he said, addressing the brunette. 'I noticed you in the audience when that speaker was on. I was glad you asked the question about that hairdressing product. In fact, I was just about to do that myself. Do you mind if I ask what your role is?'

The brunette looked at him and smiled. Brady could tell that she was flattered by his interest in her business knowledge. But there was more than that. He knew by the way her face lit up that the attraction was mutual.

'I'm the sales rep for a large distributor,' she replied, the smile still lingering on her lips.

'Oh yeah, who's that then?'

'Brigitte Beauty,' she said.

Brady recognised the name straightaway. She was right, they were a large distributor, which gave him even more reason to want to get to know her better.

'I'm the sales manager with Repertoire,' he said, hoping she'd be suitably impressed. The firm might not be quite as big as the one she worked for, but the role of sales manager trumped that of sales rep, he decided. 'I could tell from your knowledge that you were with a major player. I'd love to chat to you more,' he said, pulling out a seat at the table without waiting for an invitation.

There were no complaints from any of the other girls at the table and they turned away and made conversation among themselves while the brunette's attention switched to him. Brady felt a satisfied buzz knowing she was his for the taking.

Brady turned over in bed and he felt the shape of someone next to him. Then he opened his eyes and noticed the girl lying on her back with her abundance of brunette hair splayed around her shoulders. He searched his brain, failing to recall her name, but memories of the previous night's activities came flooding back to him. She had been good. She had been *really* good.

A self-satisfied grin played on his lips till she woke up and he was suddenly seized by an attack of conscience, remembering the wife he had left at home. The girl reached over and grabbed his arm. 'You're not getting up already, are you? Why not spend a bit more time in bed?'

'No!' snapped Brady, flinging the duvet off him and

swinging his legs out till his feet found the floor. 'I need to get a shower. Time's marching on.'

'What time is it?' she asked.

'Eight.'

'Oh, that's fine. It doesn't matter if we're a bit late. Nobody attends everything anyway.'

'There's a workshop I don't want to miss, actually.'

'Oh, yeah. Which one's that then?'

'I can't recall the name, but it was in the agenda.'

'Who's running it?'

'I told you, I don't remember.'

He noticed her eyes roaming up and down his body and he turned towards the bathroom. Before he reached the door, he swivelled round and asked, 'Well, aren't you getting up, then?'

'I'll wait till you've finished in the bathroom then I'll take a shower.' A seductive smirk lit up her face. 'Unless you want me to join you?'

'No, I don't,' he barked. 'And what's wrong with the bathroom in your own room?'

She sat up in bed, a pained expression now on her face. 'Oh, I get it. I've served my purpose, have I? You were alright last night when you were trying to get me into bed.'

'As I recall, you weren't making any complaints.'

'Fine, suit yourself.'

The girl was up now, and frantically searching for her discarded clothing. As he walked into the bathroom, she was pulling on her underwear and chuntering to herself. He shut the door to drown out her complaints.

Two minutes later Brady was standing underneath the shower, letting the hot spray caress his body, when the bathroom door flew open and the girl popped her head inside.

'Fine. I'm off now, you cheeky bastard! Oh, and just for the record, you were shit in bed anyway.'

Brady felt the sting of her words, but it amused him. That's not what she'd been saying the previous night when he had brought her to multiple orgasms. They were obviously just the complaints of a scorned and bitter woman. But it didn't worry him. She was done with, just a one-night convenience which he had now discarded. And he would soon put the experience out of his mind and act like it had never happened.

8

While Brady was away, Beth arranged for her friend Sally to stay with her on Friday evening. She and Sally had attended secondary school together and remained friends ever since. Unlike Beth, Sally was the eternal singleton. She'd had plenty of partners, none of whom she stayed with. Sally loved the buzz of a new relationship, but when that wore off, she became bored and itched to explore something new.

Despite her record with men, she was a great friend, and the two of them usually had each other's backs. It hadn't always been easy to maintain the friendship though. As soon as he met Sally, Brady took an instant dislike to her, telling Beth she was too flirtatious. And whenever Beth wanted to arrange a night out with her, he told her she was a bad influence. Although Beth tried to reassure him that she wasn't like her friend, and would stay faithful, he remained disapproving.

Nowadays, the friendship mainly consisted of lunchtime meetings and telephone conversations where they would share confidences. Nights out were rare, so tonight was a good opportunity for Beth to share some valued time with her friend and have a good catch-up.

Like Beth, Sally was blonde and attractive, but that was where the similarities ended. She was much more brash than Beth. Her mousy blonde hair was dyed in a trendy silver colour and styled in long waves. Sally's lips were full thanks to regular filler injections, and she enjoyed wearing low-cut tops to display the huge, rotund breasts that she had invested in.

Sally craved attention, especially from men, and went to great lengths with her appearance to make sure she got it. But that was only one aspect of her character. Beth knew that this craving for attention masked a hidden insecurity and, insecurities aside, she was one of the most caring and likeable people Beth had ever met.

They had decided to go out locally. As they made their way by taxi to the centre of Marple, Beth's mind flashed to the man who owned The Amber Room, but she dismissed the thought straightaway. She wasn't going into Marple to see *him*, she told herself. She was going for a night out with her friend.

The two women started out at an older pub, Beth having decided that they would avoid The Amber Room and do a tour of the other pubs and bars in the area. Later that night, as they were making their way along the road on the opposite side to The Amber Room, Sally noticed it.

Two trendy young couples had just walked inside, and as the door opened Sally caught a glimpse of the plush interior and heard the sultry tones of Sam Cooke carried out into the street.

'Ooh, that looks nice,' she said. 'Why don't we go in there?'

The sight of two fit, twenty-something men entering the

bar sealed the deal for Sally, and before Beth could protest, she was crossing the road. 'Come on, slow coach,' she shouted over to her.

Beth rushed across the road, trying to think of a reason she could give her friend as to why they should avoid the bar. But Sally didn't wait for her to get to the other side. When Beth touched down on the pavement Sally was already inside, and by the time Beth entered, she was at the bar ordering their drinks.

And then she saw him, Martin, occupying his usual seat at the end of the bar, his bulging biceps spilling out of a tight-fitting, short-sleeved shirt. The breath caught in her throat and as she walked over to the bar, she tried to regain her composure.

But he had already noticed her, and he flashed a smile, displaying his perfect white teeth. She could feel his blue eyes studying her as she approached, and her stance became awkward and self-conscious. *Why don't you just fuck off and stop staring?* she said to herself, but a contradictory internal voice on auto control told her she was secretly loving it.

Sally was at the same end of the bar, flirting with the barman as she ordered a Sex on the Beach and a Pornstar Martini. As the barman went to fix the drinks, Sally's eyes flashed over to the man at the end of the bar, following his gaze to find it settling on Beth.

As he beamed at the two women, Beth managed a tight smile. 'You took your time!' announced Sally. 'This place is great. I don't know why we didn't come here at the start of the night.'

Beth cringed, knowing that she had spoken loudly enough

for Martin to have overheard. 'Oh, I wanted to show you the other bars first. I was going to bring you here later,' she claimed.

Martin's smile had turned to more of a snigger as though he knew she had been trying to avoid him.

'I've ordered us a Sex on the Beach and a—'

'I know. I heard,' Beth cut in. Then, feeling Martin's eyes still appraising her, she said, 'I'll find us some seats while you're waiting for them.'

The place was packed. Beth had intended to sit as far away from Martin as possible, but the only free tables were within view of the bar. She picked a seat facing away from Martin, leaving the other one for Sally.

'Eh, you're getting a bit of attention,' Sally babbled excitedly when she walked back to Beth, proudly carrying the two cocktails and bending provocatively as she placed them on the table. 'Who *is* that hunk at the end of the bar? He hasn't taken his eyes off you since we came in.'

'He's the owner,' Beth replied casually.

'Well, he's definitely interested in you. Do you know him?'

'Not really. I've only seen him once.'

Sally giggled. 'Play your cards right and you could be well in there.' As she spoke her eyes roamed around the bar. 'There's plenty of other talent in here, as well.'

Beth tutted. 'Sally, you're incorrigible. I'm a married woman, don't forget.'

'I know. I'm only joking. 'Course you are. To the fantastic Brady.' Then she chuckled. 'But there's nothing to stop me.'

Beth noticed the sarcasm in Sally's voice when she referred to Brady. She could tell Sally wasn't keen on him although she'd never said anything outright. Beth therefore let it go; it wasn't worth falling out over. For a while they sat chatting, but Beth noticed that as they spoke Sally's eyes continued to roam around the bar, and their conversation was punctuated by Sally's commentary about what Martin was doing and about the other men that had caught her interest.

Suddenly, Sally shot out of her seat and announced, 'I'm going to the bar.'

'But it's my round,' said Beth.

'It's OK. I'll get this one. You can get me one later.'

Curious, Beth couldn't resist turning round to see what had caught Sally's interest. She noticed Sally sidle up to a good-looking guy at the bar, and she smiled to herself in amusement. Her friend would never change. Then she noticed Martin smile back at her. She blushed and turned around quickly, hoping he hadn't thought her smile was aimed at him.

Sally spent an age at the bar, so Beth sat patiently waiting and sipping at her cocktail. All at once she started to feel ill, and she had barely registered the feeling of nausea when the desire to vomit became overwhelming. Feeling embarrassed and afraid that she might not find a free cubicle in the ladies', she raced for the door with her hand covering her mouth.

To her shame, she was no sooner outside in the cool air than she vomited onto the pavement, attracting scornful glances from a group of girls passing by. Beth continued to retch for a while, willing it to be over. Damn Sally and her cocktails. She must have drunk more than she had realised.

Beth hated getting this drunk. She couldn't remember the last time she had been so wasted that she'd actually vomited, probably when she was still a fresher at uni. She was anxious to get back to Sally and hopefully persuade her to leave the bar and come back home with her.

Once the vomiting had stopped, she turned around intending to go back inside, but before she had a chance, she saw the powerful form of Martin stepping outside. He came straight over to her, handing her a serviette that he must have quickly grabbed off the bar.

'Are you alright?' he asked. She could see his expression of concern, making her feel even more uncomfortable in his presence. He probably thought she was just a foolish bit of a kid who couldn't handle her drink, and she held the serviette to her face to smother her embarrassment.

'Yes, yes, I'm fine,' she said. He was standing so close that she could feel the heat of his body, and she cast an awkward glance across the pavement as another group of patrons eyed her critically.

Martin spotted them too. 'Come here,' he said, putting his arm around her in a reassuring gesture and drawing her across the pavement until they were standing under the overhang of a neighbouring shop.

It wasn't until she had crossed the pavement that Beth realised how willingly she had submitted to his gentle coaxing. Martin must have read the concern on her face as he pulled his arm away and added, 'Sorry. I noticed you'd got an audience. I was just trying to get you away from them, that's all.'

Then he flashed that disarming smile. 'Don't worry, I'm not going to do you any harm. I was just worried about you. Are you OK?'

'Yes, I'm fine,' she repeated.

He then reached for her hand. As she unwittingly held it up to his touch, he took the serviette and tenderly wiped around her mouth. 'Sorry, you missed a bit.'

Beth could tell he wasn't sorry at all. He was enjoying having the opportunity to bestow his attention on her. Beth began shivering and remembered she had left her coat inside. 'I–I need to get back,' she muttered.

'Sure, come on. I'll get you a cup of tea or something. It might settle your stomach.'

As Beth stared into his beautiful blue eyes, she felt a warm glow despite the cold. He held her gaze for some moments, unsettling her as she felt a rush of something indefinable. Sexual chemistry? Attraction? Lust? Although she knew it was wrong, she was unable to break away, until Sally burst out of the door and the moment was lost.

'There you are! Are you alright, Beth?' she asked.

'Yeah, I'm just...'

'She was ill,' said Martin. 'But she's fine now.' And there was that smile again. 'I'm just going to make her a cup of tea to settle her stomach.' Then he turned to Beth. 'I'll leave you to it for now.'

Once he had disappeared inside, Sally flashed an inquisitive glance at her friend.

'Oh no, you're barking up the wrong tree there,' said Beth. 'Like he said, I was ill, and he came outside to look after me.'

Then Sally noticed the vomit on the pavement. 'Ew! Is that yours?'

'Yeah, we must have drunk more than I realised. No more cocktails for me. I'll settle for the cup of tea Martin's making for me.'

'Personalised service, eh? I told you he couldn't take his eyes off you.'

'Give over, Sally. Like I already said, I'm a married woman. I can't help it if the guy's got a thing for me, but as far as I'm concerned, it isn't reciprocal.'

Sally gave her a knowing look and said no more.

9

The following morning Beth dropped Sally at the train station then she carried on to the local shopping precinct. There was something she needed to buy while she was out.

Once she was back home, she sat down to open the small packet she had purchased. She was still nauseous, and only this morning it had occurred to her that the cocktails might not be the only thing responsible for how she was feeling.

Beth went up to the bathroom to use the pregnancy testing kit she had bought. As she waited for the result, she convinced herself that it couldn't possibly be positive. They hadn't been trying for a baby for long.

The test result proved otherwise, and she stared at the two red lines, hardly able to believe it. Once she got over her shock, she had mixed feelings about the situation. On the one hand, she was delighted because it was what she and Brady both wanted eventually, but then she was beset with guilt. She had been pregnant when she'd gone out drinking and she hoped to God it wouldn't have harmed the baby.

But then all the other worries and concerns started to crowd her mind. What would happen about work? Should she still go for the promotion? When should she make the announcement? And what would the future be like when she had a baby to look after?

Later that day, Beth heard Brady's key in the lock, and she rushed to meet him in the hall.

'Hi, love. How did it go?' she asked as she flung her arms around her husband then kissed him on the cheek.

When Brady broke away, he looked at her, his face full of enthusiasm. 'Brilliant! I made loads of new contacts. There are a couple of new suppliers I want to try out, actually. I'm going to mention it to Dodds when I get in work on Monday. Oh, and a couple of the talks were great, really informative...'

Beth listened to him gushing about his time at the trade show. It was lovely to see him like this, and although she was itching to tell him her own news, she waited until he had finished.

Eventually he paused and asked, 'How have you been? Did you have a good night with Sally last night? I hope she didn't lead you astray.'

Beth felt a momentary attack of guilt. As she thought about Martin, she could feel her blood heat up and she hoped it didn't show on her face. But then she checked herself. She'd done nothing wrong. And she had already decided that in future she would avoid Martin as much as she could and give him as little encouragement as possible.

'I've been fine, thanks. I've missed you of course, but I've been OK.'

'And how is Sally?' he asked, and she noticed the subtle change in his tone.

'Oh, you know Sally, she doesn't change. But it was good to have her company. Anyway, enough of that. I've got some news I want to share with you. I'll put the kettle on while you take your case upstairs, and then we can sit and have a chat.

'Sounds interesting,' he said, grabbing her again and giving her a passionate kiss on the lips. 'I've missed you too, so-o-o much!'

'Eh, there'll be time for all that later,' said Beth, giggling. Then she gave him a teasing pat on the backside. 'Now do as you're told and go and take your case upstairs.'

'Yes, sir!' he said, returning her playfulness and raising his hand to his head in mock salute.

Beth walked through to the kitchen. For some reason she suddenly felt an attack of nerves. She couldn't understand why, but then she supposed that it was due to the enormity of the news she was about to impart. Her life was about to change irrevocably, and she was very aware of the vast contrast between the girl who had enjoyed nights out with Sally, relishing attention from interested males, and the person she was about to become: a mother with a whole new set of responsibilities.

When they were both sitting in the living room with their coffees in front of them, Brady said, 'Well then, out with it.'

'I–I think I'm pregnant,' she said.

Brady stared at her, stunned into silence for a moment. But then he got up from his seat and enveloped her in a passionate hug. 'That's brilliant! Jesus, I can't believe it.' He stood back and looked at her admiringly.

'Well, it's true.'

'How did you find out? Have you missed a period? Have you done a test?'

'I must have missed but I didn't realise. I've been so busy with the new job and everything. It wasn't until I was sick last night that the penny dropped. Then I did a test this morning after I'd dropped Sally at the station.'

'Oh wow! That's great. You must be then. These tests are pretty accurate, y'know. Oh, but we must get you checked out at the doctor's.'

He was gushing again, and Beth couldn't help but smile. Then he said, 'Come here, for God's sake.'

She got up from her seat and he twirled her around the living room before letting her go and watching her take her seat again.

'Sorry, but it's just so wonderful. I can't wait to tell everyone!' he gushed.

'Well, maybe it would be best to wait a while.'

'I know, I understand. Let's see what the doctor says first and make sure it's 100 per cent definite.'

'Well, it's not only that,' she said. 'There's my work situation to consider.'

'What do you mean?'

'The promotion.'

'Oh yeah, I see. Well, it's probably best to wait until the job's officially yours before you tell them you're pregnant. We don't want them changing their minds, do we? Once the promotion's official, you can tell them what the hell you like. But that won't stop us from telling our families in the meantime, oh, and close friends too. We can ask them to keep it to themselves until you get your promotion.'

'I think it's a bit early yet to tell anyone,' she repeated.

'What do you mean?'

'Well, I'd rather wait and make sure everything's OK.'

'Don't be so negative, Beth. Jesus, we're talking about our families. Surely they should be able to celebrate the news with us!'

'OK, let's tell our families then but keep it from everyone else for a while.'

Although Beth was looking forward to announcing the news to their families, her thoughts were still on work. 'But would it be fair to take the job knowing I'll be leaving in a few months?'

Brady sighed, and Beth felt bad for spoiling the moment. 'We've been over this. You were offered the job fair and square, so why should you not take it just because you're pregnant? That few months' experience at a senior level will come in handy once you decide to go back to work.'

'Yes, but what about the other staff? They're not going to be happy about it, are they?'

'Stuff them! You won't have to deal with them for long anyway.'

'But I like dealing with them, they're a really nice bunch.'

'Beth!' said Brady, looking exasperated.

He didn't add anything else, but his tone and expression told Beth that the subject was closed. And she supposed that he did have a point. This was about them and their future as a family, and maybe she wasn't being fair by making it about her friends at work.

She bit her tongue and listened while Brady started to talk about the best way to celebrate the good news given that Beth could no longer drink alcohol, and made suggestions for transforming the spare room into a nursery.

10

A few weeks later, Beth and Brady were at the Repertoire Christmas party. It took place every year, and Beth normally enjoyed it, but this year it was different because she was expecting. She'd had her due date confirmed and was now twelve weeks gone, which meant she must have got caught a few weeks before she started work at Vixus. She was beginning to show, and had taken to wearing less fitted clothing to disguise the rounding of her stomach.

Ever since she found out about her pregnancy, Beth had suffered from terrible sickness, not only in the mornings but at varying times of the day. She vomited so frequently that it had been difficult to keep her condition a secret from her work colleagues. It was awful feeling so ill most of the time, and it put added stress on Beth because she never knew when she would have to dash to the nearest bathroom.

She had almost backed out of the party, but Brady managed to persuade her by telling her he would look stupid on his own and people would ask questions. They arrived late and walked into the room to find that people were already seated at tables ready to be served their food.

Brady made their apologies and they joined some of his colleagues. As they passed near the kitchen, Beth caught the aroma of roast turkey and Brussels sprouts, and her stomach roiled. Brady made polite chit-chat with his colleagues, trying to bring Beth into the conversation, but her mind was on other things. How was she going to get through this meal without vomiting?

She watched as Brady grabbed the bottle of wine in front of her and filled his own glass, turning to Beth as he did so. 'I'll ask the waitress for some water for you.'

'Are you not drinking?' asked Mr Dodds.

Beth had already anticipated the question and had her answer ready, but Brady beat her to it. 'She's on tablets off the doctor so she's not allowed to.'

'Aw, poor you,' said Mrs Dodds. 'It must be awful not being able to have a drink at Christmas.'

Beth managed a smile. 'Oh, it's OK. I'll have finished them by then.'

Brady quickly changed the subject before Mr Dodds' over inquisitive wife began asking for details of Beth's illness and the medication she was taking. They had agreed on the cover story before they left home, figuring it was best to tell as few people as possible until Beth had announced her news to the staff at Vixus once her promotion was official.

The waitresses, carrying dishes of roast turkey and vegetables, drew closer to them. The whiff of Brussels sprouts assailed Beth's nostrils once again and the familiar feeling of nausea entwined her insides. She fought not to retch as the food was ladled in front of her.

While everybody else tucked into the meal Beth hesitated, until Brady flashed her a look that told her she mustn't give the game away. For several minutes she took tentative forkfuls of the food, fighting to hold back the feeling of sickness. But it was becoming more difficult.

Beth had managed to clear half of the food on her plate, and she was toying with the idea of leaving the rest and claiming she was full. But as she swallowed down a portion of mash, the desire to vomit became stronger than ever, and she couldn't stop the retching that followed. Brady shot her another look as the retching sound reached his ears. But there was nothing Beth could do now other than drop her cutlery and run to the ladies'.

It took a while until the vomiting stopped, and Beth tidied herself up, clearing the regurgitated food from round her mouth and combing her hair before applying some more makeup to disguise her ashen complexion. By the time she returned to the table, the party guests had almost finished their sweets and Brady had a cup of tea waiting for her.

The guests made a fuss but didn't ask any more questions, and she was relieved that Brady must have told them a convincing tale about her illness. Now that the sickly feeling had passed, Beth found herself beginning to relax, and she was glad when they left the table and began to mingle with the other guests, Brady anxious to show off his beautiful wife at every opportunity.

When a man in his thirties approached them, Brady shook his hand vigorously. 'Preston! So glad you could make it,' he said. 'This is my lovely wife, Beth. And Beth, this is Preston Watts from Sevran Cosmetics.'

Preston eyed Beth appreciatively. He was a moderately attractive man with a slight frame who, despite his small stature, oozed confidence and charm. 'Lovely to meet you, Beth,' he said, planting a bold kiss on her cheek before asking, 'What's a lovely girl like you doing with a rogue like him?'

He chuckled and Beth spotted the annoyance on Brady's face. She wrongly assumed it was because Preston had taken liberties in kissing her. 'Great show that, wasn't it?' continued Preston.

'Yes, very productive,' Brady said loudly before turning to Beth. 'I met Preston at the trade show. He's one of the new suppliers I introduced to Mr Dodds.'

For a few minutes they talked business while Beth stood there, feeling bored but trying not to show it. As she watched the two men talking, she could feel Preston's eyes on her, and a curious smirk played on his lips.

Eventually he went to talk to somebody else. 'What was all that about?' Beth asked Brady.

'All what?'

'All that about you being a rogue?'

'Oh, that.' Brady shrugged. 'I suppose it's because I cut a raw deal with him, and he secretly doesn't like it. But really, I've done him a favour. It's an up-and-coming new company and he knows deep down that he's lucky to be doing business with a major player like Repertoire.'

Beth nodded, satisfied with his response because whatever Brady told her, she believed.

Brady was sweating; he hoped Beth hadn't noticed. He couldn't believe that dick Preston had nearly let the cat out of the bag. Everybody knew that you didn't mention what went on at trade shows in front of the missus. But Brady had the distinct feeling that the guy had done it on purpose, perhaps because he had designs on Beth himself, judging by the way he had been looking at her and had kissed her on the cheek.

He waited until he saw Preston go to the gents', then, making his excuses, he set off after him. Brady arrived to find Preston shooting a stream of urine against the steel trough. Heedless of any embarrassment he might cause, Brady sidled up to him.

'What the fuck were you playing at before?'

Preston looked at him in mock confusion. He casually shook the end of his penis free of any remaining drops of urine, then put it away and pulled up his zipper. While he washed his hands, he spoke to Brady over his shoulder.

'What are you talking about?'

'You know what I'm fuckin' talking about. You nearly gave the game away. What happens at trade shows stays at trade shows, OK? You don't go telling the fuckin' missus about it!'

'I wasn't telling the missus anything, just saying what a good time we had. If you've got a guilty conscience, then that's your problem. Personally, I don't see why you'd need to mess around when you've got a wife that looks that good.'

A man walked into the gents' at that point and went into one of the cubicles. Not wishing to be overheard, Brady moved closer to Preston and hissed into his ear.

'What I do in my private life is my own fuckin' business, and there's no need to go shooting your mouth off about it.'

Preston looked up at Brady who towered above him. Then he grinned, seemingly unfazed by Brady's overt aggression, and said, 'Don't worry, your secret's safe with me. I won't tell your wife a thing.'

He had spoken too loudly for Brady's liking and Brady flashed a warning glance at the cubicle the man had entered. Adopting a low, fierce growl, he said, 'It better fuckin' had be.'

'Yeah, sure. You'll have to give me an incentive, though, to keep schtum. How about we renegotiate the contract and reach a more favourable price?'

Brady tensed and snarled at Preston. For a moment he felt like hitting him. But Preston had him by the short and curlies and they both knew it. While he was deciding how to react, the other man came out of the cubicle. Brady and Preston stayed silent while he washed and dried his hands and then left.

By this time, Brady was grateful for the diversion. It had given him a chance to calm down before he did anything rash. Trying to hold his temper, he said, 'Right, I'll speak to you on Monday, but don't push your fuckin' luck too far or there won't be any contract!'

Martin hadn't seen the girl from The Amber Room since that night when she had vomited and that had been about a month ago. He thought maybe he had come on too strong and frightened her off. Nevertheless, during most of that time he had hung around the place like a lovesick teenager hoping to catch a glimpse of her, even if she was with that prat of a husband.

But then he'd had a word with himself. What the hell was wrong with him? At the end of the day, she was someone else's wife. And she probably wasn't interested in him anyway. After all, he looked nearly old enough to be her dad. She was so young-looking and it gave her an air of vulnerability that made him want to look after her. But he would have to resist because he knew no good would come of it.

11

The following Thursday was Christmas Eve and the Vixus offices were alive with excitement. Not only was it the last day in work before Christmas, but it was also Anita's final day altogether.

Anita had chosen to retire before the year end rather than waiting the few weeks it would take till she reached her retirement age. Following this, the management decided to host a party in honour of her and to celebrate Christmas.

Fortunately for Beth, it was one of her better days, although she had vomited up her breakfast that morning before coming to work. She was now thirteen weeks pregnant and couldn't wait until the misery of this constant nausea was finally over. She'd been told that the first three months were the worst so she hoped she wouldn't have long to wait.

Because she knew it was a special day at work, she had bought a new dress. It was low cut and gathered under the bust with layers of chiffon that flowed from the gathers to just below her knees, so it did an excellent job of disguising her slight bump. The dress would also come in handy for something to wear over the Christmas holidays.

'Bloody hell, you're looking hot,' Nicola had commented

when she'd arrived at work. 'You kept them under wraps, didn't you?'

Beth chuckled and could feel herself blush as she became aware of her swelling breasts.

Just after lunch Mr Worthing came round and announced to the staff that there would be an early finish and that the party would be held in the conference room at three-thirty. There was a buzz around the office and staff began clearing their desks, aware that they didn't have long to go till the party started.

By the time Beth, Nicola and the other management secretaries arrived on the fifth floor, there was already a horde of staff milling about outside the conference room and waiting for the management to open the doors.

They dashed inside, Beth trying to hold back as she didn't want anyone bumping into her. She chatted with some of the other staff who also seemed in no hurry to get inside, while Nicola rushed ahead. Once inside, Beth could tell where the drink was due to the crowd of people gathered around a particular table.

As she looked at them, Nicola emerged from the crowd and came over carrying two plastic cups, which Beth assumed were full of wine. 'Here, slow coach, I've got us one each.'

'Oh,' said Beth, feeling the bile rise as she caught a whiff of the wine. 'Not for me, thanks.'

'What? Why's that?'

'Oh, I'm erm… I'm on tablets.'

'Really? You never told me that. What for?' Nicola asked.

'It's a stomach bug, a bacterial one.'

'Aah, right. I thought you'd been looking a bit pasty lately and rushing to the loos a lot. You should have told me. Are you OK?'

'Yeah, not too bad now the tablets are kicking in, but they're strong ones so I can't drink with them.'

Beth hoped her friend would be happy with that but she persisted. 'Really? What are they called?'

'Oh, erm. I've forgotten.'

'Never mind, as long as you're alright.' Then Nicola added, 'Eh, you sure it's an infection? You're not pregnant, are you?'

'What? No, no, the doctor checked for that.'

'Oh, so you're trying then.'

'Not really. The doctor just wanted to rule it out.'

Beth felt awful for telling the lie and was glad when Nicola changed the subject.

'Eh up, here we go.'

Her eyes flashed to the top of the room where Mr Worthing had placed himself and was now calling for everyone's attention. Once the room had quietened down, he started speaking.

'Welcome everyone and thanks for attending. We're here to celebrate Christmas and the end of a successful year for the company despite the challenges. But, not only that, we're here for another reason.' He paused for dramatic effect then seemed to gather himself. 'We're here to celebrate the retirement of Mrs Anita Bain who has given twenty-seven loyal years of service to the company, fifteen years of that time as my personal assistant. I for one...'

As he outlined Anita's career with the company, Beth's mind drifted. She was thinking about her own imminent news, which she was at pains to protect until the time was right to announce it.

Mr Worthing's speech finally drew to an end and Beth, along with the rest of the staff, watched avidly as Anita was given a beautiful bouquet of flowers and a Lladro figurine, which she was known to collect.

Anita became emotional as she thanked him and the rest of the management team, and Mr Worthing gave her a moment to gather herself together. Then he continued. 'It is with Anita's blessing that I am about to make another announcement. I have already decided who is going to replace Anita and I am pleased to say that that person is Beth Harris.'

The words were out before Beth had a chance to take them in, and as he rambled on about what a suitable replacement she would be, Beth felt the eyes of the staff on her. But those of one person in particular were cold with resentment, and as she looked across at Nicola, she could see her friend wasn't happy at all.

Beth awoke in the middle of the night drenched in sweat, her heart thudding in her chest. It was that same nightmare again. As she came to, she willed her shaking limbs to steady, telling herself it was just a dream. It was all in the past now. He couldn't hurt her anymore.

She tried to stay quiet and checked the time on the bedside clock. It was 4.50 a.m., and Beth realised it was now Christmas day. She peered across at Brady, not wishing to wake him up. But it was too late. 'What is it?' he asked. 'Is it the nightmare again?'

Beth nodded sadly and Brady turned towards her, wiping the sleep from his eyes.

'For God's sake, Beth! You really should see someone about these nightmares, y'know. It can't be good for the baby, not to mention the effect it must be having on you... well... on both of us for that matter. It gave me a right fright waking up to see you staring at me like that.'

She didn't say anything, but her mind drifted back to the party, and she wondered if it was the upset that had provoked the nightmare. After Mr Worthing's announcement, Nicola had quizzed her as to whether she knew about it. Beth admitted that although she hadn't known Mr Worthing would announce it that day, she had known about the promotion for a while but had been asked to keep it quiet.

Once she had gleaned the facts from her, Nicola turned away, leaving with a dig about her being the person who had taught Beth everything. Then she'd gone to talk to a group of staff standing in a huddle. Beth had looked around only to notice other staff also turning away. They were the people who had overheard Nicola's comments or had picked up on her ill feeling.

For a few minutes Beth had wandered around the room, exchanging brief pleasantries with people from other departments or accepting their congratulations. But none of them engaged with her for long, so eventually she slipped away unnoticed and headed for home. There had been a devastating change in her friendship with Nicola, and she wondered whether it had been worth it for the sake of a few months' promotion.

'Well?' Brady asked irritably, snatching her away from

her thoughts. 'Are you going to see a doctor about your nightmares?'

Beth nodded again. 'We'll see.'

Satisfied, he turned away from her, not bothering to wish her a happy Christmas, and pulled the duvet up over his shoulders. But Beth knew she wouldn't concede to his wishes. How could she? Because if she did then she'd have to explain the nightmares, and the whole sorry truth might come spilling out. And she couldn't handle that, especially now she was about to start a family. She had to hold things together for the sake of the baby.

12

Martin hated the Christmas period. Apart from reminding him how alone he was, it was a time when chaos erupted. At that time of year, Virtuoso was always full of pissheads who couldn't hold their drink, and he was usually short-staffed as bouncers and barmaids called in sick at the last minute because they'd had too much booze the night before.

He therefore liked to make sure he was around in Virtuoso at that time of year to handle any problems that might arise. His bars were a bit more civilised, but he kept his phone with him nevertheless, in case he got any calls that he needed to attend to.

Tonight, he was thankful that he hadn't heard from the staff at any of the other bars as he had his hands full with the club. He was so short of bouncers that he'd had to step in himself, and had already calmed down one heated situation and thrown a young lad out who was having trouble staying upright. Before he'd turfed him out into the street, he'd made sure he helped him call a cab.

Now as he looked across at a young couple, it appeared that trouble was about to erupt again. It was obviously a domestic, and at first he decided to leave them to it and see if it fizzled out. They were only young. She was a pretty, petite girl with a curtain of dark hair, and the boyfriend was of medium height with a slight build, but he had a nasty air about him.

When the girl began yelling obscenities at her partner, Lloyd, Martin decided it was time for him to step in. He hadn't quite reached the girl when her partner swiped her across the face with his bare knuckles. She screamed and clutched her mouth where the lad had caught her with his fist. Martin sped over, then squared up to the lad.

'Eh, there was no need for that.'

While he spoke, he took gentle hold of the girl's hand and pulled it away so he could examine her injuries. Martin was perturbed to find that her lip was already swelling, and it was evidently painful as she was struggling to contain her tears.

He had a flashback to another time, when he was just a kid. He'd stood rooted to the spot as his father yelled at his mother because she hadn't kept his tea warm while he'd been at the pub. When his father started laying into her with his heavy fists, Martin had fled up the stairs, petrified. Later that evening he noticed her split lip and black eye. But he'd kept his mouth shut, frightened that if he said something his father would turn his anger on him. Since then, he'd vowed to never let a man get away with hitting a woman.

'She fuckin' asked for it!' snarled Lloyd. 'She's always bending me fuckin' ear.'

Martin was becoming annoyed. His head shot forward till it was only centimetres from the lad's face and he hissed, 'No woman deserves to be hit by a fuckin' man, especially not by a little tosser like you!'

Martin was so angry by now that the tendons in his neck were taut. His eyes were protruding like fiery, hate-filled orbs and his breath was coming in frenzied gasps. Lloyd stepped back in shock but still wasn't ready to back down.

'It's none of your fuckin' business anyway. You should keep out of it, you nosy old fucker!'

Martin snapped and grabbed Lloyd by his shirt collars, ready to throw him out of the club. His girlfriend now seemed less concerned with her throbbing jaw as she raised her hands in an attempt to push Martin off him.

'Leave him alone!' she squealed.

'Take care of her!' Martin shouted to Billy, who he could see approaching. 'Make sure she gets a taxi.'

Martin knew he could trust Billy to make sure she was out of the way while he dragged her boyfriend through to the alleyway. Normally, Billy would have been the one dishing out the pastings and Martin would have seen the girl safely on her way home. But he would handle this one himself. Not only had the little shit hit a woman, but he'd also shown no remorse, and on top of that, he had disrespected him.

As he hauled him towards the back entrance, Lloyd continued firing abuse at him. By the time they were outside, Martin's temper had calmed a little.

'Right, I'm gonna give you a chance,' he said. 'You're gonna apologise for disrespecting me or else you're gonna learn a lesson.'

'Oh yeah, hard man,' sneered Lloyd. 'And what lesson do you think you can teach me? You're a nobody, just a fuckin' thug.'

Martin could feel his fury rising again. 'You're gonna

learn what happens to wimpy little bastards like you who think it's OK to hit a woman.'

As he spoke, Martin's hand moved to the lad's throat, and he tightened his grip to emphasise his point. 'Right, are you gonna apologise for disrespecting me?' he asked, squeezing Lloyd's larynx till he heard choking sounds, then easing his grip again.

The look of panic in Lloyd's eyes gave Martin a feeling of satisfaction and he nodded as the lad tried to indicate his compliance by shaking his head up and down. Martin took his hand away but still kept a rough hold of Lloyd's arm while he waited for him to speak.

'OK, I'm sorry,' he babbled.

'Right, that's a start. Now I want you to apologise for hitting your girlfriend.'

'Yeah, yeah, I'm sorry. I shouldn't have hit Jodi, but she was pissing me off.'

'A man should never hit a woman, no matter what she says or does and no matter how much he's had to drink.'

Panic was still in Lloyd's expression as he gushed, 'OK, I know.'

'Good. I hope you fuckin' do. And I hope you'll make sure that it never happens again.'

'I will.'

But his response had come too quickly for Martin, who knew Lloyd was just complying so that he could get away from him. As far as he was concerned, it wasn't good enough. He wanted to scare the crap out of the lad so that he'd think twice next time he was about to lift his hand to a woman.

'Right, now say after me, "I promise I'll never hit a woman again."'

'I've told you, I've fuckin' told you I won't. What d'you want from me, you fuckin' weirdo.'

Martin retaliated to the insult with a swift smack to Lloyd's jaw, then his hand was up at his throat again. 'I said, say after me, "I promise I'll never hit a woman again."'

'Alright,' Lloyd gurgled till Martin released his hand and the youth repeated his words.

Martin nodded. 'OK, now I might let you go.'

Lloyd looked as though he was about to break away, so Martin grabbed him quick. 'Not so fast. You've not learnt your lesson yet. I want to make sure it's one you'll never fuckin' forget.'

He laid into Lloyd with a series of practised punches, just enough to drive his message home but not sufficient to cause him any real damage. Then he stood back. 'Right, *now* you can go.'

The youth straightened up painfully and started to make his way up the back alleyway. Feeling that he had finally got through to him, Martin turned to make his way back into the club, and it was as he turned that he heard Lloyd curse, 'Fuckin' old cunt.'

Martin felt a rush of anger and shot after Lloyd then pinned him up against the wall. 'Right, you little bastard! I told you not to disrespect me. Now you're really gonna fuckin' learn your lesson.'

13

Beth was lying in bed, still awake, while Brady slept beside her. It was the Wednesday between Christmas and New Year, and she was glad she had taken a break from work because her sickness had persisted. If it hadn't been for that, she would have had a really enjoyable time.

They had been to visit her parents on Christmas Day and Brady's family on Boxing Day. Christmas dinner had been a struggle with her sickness; fortunately her parents had been understanding, although concerned. Boxing Day had been a running buffet, so it was easier to disguise how much she had eaten without attracting comments.

Brady also helped to make Christmas special, buying her a beautiful, silver-plated jewellery box and a designer makeup palette. Then, in a separate present addressed to *The Bump*, he had given her a set of unisex Babygros.

They hadn't made plans for New Year other than to stay in and watch TV. She was due back at work the following Monday. As she thought about work, she couldn't help but dwell on Nicola's reaction on hearing the news of her promotion. It felt so awful to have people turn against her, and Beth hoped that by the time they returned to work Nicola might have come to accept things. But there was still the pregnancy to announce, and she had a feeling that things were about to get worse rather than better.

Once he had let loose on Lloyd, Martin found it very hard to calm down. The lad's wanton disregard of the opposite sex, teamed with his cocky attitude and general disrespect, had really got Martin's back up. He punched him repeatedly, his large fists causing Lloyd's flesh to swell and his nose to explode like a burst pipe, the blood flooding from him. Lloyd was no longer disrespecting Martin. Instead, he was screaming and begging him to stop.

When it became obvious to Lloyd that Martin wasn't about to stop, he bent his head forward, trying to protect his face from further damage. Martin carried on regardless, his punches now landing on the top of the youth's head, till he changed tack, combining uppercuts with body blows. But Lloyd was no longer yelling in pain as a savage blow to the back of his head had knocked him unconscious.

Realising that he was now wasting his efforts, Martin stood back to regain his breath and the youth tumbled to the ground. 'Dirty piece of fuckin' scum!' Martin cursed, even though Lloyd wouldn't hear him.

Billy then walked through the back door and into the alleyway, a grin breaking out on his face. 'You done with him then? I've packed the girl off into a taxi. Silly bitch was yelling to get back into the club to see him, but I told her there was no chance.'

Martin responded with a scowl. 'Yeah, it's time the little fucker was on his way too.' He grabbed Lloyd's shoulder and shook it but there was no response. 'Get us some water, will you, Billy? And make sure there's plenty of it. Let's give the little shit a good soaking then he'll come round.'

Billy was soon back in the alleyway carrying a pail of water. A quick nod of the head from Martin and he launched it over Lloyd, drenching him. Billy grinned in amusement as Martin watched the spectacle, but there was no response from Lloyd.

He shook the lad's shoulder again and flashed a look of concern at Billy, whose grin had been replaced by a grimace. But Lloyd still didn't react. Panic was now setting in and Martin shook him repeatedly, trying to get a reaction.

'Boss, boss, leave it!' said Billy.

He grasped Martin by the shirt sleeve and gently pulled him away. Then, without speaking, Billy walked over and took Lloyd's pulse. Martin couldn't tear his eyes away as Billy's fingers moved from the youth's wrist to his throat, before kneeling on the ground and putting his head to his chest. Suddenly Martin felt the chill of the night, and he shivered as a feeling of dread shook him.

'For fuck's sake, is he breathing?' he asked.

Billy stood up and shook his head. 'No, boss. He's gone.'

'Shit!' said Martin, covering his face in his hands.

He couldn't believe it. He'd been in plenty of fights in his life, but he'd never killed anyone before. As the enormity of it hit him, he yelled, 'Shut the fuckin' door. I don't want anyone coming out here and seeing him.'

Billy did as ordered, then came back to stand by Martin's side. 'What now?' he asked, and Martin couldn't help but notice his calm demeanour.

How could he be so composed at a time like this? But

then, he thought, Billy wasn't the one who had just killed someone.

Martin was trembling, his voice was shaking as he replied to Billy, 'We'll have to get rid of him. Will you help me?'

He had always trusted Billy's loyalty in the past and saw no reason to doubt it now. But then Billy said, 'You're asking me to cover it up?'

Martin nodded solemnly, then he noticed a big grin spread across Billy's face. 'Yeah, sure,' said Billy, 'But it'll cost. How about ten grand and I'll see to it that no one will ever trace him back to you?'

His words had the impact of a hammer blow. 'Are you fuckin' serious?' he asked.

Billy held up his hands. 'OK. Suit yourself. I'll leave you to it.'

He made to walk away but Martin stopped him, suddenly seized by panic. He couldn't think straight. His mind was clouded by what he had just done. He'd killed a guy! And the girlfriend had seen him march the lad out of the back of the club.

The police would be onto him in no time. What would he tell them? There was no way he would make them believe he was innocent. He was finished. And at his age he would probably spend the rest of his days in prison, or the best part of them anyway.

But here was Billy offering him a lifeline. 'What will you do?' he asked, his voice little more than a murmur.

'I've told you; I'll make sure no one traces it back to you. I've done it before.'

Martin wasn't surprised to hear that. He'd heard the rumours about Billy. In fact, he'd hired him based on the fact he could handle himself. But the way he was almost bragging about it made Martin feel sick to the stomach.

'Tell me if we have a deal then I'll give you the details,' Billy added.

Martin sighed. 'OK.'

Billy was the one in control now. 'Shake on it,' he ordered, and Martin offered his trembling palm.

As soon as they had shaken on the deal, Billy became animated. 'Right, for a kick-off, we need to make it look as though he's wandered off after he left the club. We can't afford to leave him there. It's too near to the club. We want the cops to assume he was jumped after he left here. I'll dump the body elsewhere. Then, when the cops call, we tell 'em we kicked him out, nothing more, but that the lad was pissed, and he staggered away. Oh, and we'll have to get some bleach down, clear away any traces of his blood.'

Martin hardly took in Billy's words as he detailed what they were going to do. He was still in shock, so he let Billy take the lead, putting his trust in him and hoping it would work out.

At Billy's suggestion, he returned to the club, leaving Billy to handle things. As the club's owner, people would notice more if he went missing for a while, Billy had said. Martin walked straight over to the bar and downed a double brandy to settle his nerves.

Eventually the fuzziness in his mind diminished and he began to see things more clearly. He was hit by the fact that he'd just been blackmailed, and he had willingly let it happen, too stunned to react otherwise. The thought angered him. There was no way Billy or anyone else would have got away with that under normal circumstances.

Billy had really shown his true colours tonight, and Martin had an uneasy feeling that it wouldn't be the last of it. Now he had got away with it once, chances were he'd do it again. It was evident to Martin that he was dealing with a very ruthless man.

14

Beth wasn't in the best frame of mind when she returned to work that Monday. The sickness had persisted all through the Christmas break and into New Year. Added to that were her feelings about facing Nicola since the announcement of her promotion; she hoped she had come round to the idea. Beth had tried telling herself that she got the job on her own merits and therefore deserved it no matter what Nicola thought, but it didn't alter the fact that her promotion may have tarnished their friendship.

One look at Nicola's face told Beth nothing had changed. When Beth bid her good morning, she deliberately turned and faced the other way. To make matters worse, the other staff gave her a lukewarm reception.

Trying to ignore their reactions, Beth went straight in to see Mr Ballantyne. There was no point delaying her news any longer.

'Aah, Beth. Welcome back. I hope you had a lovely Christmas.'

'Yes thanks, you too.'

'Yes, yes, very nice thank you. Mr Worthing would like you to start as soon as possible now Anita has left, so it's just a matter of moving your things over to your new desk.'

Beth decided to cut in before he went any further. 'I erm… I've got something to tell you,' she said.

Mr Ballantyne said jovially, 'You've decided to turn down the promotion because you couldn't bear to leave my employment?'

Beth obliged him with a giggle then said, 'No, it's something else. I'm pregnant.'

Mr Ballantyne's eyes and mouth grew wide in surprise, but he quickly righted himself. 'Oh, I see. Well, I suppose congratulations are in order.'

She managed a weak smile. 'Thank you.'

'You're welcome.' He was pensive for a few moments before saying, 'Do you mind if I ask how many weeks you are?'

'Fifteen,' said Beth.

'Aah, right. So you were expecting before you started work at Vixus?'

'Yes, but I didn't know.'

'OK, well, do you realise that means you won't qualify for SMP?'

'Yes, I do.' Beth had already gone through all the dates with Brady.

'I don't suppose you've any idea when you'll be finishing for maternity leave?' added Mr Ballantyne.

Beth knew exactly when she would be leaving, as Brady had sat and worked it out with her, so she gave Mr Ballantyne the date of 15 May.

'I see, well, that means you'll only be with us another four months. Mr Worthing will need to be informed. He'll have to find a replacement, at least to cover your maternity leave, depending on whether you decide to return or not.'

Beth gave a pained expression. She was feeling guilty for her decision to announce her pregnancy after she got the promotion, although it was good that Mr Ballantyne was open to her returning to Vixus after she'd had the baby.

'It's fine,' said Mr Ballantyne. 'I can let him know. We'll sort something out, don't worry.'

Unfortunately for Beth, not everybody was as receptive to her news as Mr Ballantyne. Expecting a backlash, she decided to get it out of the way as soon as possible, starting with Nicola. Beth walked over to Nicola's desk and after standing there a few seconds Nicola turned round to face her.

'I've got something to tell you,' said Beth.

Nicola sniffed, disinterested. 'What?'

'I'm pregnant.'

Nicola's head flew back as though somebody had just slapped her. 'You what?' she asked, her mouth agape.

'I said I'm pregnant.'

There were no congratulations from Nicola. Instead, she asked, 'How far gone are you?'

'Fifteen weeks.'

Beth could see her doing mental calculations. 'You knew!' she said accusingly. 'You knew when you took that promotion.'

'Well, erm…'

Nicola didn't give Beth a chance to continue, 'No wonder you weren't fuckin' drinking at the office bash. When you told me you were ill, you weren't ill at all, you were fuckin' pregnant all along. And you accepted that promotion, the promotion I should have got, knowing full well you were pregnant.'

Beth tried to speak again, but Nicola wasn't finished with her yet. 'Don't even bother trying to deny it,' she snarled, 'because I don't trust a word that comes out of your mouth from now on.' Then, after a brief pause, she asked, 'Will you be leaving?'

'Yes, I think so.' Trying to placate her, Beth added, 'You'll probably get the job once I've gone.'

'Even if I do get it, it won't make up for the humiliation of everyone knowing you were picked first.'

'I'm sorry, Nicola.'

'So you should be. Now go away, and leave me alone.'

When Beth returned to her desk, she felt awkward. She'd seen the rest of the secretaries watch her walk back from her confrontation with Nicola, knowing they'd witnessed every word of it. The atmosphere in the office was terrible for the rest of that morning. Every time she glanced over, Nicola looked away, until finally lunchtime arrived.

Beth hoped Nicola may have calmed down by now. If she had a chat with her over the lunch break, then maybe she could get her to see reason. But before Beth had the chance to see whether Nicola wanted to go to lunch, she saw her leave with two of the other staff; the finance secretary who Nicola had never liked and the secretary to the head of underwriting. It was obvious to Beth that this had been pre-arranged, maybe even before Nicola found out about the pregnancy.

The atmosphere didn't improve for the rest of that week, and every time Beth arrived at the office, she had a feeling the other girls had been talking about her. It was making her feel unhappy to such an extent that she decided she would be glad when her maternity leave finally arrived.

***

Martin had hardly slept for over a week. He had kept replaying the scene outside Virtuoso in his head, full of regret and wondering if he could have handled things differently.

True to his word, Billy had sorted everything. It was the following morning when the police arrived at Martin's home telling him a body had been discovered a few streets away from the nightclub. They had been given his name, as he was seen dragging the lad out the back door.

Martin managed to stay calm while he told them that he'd left the lad staggering up the alleyway at the back of Virtuoso and that was as much as he knew. He'd also denied hitting him and only admitted to dragging him out of the club. Martin hoped Billy had done a good enough clean-up job to corroborate what he had said.

Luckily, Billy had backed him up when questioned. Martin knew the police had found the lad with his wallet missing, because Billy had deliberately taken it away to make it look like a mugging. The fact that the police hadn't been back to see Martin in the past week told him they bought his story – thank God!

He should have been thankful for that. He should have been relieved. But he wasn't. What had happened that night had made him question everything and the guilt was eating away at him. He'd already been feeling dissatisfied with his lot. It wasn't the life he would have chosen for himself; it seemed as though it was the life that had chosen him.

Martin had many regrets looking back. In the early days he'd started out with a protection racket. Times were hard when he left school. There weren't many jobs for a youngster like him with no qualifications. But he had always been a well-built lad and a fighter. In the area where he had grown up, he'd learnt to stick up for himself and had been a bit of a young tearaway into shoplifting, car theft and other petty crime like a lot of his mates.

A mate of his dad's down the pub had seen his potential, and when he offered him a job collecting protection for his firm, Martin had jumped at the chance. It didn't take much doing; most of the businesses under protection paid him the cash without him having to get physical.

As a young man with cash in his pockets, he thought he was the dog's bollocks. He'd been too naïve to realise that he was earning his living by heaping misery on hardworking pub landlords and shop owners. Things progressed from there until he was running the protection racket himself and investing in his own bars and clubs.

Nowadays, he had given up the protection. But he still had his work cut out making sure that his own businesses didn't fall foul of other rackets. He supposed he could have chosen a different line of business. But this was in his blood. Protection rackets, bars and clubs; they were all he'd ever known.

Despite how he felt, he had to put on a tough front. It didn't pay to be otherwise; there was always someone ready to take advantage like Billy had done last week. He hadn't seen Billy since the night after the incident when he'd popped into the club again to pay him the £10,000 in cash. Since then, Martin had kept away from Virtuoso. But, telling himself he couldn't stay away forever, he was now back.

As soon as he saw Billy with a broad grin across his face, a cold chill ran through him. But Martin plastered on a smile and patted him cordially on the back.

'Everything alright?' he asked.

'Sound, boss,' said Billy.

Martin saw that he was sporting a large, gold sovereign ring. A ring that he hadn't worn last week. He was sickened by the thought that his hush money had paid for it, and he could feel his temper rising.

Martin knew this wasn't finished. He had now learnt the kind of man Billy really was. Billy hadn't been shadowing him because he was fiercely loyal and wanted to protect him: he had been doing so because he wanted to find something he could use to his advantage. And now he had found it.

It was ironic to think that Martin's head bouncer, Skippy, had Billy sussed long ago, telling Martin the guy had a sly streak and he couldn't stand his constant bragging. But Martin hadn't taken Skippy seriously, thinking it was just a bit of petty rivalry between his staff. Now he knew differently, and he felt a fool.

Martin recalled Billy's face when he had handed over the cash; a smug grin had lit up his features as he thanked him insincerely and then commented, 'Pleasure doing business with you. We'll have to do it again.'

The fact that he could laugh at the death of a man was bad enough, but Martin had also seen the hidden threat in those words. As soon as the cash was spent, Billy would be back for more.

Now, as if reading his thoughts, Billy leant into Martin and said in a low voice, 'I need another five grand.'

'You what?' growled Martin, pulling away.

'You heard.'

'No, no chance. I can't raise that sort of money.'

'Come off it. A man like you with a fuckin' big nightclub and loads of bars.'

'I told you; it's not happening.'

Martin made to walk away but Billy stopped him with a hand on his forearm. 'Do you really want people to know what happened that night?'

'You won't, you'd be implicated as well.'

'Oh, I don't think so. All I need to do is tell the cops about how the lad was unconscious last time I saw him. Of course, I wanted to tend to him, but you ordered me to leave him there. I mean, everyone knows that what you say goes around here.'

Billy's voice then took on a pitiful tone, as though he was trying to ingratiate himself with the police, as he continued, 'Ever since I was told about how his body had been found somewhere else, I've been beating myself up wondering how that could have happened. And now I can't keep my mouth shut any longer. My conscience can't deal with it, you see.'

His convincing lies angered Martin, who hissed, 'Go fuck yourself. You're not getting another fuckin' penny.'

Then he wrenched Billy's hand away from his arm, slapped it down and sped away.

But, despite his show of resilience, Martin was shaken. What if Billy did dob him in to the police? After what he had seen of Billy's recent behaviour, he knew he was capable of it. And tonight confirmed that.

Martin had already spent countless sleepless nights churning things over in his mind and wondering what to do about Billy. And now he knew he would have to put a stop to him. He had finally reached a decision. And he knew how he would do it.

15

Beth had come home earlier than Brady that evening. He had an after-hours meeting to attend so she'd rushed ahead of him and prepared that evening's meal. When Brady arrived home, she took the shepherd's pie she had been keeping warm out of the oven. But one look at it sent her heading for the bathroom.

She emptied the entire contents of her stomach, and when she had finished retching, she looked up to see Brady standing at the bathroom door watching her. She felt embarrassed, having her husband see her looking like this and reeking of vomit, and she made her way to the sink to clean her face.

'This isn't good, Beth,' she heard him say. 'I honestly thought you would have been feeling better by now.'

The way he said it made her feel inadequate, as though he felt she was somehow at fault. 'I can't help it!' she snapped.

'I know,' he said, adopting a sympathetic tone, then draping his arm around her shoulders. 'I'm only thinking of you, babe. And that little chap in there.' With his other hand he pointed at her growing bump in case she was in any doubt as to who he was referring to.

Beth felt guilty for snapping at him, but she was fed up

with it. She was seventeen weeks pregnant and thought the sickness would have been over by this stage. But it was as bad as ever.

'I'm sorry,' she said. 'I didn't mean to take it out on you, but I hate all this sickness and I don't like you seeing me like that, all blotchy faced and full of vomit.'

'I'm concerned about you,' he said. Then, after a pause, he added, 'I tell you what, why don't you finish work early?'

'Really?' Beth asked.

'Yeah, why not? I mean, I've got my promotion now, so what difference will a couple of months make? Besides, you don't qualify for maternity pay so we're not missing out there, are we?'

Beth thought about the timescale. 'I'll have to give them a month's notice, which means I'll be twenty-one weeks by then. The sickness should have stopped.'

'Yeah, and it might not. It should have stopped by now really. But it's not only that, you look exhausted, if you don't mind me saying. And twenty-one weeks, well, it's not that long before you were due to finish anyway, is it?'

'I was going to finish at thirty-three weeks, so it's twelve weeks early.'

'So? Like I say, I've got my promotion. We can afford it.'

Beth thought about the atmosphere at work which had persisted ever since she'd returned after the Christmas break. It wasn't pleasant and neither was the sickness. The more she thought about it, the more she was warming to her husband's suggestion. She gazed at Brady and sighed. 'I'll think about it.'

★★★

Death was a frightening proposition. Martin had previously seen it as something to be avoided. Good men weren't killers. You could come over as menacing, push people around, even rough them up a bit. For him it had always been part of the job description. But you didn't kill them.

Then it had happened, and it made him realise that there was a tenuous line between life and death. One moment the lad was alright, and the next he was gone. The line Martin had been avoiding all this time had now been inadvertently crossed. He had done it once and he now realised that, if necessary, he could do it again.

He had been trailing Billy for a couple of weeks. He knew that he drove a battered, old red Toyota Yaris and parked on a patch of land about half a mile from the club then walked the rest of the way. It was clear to Martin that he probably did it to avoid paying the exorbitant parking fees in the city centre. Then, when the club was shut, Billy returned to the patch of land and got back in his car.

Martin had also tracked Billy to his home, a terraced house in Levenshulme. The area was built up and there was always plenty going on at the weekend, even in the dead of night: late parties, people being dropped off by taxis and one guy who regularly left home at four in the morning, probably to work the early shift.

After two weeks Martin had reached the conclusion that the best place to strike would be the barren patch of land. It was out of the way, in a part of the city with no pubs and clubs, just a few warehouses, abandoned buildings and wholesale businesses that only opened in the daytime. And there was no CCTV.

Now was the time. Martin had been putting it off. Even

though he'd resigned himself to being a killer, the thought of doing it again was still daunting. But tonight, Billy had threatened him again and demanded the other five grand. And that had made Martin's mind up for him because he didn't want the word to get out about what really happened that night.

Martin left work before Billy. Exercising caution, he wore a cap and made sure he kept his head down. Then he caught a taxi from a nearby rank and asked the driver to drop him off near where Billy's car was parked. He couldn't risk being seen on foot or having his car picked up on CCTV as it headed out of the city centre in the same direction that Billy walked every night after the club.

Once he was there, Martin did a quick check to make sure no one was around. He took some latex gloves out of his coat pocket and slipped them on. Then he approached the Toyota Yaris and broke in easily using a wire coat hanger, a trick he'd learnt during his misspent youth. Martin then snuggled into the footwell of the back passenger seats and waited for Billy to arrive.

It was cold in the Yaris and cramped in the footwell, so after waiting for ten minutes, Martin stretched out and sat on the back seat while he looked out of the windows for Billy's arrival. It was another five minutes before Martin saw him appear from behind an old factory wall.

Martin ducked down quickly and waited for Billy to get inside and put his keys in the ignition. As soon as he had Billy where he wanted him, Martin shot to his knees and held the gun to the back of his head.

'Don't move an inch or I'll blow your fuckin' head off,' said Martin.

Sensing Billy's fear as he sat rigid in his seat, Martin felt relieved now he was back in charge.

Recognising his voice, Billy asked, 'What the fuck's this about?'

Martin drew huge satisfaction from hearing the fear in his tone. 'I'll tell you what it's about. It's about you taking fuckin' liberties. As if the ten grand wasn't enough, you had to ask for more, didn't you?'

'Alright, alright. Forget the other five grand,' said Billy. 'You can't blame me for trying.

Despite Billy's fear, Martin could still sense his smugness and it angered him. He obviously thought he wouldn't pull the trigger. Did his reputation count for nothing? 'Don't fuckin' underestimate me!' he threatened.

'I wasn't, honest boss. OK, maybe I got a bit carried away. It was the lure of the cash. I promise it'll never happen again. Please, don't do anything you'll regret. We're in this together.'

'Dead right it won't happen again. Now get out of the fuckin' car!'

'You what?'

'You heard! Get out of the car.'

Martin could sense Billy's confusion now. He didn't know where he was going with this and there was no way he would tell him. Shadowing Billy's movements, Martin also slid out of the Toyota then pulled himself quickly to his feet and aimed the gun at Billy's back.

'Right, now walk!' he ordered.

Billy took a few unsteady paces then broke into a sprint. But Martin had pre-empted him. He wanted Billy to put some distance between them; he couldn't risk having his clothes stained by the spray of blood. But he was still close enough. Martin pointed the gun and took a shot, then another and another. On the second shot, Billy's back opened up like a crimson starburst, and he dropped to the ground.

Martin raced to the spot where he had fallen. Taking care not to contaminate himself with Billy's blood, he knelt down and took his pulse. Satisfied there was no life left in him, Martin took to his heels and dashed through the backstreets, away from the city with its cameras, making sure he kept his head low.

Once he was well out of the city, Martin hailed a cab to take him back to the club. Ten minutes later he snuck in through the back door of Virtuoso and made his way to the bar, the place now empty. Then he poured himself a double brandy to steady his nerves.

It was over. And now there was just the gun to deal with. He was glad he'd kept hold of it after he'd confiscated it from the cocky youth in The Amber Room a couple of months previously. He'd make sure he hid it somewhere nobody would ever think of looking for it.

Taking Billy out hadn't been pleasant and now he had two killings on his conscience. Shooting wasn't his style; it was the first time he'd done it and he felt sickened to the stomach but also relieved to have regained control. He knew that if he hadn't dealt with Billy, he would have held power over him, and he couldn't let that happen.

It hadn't been as bad as the first killing though. Death may have been a frightening proposition, but murder was easier the second time round.

16

It had been a little over a week since Beth finished work. Her boss, Mr Worthing, recognising that she wasn't at all well, hadn't insisted on her working a full month's notice. Instead, he agreed to release her after only two weeks, giving her enough time to hand over the reins to her replacement and show her what was what. That replacement happened to be Nicola.

On hearing that she would be leaving so soon due to ill health, Nicola had mellowed towards her. For two weeks they worked together amicably. Nicola even arranged a collection and made sure they gave Beth a good send-off with baby gifts and a get-together in the pub after work.

But, for Beth, the way she had been treated prior to that had soured her resignation. She'd played along, but secretly she yearned for the day of her departure to come round. And once it arrived, she felt truly happy as she said her goodbyes to people she had known for the past few months and prepared herself for this new phase in her life.

Ironically, during the last week at work her sickness eased, and for the past ten days she'd had no sickness whatsoever. It made a huge difference to her. For the first time she was able to enjoy her pregnancy and start making plans for the future with her little family.

Tonight, she would pull out all the stops and make a lovely meal for her and Brady complete with candles and wine; non-alcoholic for her. After being so considerate towards her in suggesting she finished work early, she felt he deserved a treat.

She'd been poring through her cookery books and decided on French cuisine: a starter of pâté, beef bourguignon for the main course and an apple and ginger tarte Tatin for dessert. She had already prepared the sweet and was feeling rather proud of herself as it had turned out well considering it was her first time.

Beth still had plenty of time left before she needed to start preparing the main course, so she pulled out the hoover ready to do a bit of housework first. She had finished the lounge and was just working her way round the kitchen when she spotted something on the floor.

She switched off the hoover and examined the item. It was a piece of apple. She tutted at herself; she must have dropped it while she was preparing the sweet. Beth bent to retrieve it, but as she did, she felt a pain in her stomach. She straightened quickly and took a deep breath, then held her stomach till the pain eased.

Dismissing it as just a twinge, she put the piece of apple in the bin then returned to her hoovering. But only a few seconds later she felt another pain. This time it was so sharp that it made her suck in her breath and both hands shot instinctively to her stomach.

But the pain didn't ease. In fact, it shot through her, and

she bent forward, clutching her stomach, her eyes misting with tears. Trying to take control, she took several deep breaths till the pain subsided a little, then she fled to her phone and dialled 999.

Brady was in a meeting when he got the call. He'd set his phone to vibrate but sneaked a peek at it and saw Beth's number flash up on the screen. He slid his phone back into his pocket intending to ring her back later. But then it vibrated again so he had another look. When Beth's name showed up for a second time, he became concerned. It wasn't like her to be so persistent.

When he looked up, he noticed several members of the team looking at him expectantly. Mr Dodds, in particular, didn't look so happy. 'Mr Harris, when you've finished checking your messages, perhaps you'd like me to repeat the question.'

'Oh, yeah. Sorry,' he muttered.

Mr Dodds then carried on speaking and Brady was just getting his head around the question when he felt his phone vibrate again. This time he knew there was something wrong.

'I'm so sorry. I need to get this,' he said, pulling his phone out and noting Beth's number on the screen for the third time. 'It's Beth and, well, in her condition...'

'Very well. Please don't take too long,' said Mr Dodds.

Outside in the corridor, Brady hit the call receive button. 'This had better be good, Beth. I've just had to leave a meeting to take this call.'

As soon as he heard Beth on the other end of the line, he knew she had been ringing him for good reason. Her breath was coming out in shallow gasps, and she spoke as though she was in pain and struggling to get her words out.

'I've rung an ambulance,' she said. 'They... ouch... aah... they've told me I need to go to hospital.'

'Why? What is it? What's wrong?'

'I don't know... aah... I just started getting pains... they're really bad.'

'OK, OK, don't wait for me. You go straight there in the ambulance. I'll meet you at the hospital. Oh, and don't let them take too long. Ring them back if they've not arrived in a couple of minutes.'

Without waiting for Beth to reply or giving any explanation to his boss, he cut the call and dashed from the office, ran across the road to the car park and then to his car. Then he raced out of the city centre in the direction of Stepping Hill hospital.

It was difficult for Brady to find a parking space when he arrived at Stepping Hill. Determined not to waste time circling round the car park, he parked up in a disabled bay and ran to the entrance. Then, searching frantically for the maternity ward, he zoomed through the corridors and straight to the ward until a nurse stopped him.

'Who are you here to see?' she asked.

'My wife, she's been rushed in,' Brady panted.

'What's her name?' asked the nurse.

Brady gave her Beth's name and she pointed to a waiting room. 'Can you wait here, please?'

'But, but, I need to be with her. She might be losing the baby.'

'I'll come back to you as soon as I find out what's happening,' said the nurse, and to Brady it seemed that her tone was patronising.

After five minutes when the nurse hadn't come back to him, Brady left the room in search of another nurse so he could find out what was happening. He came to an office where there was only one nurse sitting at a PC and leafing through paperwork. It wasn't the one who had led him to the waiting room. She was younger, but this one was middle-aged and weighty.

'Excuse me!' he said, but the nurse ignored him.

Becoming annoyed at her lack of response, he turned away from the office and carried on up the corridor. Sod them! If they weren't going to take him to Beth, then he would find her himself.

He was heading for a set of double doors when he heard someone call behind him. 'Excuse me! Where do you think you're going?'

Brady turned round to see the older nurse addressing him, and she didn't look very happy. He walked towards her. 'I'm looking for my wife. She was brought…'

'Wait a minute!' she snapped. 'What is your wife's name?'

Brady was now standing next to the nurse. He tutted. 'Beth Harris. I've already given it to another nurse. She was supposed to come back to me ten minutes ago and I'm still bloody waiting.'

'Now,' said the nurse, 'I've already been made aware that you're waiting. I'm sure you can see how busy the hospital is at the moment. We're short-staffed but we're doing everything we can. Now if you'd like to go back to the waiting room, I'll see what I can find out, and we'll come back to you.'

As she spoke, she put her arm around Brady's shoulders to guide him. He became angered by her patronising manner and shrugged her off. 'I'm quite capable of finding my way there myself, thank you. But I don't want to be sat there all day. I need to be with my wife. It's my right as her husband!'

'Yes, yes, I understand how you must be feeling. As I said, we're doing everything we can.'

'What the hell does that even mean? Has she lost the baby or what?'

The nurse pursed her lips and inhaled sharply through her nostrils. 'It's too early to say at the moment. Like I said, I'll come back to you as soon as I can.'

Another ten minutes and Brady was still sitting in the waiting room. He was becoming increasingly agitated. What the fuck was wrong with these nurses? He should be with Beth. It was his child too, for fuck's sake.

He left the room again in search of the staff, but this time the nurse's office was empty. For a moment he hovered, staring at the double doors at the end of the corridor. He was tempted to go through them. But then he remembered the nurse's gruff manner when she had told him not to. He couldn't risk it. What if they called security and had him chucked out?

So he returned to the waiting room and sat there, tapping his feet impatiently. The time dragged. He couldn't even look out of the window as there were none. There were a few magazines scattered on a table, but they were all women's ones, and he didn't want to be reading crap like that. He probably wouldn't be able to concentrate anyway.

Then Brady recalled how he had dashed out of the office without telling anyone where he was going. He took out his phone and fired off a text to work explaining that Beth had been rushed to hospital and he was still trying to find out how she was. Then he shuffled through social media until, eventually, the door opened, and the overweight nurse stepped inside.

He noticed straightaway that her features had softened and then she spoke, her voice calm. 'We're ready for you to see your wife now, Mr Harris.'

Brady shot up out of his seat. 'Where? Where is she?'

'I'll take you through,' said the nurse. 'But before we go, I need to warn you that it isn't good news, I'm afraid. Your wife lost the baby. She's very upset. I think she'll need your support.'

She looked at him for a reaction and he nodded sombrely at her unspoken question. Brady knew she was asking him not to kick off for Beth's sake. He tried to speak but no words came. The thoughts were whirling around inside his head. Beth had lost the baby. Their baby! And all the time he had been sat here in this fuckin' waiting room on his own.

When he reached Beth, she was sat up in bed, her face stained with tears. He dashed over and flung his arms around her. For a few moments they sobbed in each other's arms. Neither of them spoke but thoughts were still racing around inside Brady's head. Their baby was gone!

Beth wasn't to blame; he knew that and yet he felt anger among his sorrow. Anger at the hospital staff who had kept him away while all this was happening. Beth had lost his child. And all that was left for Brady was a strange sense of resentment.

17

It was Beth's fourth day back at home, and the only day since the miscarriage when she hadn't cried. The loss had hit her badly, especially since she had been so far on in the pregnancy. Feeling that it was about time she did something other than moping about the house, she took out the duster and began tackling her bedroom furniture. While she worked, she played some music, which was a mix of twenty-first-century tunes from Ed Sheeran, Sam Smith, Bruno Mars and others. It helped to take her mind off things.

When she finished in there, she went to one of the other bedrooms. Beth knew it was a bold move. This was the one they had chosen for the baby. They hadn't started decorating yet, but they'd had plans to do so in the next few weeks.

Although none of the furniture and furnishings had changed, Beth had planned it all out in her head. As she looked inside the room, she pictured the cot in the centre with a small wardrobe and chest of drawers against the wall, which was to have been decorated in a neutral paper featuring bunnies and other cuddly animals.

At the moment there was only some old furniture there and she saw no need to change it, not yet anyway. As she got carried away in her thoughts, something caught her eye. It was a carrier bag on top of the chest of drawers, which had been placed on its side, its contents slim and flat.

Beth couldn't remember putting it there and she crossed the room to see what it was. She picked up the bag and pulled out a present wrapped in Christmas wrapping paper, which had been opened along one edge and then the contents pushed back inside. She pulled it out and remembered what it was, once half of it was exposed. But she couldn't resist tearing it fully out of the wrapping paper and looking again.

She gasped when she saw the minute Babygros; a pack of four in assorted colours. Her mind switched back to Christmas day when Brady had passed it to her and watched in animation as she tore at the paper.

She wept, not only for the baby she had lost but for the change in her husband. Since she lost the baby, he had been distant. She had tried to be patient, knowing that he would be feeling the loss just as much as she was. And it *was* early days yet. Hopefully, they would soon get back to normal and try to get on with their lives. But she knew that until then they would both be grieving.

Later that day, Brady came home from work, but she no longer felt excited to see him because she knew he would be miserable, his presence a constant reminder of their loss. Unlike the first three nights after the miscarriage, she had cooked him a meal, but she'd opted for a spaghetti Bolognese because it was easy. She couldn't seem to find the heart to do anything anymore.

Seated at the table in the dining room, they ate in silence. He didn't discuss his day, and she didn't have a day to discuss now that she spent hers at home. Beth's parents had been round to see them after it happened but they both had busy jobs so they couldn't be with Beth all the time.

Once the meal was over, Brady pushed his plate away. Beth got up to shift it, but he stopped her. 'That can wait. I need to ask you something.' He paused a moment while Beth looked at him expectantly. Then he carried on. 'How long did the ambulance take to get here?'

Not this again, thought Beth. It was the third time they had been over the details and, although she was trying to be patient with him, it was becoming trying. 'I told you, I can't remember. I was in a lot of pain.'

'OK, so did you lose the baby here or at the hospital?'

Beth sighed and gave him his answer. He carried on asking all the questions he had already asked, then finished with the now familiar complaint about the nurses not letting him in to see her.

'It wouldn't have made any difference!' Beth finally snapped. 'I was already losing the baby by then and would you really have wanted to see me like that? You'd have probably felt even worse than you do now.'

'Well, apologies for caring!' he snapped back. 'Just 'cos you haven't got a clue what it feels like.'

His words hit Beth like a slap in the face. 'I haven't got a clue? Are you fuckin' serious? I was carrying our baby. I had to go through the pain of losing it, physical and emotional. And you're telling me I haven't got a clue?'

'Oh yes, I'm forgetting,' he sniped. 'You're the mother so that gives you all the rights to grief, doesn't it? But we both know I was the one who wanted this baby. You weren't even fuckin' interested till I brought you round to the idea.'

Beth couldn't believe what she was hearing. 'Just because I was undecided at first does not mean I loved our baby any less than you. Has it not occurred to you how emotionally attached I became to our child while I was carrying it?'

'Oh yeah, here you go again, playing the mummy card.'

He stood up and pushed his chair back then stormed off to the kitchen, leaving Beth in tears. Why couldn't he understand how she was grieving too? She had wanted this baby just as much as he had. Once she had come round to the idea, she was committed to it, and she had looked forward to having a family together.

As she thought about all their plans for decorating the nursery, how they had discussed the baby's sex, their favourite names and their aspirations for their child, her tears flowed. In the background she could hear Brady slamming around the kitchen, and she decided not to clear the dishes until he had finished.

She watched as he came back into the room carrying a wine glass and a full bottle of red. He walked straight past her, heading for the other door which led out of the dining room and into the hall en route to the lounge. Beth knew that, yet again, he would spend the evening drowning his sorrows. She noticed how he had only fetched one glass and tried not to let it bother her that he was shutting her out.

He had almost reached the door when he turned around and shot her a look of pure venom. 'By the way,' he snarled. 'I think it's about time you looked for a job. Now that you've lost the baby, there's no excuse to be lazing around at home. And there's no fuckin' way you're sponging off me!'

Then he was gone, leaving Beth dazed by his attitude. She couldn't believe the change in him since she'd lost the baby. She needed support with what she was going through, not condemnation. She should have been able to go to him for comfort. They could have helped each other.

But instead, he was holding it against her. And it hurt! Was this really the man she had married? A man so unfeeling that he couldn't see how much the loss of their baby had affected her. But, more than that, he was actually adding to her upset.

She decided to stay away from him for the rest of the evening. She would watch TV in bed instead. Then, when it was time for him to join her, they would dim the lights, turn their backs to each other and sleep as though alone like they had done every night since the miscarriage.

18

It was a few weeks later when Beth walked into the bedroom to find Brady sitting up reading a book. She groaned inwardly, disappointed that he wasn't already asleep. When Brady put his book down and looked up at her, she knew what he wanted, and she felt obliged to comply. Maybe it was a sign that the recent atmosphere between them was about to change.

She shuffled down under the duvet and Brady got straight on top, showering her with eager kisses. Then, after a perfunctory grope of her breasts, he got down to business. Beth wasn't ready for him, and it felt uncomfortable, but she gritted her teeth knowing it would be over soon.

It wasn't long before Brady gave a groan and Beth felt the stickiness on her legs as he withdrew. Then he turned over, wished her goodnight and switched off the bedside lamp.

Beth lay there weeping quietly for some time. Although things were much better between her and Brady than they were in the early weeks of her miscarriage, they still weren't back to how they had been before. But they were making progress, so she hoped that in time her husband would go back to his old self. She also prayed that the man she had married was the real him, and not this hostile, insensitive being that currently inhabited their home.

At least they were speaking now, and sometimes he even shared his day with her. For the first two weeks she hadn't been able to reach him at all. It was as though he had built a wall of ice around himself. Then the wall melted a little when they attended a concert with two of his friends. The concert had already been booked so Beth supposed he hadn't wanted to cancel.

After that, they went to dinner with one of Brady's clients, because Brady had said it was good for business. On both occasions it felt like he was putting on a happy act, then once they were on their own his mood would shift again.

But the worst part of his behaviour for Beth came at bedtime. At his suggestion they were trying for a baby again. Beth felt it was too soon, but she couldn't put up a convincing argument against his persuasion, so she had gone along with it. Things weren't the same in the bedroom. They no longer made love. Instead, Brady seemed to want it over with as soon as possible, his sole intention to impregnate her. And it was nights like tonight when Beth really felt let down.

They had arranged to go out the following evening, just the two of them to a few local pubs and bars. Beth took it as a positive sign that Brady might want to get things back on track between them. He was still moody a lot and she sensed a festering resentment towards her. She knew she needed to speak to him about it, but she had felt too nervous to broach the subject since his outburst a few weeks prior.

Now, though, she was determined to have it out with him. Tomorrow evening would be the ideal opportunity when they were out alone with nothing to distract them. And, if she were honest with herself, a few drinks would give her the courage, that and the fact that he wouldn't react so vehemently if they were in a public place.

Martin was sitting in his place at the end of the bar in The Amber Room. It was the place where he could be found most evenings although he didn't always drink. He liked to keep his wits about him.

Ever since that night two months ago when he shot Billy dead, he had become a different person. He was often morose, bordering on depression, although he did his best to hide it. Martin didn't want to do anything to arouse suspicion so he still visited Virtuoso occasionally, even though he could no longer stand the sight of the place.

The weeks since the killings had been difficult. Two killings connected to the same nightclub had been too much of a coincidence for the police who had visited him several times. But Martin didn't crack. He was made of stern stuff, and he got through each day by telling himself he had done what he had to do.

Every time his conscience pricked him, Martin shook it away. He couldn't afford to dwell. He had to get on with his life, such as it was. His existence seemed even more meaningless than before; he now felt that he was no more than a murdering thug who owned a few bars and a nightclub. Even the name of his club was a joke: Virtuoso. There was nothing virtuous about the place.

Martin wanted more. He wanted to be a good man, someone who was respected, not out of fear, but because of the good things he did. Maybe it was because of the young woman he had met a while back. She seemed so pure that it made him want to be a better person.

She hadn't been to The Amber Room since that night when she had been ill and he had looked after her. It had been so long ago, and yet he still thought about her. There was something about her that drew him in. Martin could tell there was a feisty female under that untainted veneer, and it intrigued him.

Beth and Brady made their way inside The Amber Room. They'd already done a tour of the other pubs and bars in Marple, and Brady had finally decided that they should finish up here.

When they walked in, Beth noticed Martin sitting at the end of the bar. She smiled weakly then looked away as a blush crept up her cheeks. She was glad Brady hadn't noticed, otherwise he would have been bound to ask questions, and she was relieved when they left the bar area and found a table in the centre of the room.

Beth still hadn't tackled Brady about his attitude towards her, but after a few drinks she was feeling more confident. She was just about to raise the subject when Brady asked, 'How's the job hunting going?'

Beth's eyes flickered shut for a moment. *Not this again, please!* For the past few weeks, Brady had been pestering her to go back to work, telling her they were going to need the extra income for when the baby came. It had occurred to her as strange that they hadn't needed additional income when she was pregnant, and yet now they did.

It seemed to Beth that Brady wanted everything. Even though he would like her to get pregnant again as soon as possible, he still wanted her to work in the meantime, even if it meant she would lose the job once her pregnancy came to light.

Despite her feelings, Beth had tried to find work. But her heart wasn't in it. She was so distraught over the loss of her baby and the change in her husband that she found it difficult to sell herself. The job applications became a chore, and in the two interviews she had managed to secure, she felt that her potential employers picked up on her lack of enthusiasm.

But she didn't tell Brady all this. Instead, she said, 'I'm trying. I'm sure something will come up eventually.'

'Huh, did you hear anything back from that company on Quay Street?'

'No, I think that one's dead in the water. I've still got a few others to try though.'

'Well, it looks like you'll have a busy week next week filling in applications, doesn't it?'

'Yes, I suppose so,' said Beth, sounding despondent.

'What's wrong?' he demanded.

Beth shrugged and took a giant slurp of the cocktail in front of her. 'Well, it's just... things haven't been the same between us, have they?'

He tutted. 'Here we go.'

She was taken aback by his attitude and wondered how to play this. She didn't want it to escalate into a row. 'Brady, I'm sorry, but we need to talk,' she said, taking another sip of her drink while she waited for him to respond.

When he didn't say anything, she returned to her cocktail

again. He waited for her to drain the glass then he grabbed hold of it. 'Bloody hell! You're going through the cocktails tonight, aren't you? Let me take that, I'll get you another one.'

'OK,' she said. 'And when you get back, we can talk.'

19

Martin was surprised to see Beth and her husband walk inside The Amber Room after staying away for so many weeks, especially when he'd just been thinking about her. His heart lifted at the sight of Beth, eyes following her as she and her husband walked to the bar. When he noticed her brief smile, Martin smiled back.

She looked troubled somehow, her beautiful facial features showing strain, and he wondered what had been happening in her life. He also took in the husband. He always had an air about him that told Martin he felt superior to the rest of the clientele. But tonight, there was something else. He seemed moody and full of attitude. It was in the way he strode cockily up to the bar, leaving Beth rushing to catch up with him, and in the way he spoke condescendingly to the bar staff.

Martin carried on observing the couple discreetly from his seat at the bar. Their body language was tense, and they were speaking in short sentences. There was no laughter, just sombre expressions. Martin also noticed how fast Beth was downing her drinks.

After the husband returned from the bar with their second drink, which Beth seemed to down just as quickly, they became deep in conversation. It seemed to be getting steadily more heated until the sound of the husband's raised voice reached Martin. Rather than argue back, Beth seemed to be pleading with him. Martin was tempted to go over to see what the problem was, but then they seemed to calm down again.

However, they both remained looking sullen after that and exchanged a few words until they finally got up and left. He noticed how Beth was staggering and grasping at her husband's arm to support her. There was definitely something amiss, and he couldn't help but feel concerned for the lovely young woman who seemed to have saddled herself with an utter tosser.

Beth struggled to keep up with Brady as he stomped out of the bar, and when she got outside and the night air hit her, she realised how drunk she was.

'Wait for me,' she slurred, grabbing at his arm to steady herself and almost tumbling over when he snatched it away.

'Look at you, you're a fuckin' disgrace!' he grumbled. 'Why can't you take a bit more time with your drinks instead of knocking them back like they're on fuckin' ration or something.'

Beth knew he was in a mood because she brought up the fact that he had changed towards her. This was confirmed when he said, 'Y'know, Beth, tonight was supposed to be about us. You wanted us to get back to normal and that's what I was trying to do, but all you've done is complain about how I am towards you. I'm doing my fuckin' best for

Christ's sake! It's gonna take me time to get over you losing the baby.'

Beth felt the sting of the accusation, but she wasn't giving up that easily. She wanted to address their problems, not just ignore them by backing down every time he came at her. Because of the alcohol she spoke louder than intended, 'I just wanted to talk about things and try to agree a way forward, that's all! We need to discuss what's wrong.'

'Why? Why the fuck do you need to analyse everything?'

Beth could feel her eyes becoming steamy, but she fought back the tears. 'Because I'm not happy, that's why,' she said, her lip quivering.

'Why? What the fuck have you got to be unhappy about? We've got a lovely home; you have anything you want even though you don't contribute towards any of it and then you have the cheek to–'

'The sex,' she cut in. 'It's not the same. You don't make love to me anymore. You're not interested in me, just in getting me pregnant.'

Brady stood back, his expression irate. She could tell he was shocked, and it took him a moment to respond, but when he did, he said. 'So you're criticising my performance in the bedroom now? Just how low do you want to fuckin' go, Beth?'

His face had taken on a hurt expression now, which made her feel bad for saying it. 'I'm sorry,' she sobbed. 'I didn't mean to. It's just that, I feel like I'm losing you. It's like you're not a part of me anymore, we're not like we used to be.'

Then she felt a surge of emotion which threatened to overwhelm her. 'I don't want to lose you, Brady. I love you.'

Her sobs grew louder and between tears she gasped, 'Why do I always lose those I love? I've already lost Rex and the baby, and now I might lose you.'

'For fuck's sake, Beth. You're not losing me. I think we need to get you home and get you sobered up. You're getting fuckin' maudlin.'

But Beth's drunken brain had already switched back to the night of the attack. It was always there, hovering in the back of her mind, and it didn't take much for it to emerge, drowning out every other thought like a tsunami of distressing memories.

'I need to tell you,' she sobbed. 'I need to tell you about the night that Rex died.'

'You've already told me. You found your dog dead,' he said without feeling.

'No, it wasn't just Rex,' she said. 'It was more than that.'

This last comment got his attention. Brady stopped and turned to her in the street, and as Beth thought about what she was about to say, she grabbed at his jacket lapels and clung onto him.

'I–I need to tell you,' she repeated. Then she took a sharp breath before continuing. 'When I found Rex, there was a man there. He was holding a knife with blood on it, Rex's blood.' She felt the tears gush again and paused for a moment to regain her composure.

Brady took hold of her by the shoulders and stood back, searching her features, his own expression one of shock. 'But you said Rex's death was unexplained. You said there was nobody there.'

'I lied. I couldn't tell you. But I need to now. I can't stand to keep it a secret anymore. That's what the nightmares are about, and I feel like they'll never go away until I come to terms with what happened.'

'Did the man attack you?' asked Brady, and she could hear the concern in his voice.

She held her hand up then, taking another deep breath, she began to tell him all that had happened on that fateful night.

20

Martin watched Beth stagger from the bar as she trailed after her husband. She looked really drunk, and given that and the husband's attitude towards her, it was apparent to Martin that there was something serious going on here. He couldn't resist going to the window to watch, but he hung back as he didn't want them to see him.

He heard someone approaching from behind and was so wired that he jumped. 'Everything alright, boss?' he heard, his doorman, Des ask.

Martin's head swivelled around to face him. 'Yeah, yeah, no problems. I'm just watching that couple there. The guy seemed a bit aggressive towards her when they were in here.'

'Eh, if he does anything outside The Amber Room, it's not our problem. I wouldn't get involved.'

Martin was quick to respond. 'You know me, Des. Do you really think I'd let a man raise his hand to a woman and just stand by and do nothing?'

Des nodded. 'OK, up to you.' Then he walked away.

Once he was gone, Martin resumed watching the couple through the window. He saw that Beth was now clinging to her husband by his lapels, but it didn't look as though she was doing it to steady herself. It seemed more like she was pleading with him the way she had been when they were inside the bar.

The husband pushed her away and took hold of her by the shoulders. He looked shocked and then furious, and Martin thought for a moment that he would hit her. He was prepared to go outside, but then the husband seemed to calm down as he listened to what she had to say.

She spoke for a long time and Martin saw that the husband was listening ardently now. As she spoke, she still appeared as though she was imploring him, and Martin wondered what she might have done that was so bad. Perhaps she had been unfaithful. He felt a sharp sense of disappointment at that thought, and it made him realise how much he wanted her.

Eventually she stopped talking. The husband didn't say much but when he did speak his body language told Martin that he was angry again. Martin was still tempted to go and have a word. He was worried about her, but he knew his feelings were personal rather than a normal reaction to some couple having a domestic, so he resisted the temptation. He also feared that if he stuck his nose in then it might make things worse for Beth.

Martin saw the husband step out into the street and flag a taxi down. Then they were gone, and Martin couldn't help but worry about what might face Beth when she got back home.

It was the morning after their night out and Beth woke up with a banging headache. She turned in bed, noticing that the space next to her, normally taken up by her husband, was now empty. Memories of the previous evening and her revelation came flooding back to her and she felt a rush of heat to her face. *Oh no!* she thought. *I can't believe I told him everything. As if things weren't already bad enough between us.*

She went downstairs and into the hall, then pushed the door to the living room. There was Brady, sprawled across the sofa watching a science documentary on the TV with a cup of coffee on the table in front of him.

'Hi,' she said. 'I wondered where you'd got to.'

He flicked his head back momentarily then turned straight back to the TV without speaking.

So that's how it's going to be? she thought, padding through to the kitchen in her slippers and dressing gown.

Beth grabbed a couple of paracetamols from the cupboard and downed them with a glass of water. Then she made herself a cup of coffee and went to join Brady in the lounge. Again, he barely acknowledged her presence.

'Brady,' she called to get his attention.

He turned and looked into her beseeching eyes, then tutted and pressed the pause button on the remote control. 'What?'

'About last night.' He tutted again but, undeterred, Beth carried on. 'Can we put it behind us, please?'

Brady tutted again then shook his head. 'I don't know. I don't know what to think. It hasn't all sunk in yet. I need time to come to terms with it all.'

Then he turned back to the TV and pressed the restart button on the remote control. It was obvious to Beth that he had been doing a great deal of thinking, he just wasn't ready to share his thoughts with her.

For a few minutes she sat in uncomfortable silence, trying to feign interest in the programme Brady was watching. But then she got fed up with being ignored so she stood up, hoping Brady would at least look at her. He didn't, so she went back to bed, taking her coffee with her.

She wished to God she hadn't told him anything the previous night. Somehow, she knew that this wasn't something he would get over in a hurry. It didn't seem fair that he should hold it against her, but he was. Maybe given time he'd come to terms with things as she'd had to do. And surely if he loved her enough, he would find a way to deal with it.

But deep inside, Beth didn't really believe that. It was obvious to her from the way he was behaving that there had been a drastic change in their relationship. Things were even worse than before, and she didn't know if they could recover.

21

When Beth walked inside the Vixus offices, she felt trepidatious. She hadn't wanted to come here but felt it was something she had to do. Her low self-esteem hadn't improved, and every time she got a knockback from potential employers it rocked her confidence even more.

The way Brady was acting towards her hadn't helped matters either. Ever since the revelation over a week ago he'd hardly spoken to her. Conversations were kept short and revolved around domestic arrangements with no mention of how his day had been. The only time he'd ventured onto other subjects had been to ask her how the job hunting was going.

Eventually Beth had decided to visit Vixus. At least the senior managers already knew her, so perhaps she would have a better chance of securing work there. And although she was embarrassed at having to go to them cap in hand, she felt compelled to do so. Perhaps if she managed to get work, she could regain Brady's respect and things would be alright with them again.

Beth didn't see anybody on her way up to the top floor. When the lift pinged, she felt an attack of nerves. Stepping out of the lift, she squared her shoulders, held her head high and took a deep breath. Then she walked through the double doors into the office.

Nicola was the first person to spot her. Her expression was one of confusion, which intensified when she eyed Beth's flat stomach. 'Oh, hi Beth,' she said. 'What brings you here?'

Beth gazed around at the other staff who watched eagerly, awaiting her reaction. 'Oh, I'm here to see Mr Ballantyne,' she said. 'I'll chat to you later.'

She had no intentions of telling them anything yet. None of the staff had stayed in touch with her since she left Vixus, so they weren't aware that she had lost the baby, although they had probably guessed as much by now. Ignoring their curious glances, she walked straight through to Mr Ballantyne's office then stopped and knocked on the door.

When Mr Ballantyne invited her inside, she found him much more welcoming than Nicola had been. 'Oh hello, Beth,' he said. 'To what do we owe the pleasure?'

As Beth struggled to find her words, he urged her to take a seat. Then he smiled across the desk at her, giving her the encouragement she needed, and she plonked her handbag down on the floor as she began to speak. 'I erm... you've probably noticed that I'm no longer pregnant.'

'No, I didn't, actually. Oh Beth, I'm so sorry.'

She didn't want his sympathy. It would only make her feel upset and she wanted to hold it together. So Beth cut in quickly. 'I'm hoping you can help me. You see, now that I'm no longer expecting, I need to return to work. And, well, I was wondering if perhaps I could get my old job back with you.'

She'd thought about things before she came here,

knowing that she couldn't expect the job as Mr Worthing's PA. That position had already been filled by Nicola. But maybe if she could get her old job back, then Nicola would be alright with her now that she had gained the senior role.

'Beth, I'm so sorry,' he said. 'But I'm afraid we've already found a replacement. You probably passed her on the way in, actually.'

Beth hadn't noticed; she'd been too preoccupied with getting this meeting over with. 'Are there any other positions available?' she asked. 'What about Nicola's old job?'

'I'm afraid we've found a replacement for that post too. Her appointment letter should be going out any time.'

'Oh,' was the only word Beth could muster as disappointment set in.

'I'm sorry,' Mr Ballantyne repeated. 'If I could help you I would but, like I say, all the positions have been filled. I'm sure someone with your experience will have no problems finding work elsewhere though, and I'll certainly bear you in mind if any other positions become available.'

'OK, thanks,' Beth muttered, picking her bag up and walking from his office with her head bowed low.

She didn't stop to talk to anybody. She was feeling too dejected and couldn't bear the pain of having to explain everything to them. All she wanted now was to get out of there.

Beth knew Mr Ballantyne could have given her a job if he'd really wanted to. He could have stopped the appointment letter for Nicola's replacement from going out and its intended recipient wouldn't have been any the wiser. But he hadn't, and to Beth it was apparent why. Because he didn't see the point in giving the job to her when there was a chance she would soon fall pregnant and leave again.

If only she could have shared the reality with him. There wasn't much chance of her getting pregnant again because, since the night of her confession, Brady no longer came near her. He could barely stand the sight of her now, never mind make love to her. And the way things were going she couldn't see any hope of things getting better any time soon.

That afternoon, Beth deliberated over whether to tell Brady about her visit to Vixus. It would have been lovely to have got a job and been able to share the good news with him. Perhaps they could have popped open a bottle of wine to celebrate.

But she hadn't got a job, and the more she thought about it, the more deflated she became. In the end, she decided she would tell him in the hope that it would at least prove she was making the effort. She felt bad that he was the only one working and would have loved to have taken some of the financial pressure off him.

When he came into the kitchen, she was already cooking their evening meal. He walked over to the pan on the hob, lifted the lid, sniffed and then replaced it.

'Chicken curry,' she announced. 'I hope you'll like it. 'Would you like a drink while you're waiting for it to cook?'

'No, it's fine. I'll have a drink with my dinner.'

He was about to walk out of the kitchen again when Beth called after him. 'You'll never guess where I've been today?' When he didn't reply, she added, 'Vixus. I went to see Mr Ballantyne to see if I could get my old job back.'

This pricked his interest. 'And?' he asked.

'No go. Unfortunately they've already found another replacement. Oh, but he did say he'd let me know if anything else cropped up,' she added, trying to sound positive.

'It doesn't surprise me,' he snapped.

'What? What doesn't surprise you?'

'That you didn't get the job.'

'What do you mean?'

'Well, look at you? You've become slovenly, lounging around all day in your tracksuit. He probably picked up the negative vibes from you.'

Something in Beth snapped. She'd had enough. After she had humiliated herself, practically begging for her old job just to please him, this is what she got in return.

'Do you really think I enjoyed having to go there and grovel?' she asked.

'Probably not, seeing as how you don't seem to want to work anymore.'

'That's not true, and you know it!' she raged. 'It seems like you can't wait to see me back at work even though you know everything I've been through. You're such a callous bastard and I'm sick to death of your attitude! Stop treating me like I'm diseased or something. The way you are towards me, I feel as though we might as well not even be together.'

'Well, if that's the way you feel then you know where the door is,' he said, so casually that it angered her even more. Then he added, 'To tell you the truth, after what you told me a couple of weeks ago, I'm not sure I want to stay with someone like you. What you did was bad enough, but I can't believe that you kept it from me all that time. You actually thought you could get away with it! Anyway, now that you've lost the baby, you're no longer any use to me.'

Beth was stunned by his remarks. She couldn't believe how much he had changed in such a small space of time. How could he be so cruel? He knew she was reliant on him. Without a job, how could she possibly support herself? His comments had left her speechless, and she watched with glazed eyes as he walked out of the kitchen, his harsh words still echoing in her ears.

For the rest of that evening they didn't speak to each other. Beth was too upset to continue the row and Brady had resorted to his recent pattern of behaviour. When it was time for him to go to bed, he got up from the sofa and went straight upstairs without saying goodnight.

Beth followed shortly after but was perturbed to find that Brady wasn't in the bedroom. He had chosen to sleep in the spare room. She changed into her nightwear then flung herself on the bed and cried into her pillow.

The following morning, Beth could hear movement in the house. She looked at the clock and saw that it was still only six. Perhaps, like her, Brady hadn't been able to sleep. She got up to use the bathroom, and while she was there, she heard Brady come up the stairs. His footsteps faded and she wondered if he had gone into their bedroom for his work clothes.

Beth hoped that he might have had a change of heart since last night, so she went back into the bedroom. She was shocked to find him stuffing clothes into a suitcase.

'What are you doing?' she asked.

'Isn't it obvious? I knew *you* wouldn't leave so I'm saving you the fuckin' bother. I'm going instead.'

Beth stared at him open-mouthed. She didn't know what to say. What could she say? It seemed like nothing she said or did would put things right. She'd lost his respect and there was no getting it back.

Eventually she found her voice. 'You don't need to go. Surely we can work things out. I mean, after all that we had together, surely you're not going to let all that go because of something that happened in my past.'

'Don't try emotional blackmail with me, Beth, because it won't work. You're not the person I thought you were. I've made my mind up and that's that.' As he spoke, he continued removing clothes from hangers and folding them neatly into the suitcase. Then he added, 'I need some space from you so I'm going to stay with a friend to mull things over.'

Then he zipped the suitcase closed, lifted it off the bed and pushed past her. Still in a state of shock, Beth sunk onto the bed and let the tears flow freely as she heard him dash down the stairs then fiddle with the front door catch. The last thing she heard was the sound of the front door slamming as he left their marital home.

22

Before Beth came into The Amber Room just over two weeks ago, it had been more than three months since Martin had seen her. He had thought that she was out of his system, but perhaps it was just because he had had so many other things on his mind. One look at her as she walked into his bar had told him that he was far from being over her, and he hadn't stopped thinking about her since.

She was still as stunning as ever, with her beautiful, youthful features and that classiness that emanated from her. But something had changed. She was tense all night and the husband was obviously angry with her over something. Martin wondered again what had happened.

It seemed that something drastic had taken place between the couple. Maybe it was just a one-off, but Martin didn't think so. It was evident in their body language towards each other. The husband still had his cocky strut, but he also seemed angry and just as tense as Beth.

Martin wished he knew what was going on, wished he could do something to help her. But really, he hardly knew her. And even if he were to do something, how would he find her? Apart from knowing that she was called Beth, he knew very little else about her. All he could do was hope that she was OK.

Then it occurred to him that while he had been thinking about Beth this past week it had at least diverted him from his own concerns. He would never forget the two murders he had committed but at least with time he was thinking about them less and less. And he hoped that eventually he could put them behind him.

A week after Brady walked out, Beth was sitting home alone when she heard the key in the lock. Immediately her senses were on high alert, her heart pounding like a drum roll. It was Brady. He was back. Maybe he had finally come to terms with what had happened that day in the woods. Maybe he had accepted that none of it was her fault.

She heard his footsteps in the hall and tried to gauge his frame of mind. But the heavy tread gave nothing away. Then he came into the lounge and plonked himself on the armchair facing her. One look at his staunch expression told her he wasn't here for a reconciliation.

'I've come to sort a few things out,' he said.

Beth switched the TV off so she could hear what he had to say.

'I've put the house on the market,' he began. 'Someone will be here tomorrow to measure up. Can you make sure you're in? I take it you've got nothing else planned, no interviews lined up?'

Beth heard the sarcasm drip from his tongue, and it stung. Why couldn't he understand that she had been trying her best to get a job? But it wasn't easy with everything else she was going through.

She could have bit back, but what was the point? She'd already thrashed things out with him and was now coming to realise that Brady wasn't capable of understanding. Brady lived in his perfect, untarnished world. A world full of ambition and aspiration and materialistic gain. And if anything came in the way of that he couldn't deal with it.

Instead, she stayed silent and listened to what else he had to say. 'I've also made an appointment to see a solicitor. I want a divorce.'

Beth sucked in air, trying to stay calm. She wouldn't give him the satisfaction of seeing her reduced to tears. Besides, she was now seeing him for what he was and, reluctant as she was to let him go, she realised deep down that it was for the best.

In the past week, although she had been devastated at seeing him walk away, she had felt calmer in herself. There was no longer the feeling that she was being scrutinised in everything she did. And she no longer felt as though she had to try desperately to gain his respect.

She was managing to hold it together till Brady played his trump card. 'I don't see why I should lose out because of this divorce, so I think we should agree on a settlement of five grand to tide you over till you get a job. And the rest is mine.'

Beth finally spoke. 'No! You can't do that. I'm legally entitled to half.'

'I think you'll find I can, unless you want the world to know your sordid little secret.'

His words penetrated her skull like an electrical impulse,

prompting a reaction. 'You bastard! You absolute bastard,' she yelled. 'I can't fuckin' believe you would sink so low. I trusted you with my secret and now you're turning it against me.'

'No, Beth, you didn't trust me with your secret. You spat it out when you were pissed out of your head and feeling sorry for yourself. If you hadn't been so pissed, I might never have known the sort of woman I'd married. Now, thank God, I do. And if you think I'm losing out because of you then you've got another think coming.'

He got up from the chair. 'I'll give you till five o'clock tomorrow to think about it. If I haven't received a text or a call from you by then telling me you're happy with the five grand settlement, then the word will be out, and you'll have to suffer the consequences.'

He strode across the living room, into the hall and out through the door. Beth followed behind, yelling at him. 'You won't fuckin' get away with this. You no good, sly bastard! I'll never let you take half of what I've worked for.'

But Brady carried on walking till he reached his car and got inside. Catching sight of a passing couple witnessing her distress, Beth slammed the door behind him. Then she sank to the floor in floods of tears. Although she had threatened Brady that he wouldn't get away with blackmailing her, she already knew he would. Because she couldn't face having the world know her secret.

23

It had been a tough few weeks for Beth. Since Brady decided to get a divorce, she had tried to reason with him in the hope that he might see sense and agree to make a go of things. Although she was now seeing the other side of him, she still yearned for the time when they had been happy. But the more time went on, the more unlikely it seemed that they would ever reach a reconciliation.

And now she had to sit and watch as estate agents paraded strangers around her home and pointed out its plus points. Then she'd had to confide in her parents and friends about what had happened. It made her feel such a failure, and she had hated seeing her parents' sad and disappointed faces when she opened her heart to them about the end of her marriage.

Beth hadn't told her parents everything. She couldn't bear their judgement if she were to tell all. She also didn't want to worry them about her financial situation. A sale had been agreed on the house and it was currently going through. For the moment she was living in the home, but once the sale was finalised she would have to leave, and with no income she didn't know how she would manage. Up to now she'd been living off the measly five grand that Brady let her have, but she knew it wasn't going to last forever.

Perhaps she'd tell her parents eventually. She knew they'd take her in, but she was putting it off, hoping something would turn up. Perhaps she'd finally get a job and then she would be able to rent somewhere till she could secure a mortgage. But she hadn't had much luck up to now. Despite being shortlisted twice, she had missed out on two ideal jobs. Sally had been a great support, telling Beth she was well shot of him. To Beth's amazement, her friend confided that she had never liked Brady; he was too up his own backside for her liking. She also admitted that she thought he was controlling Beth to the point where she was losing her identity. But she hadn't wanted to spoil Beth's happiness by confiding in her about how she felt. Beth had seemed so loved up that she would probably have resented the intrusion.

Beth hadn't told Sally everything. Instead, she'd given her a diluted version of events about Brady not being the person she thought he was. His attitude towards her had changed once they were married, and she could no longer cope with his selfish, money-grabbing ways. Then she'd thrown in a few sour examples of his behaviour, taking care to avoid any mention of blackmail.

When the sale of the house was finally complete, Beth would think up a convincing lie as to why she couldn't afford to buy another one, assuming she had found a job by then. The money from the settlement wouldn't even be enough for a deposit let alone all the other expenses that came with buying a home. But it would be easy to convince Sally that she and Brady had overstretched themselves with loans because of his materialistic greed.

Ever since Beth had split up with Brady, Sally had been

trying to persuade her to go on a night out. 'You know what you need, don't you?' she had said so many times that it had become a standing joke between them, with Beth pre-empting her words before she finished saying them.

Beth had finally given in to Sally's persuasion and tonight they were going out locally. To Beth's surprise, as she sat at her dressing table putting on makeup, she found herself looking forward to it. Perhaps Sally had been right; after sitting at home in her scruffs for weeks, maybe it would do her good to have something to get dressed up for.

She was putting the finishing touches to her makeup when she heard the doorbell. She dashed downstairs to find Sally at the front door with a bottle of wine in her hand. 'Eh, babe. Look at you!' she announced. 'You look stunning. In fact, you look the best I've bloody seen you for a long time.'

Beth swung the door wide and beckoned her friend inside. 'Right,' continued Sally, 'tonight you're gonna forget your troubles and we're gonna have a bloody good time. You deserve it, babe. And that tosser of an ex-husband of yours can do one. Don't forget, you're a single girl now, so you can do what the hell you like.'

'Eh, I'm not divorced yet,' said Beth.

'Why, you're not hoping to have him back, are you?'

'No, not at all.'

'Well, come on then. Let's get this bloody bottle opened and have a few. Then we'll grab ourselves a taxi and you can take me to that trendy little bar in Marple where all of them hunky guys are. Eh, you never know, your admirer might be there.'

Beth felt herself blushing. 'Who are you talking about?'

Sally giggled. 'As if you didn't know.'

Martin sat up on his stool the minute he saw Beth walk inside The Amber Room. This time she wasn't with her husband but the flirty friend he had seen on the night when Beth had vomited. He tried not to read too much into that. Even married women were entitled to go out with their friends once in a while.

As the girls approached the bar, Beth smiled widely at him and Martin smiled back. He could feel a stirring of passion within him, but he fought to contain it. He mustn't forget that she was married and there was no way he wanted to come between a married couple, especially one with the troubles they seemed to have.

But Martin couldn't help but look. From his seat at the end of the bar, he studied her. She looked the most stunning he had ever seen her with her hair tied up loosely to accentuate her beautiful features. She was wearing a red top with puffed sleeves. It was fitted and dipped slightly at the front to reveal a little of her cleavage. Her skirt was floral and mid-length with a front-side slit that was high enough to be provocative but still classy.

The friend was certainly on form as she cast her eyes around the bar sizing up the talent. But Beth, well, she was different. He watched her order the drinks then reach inside her handbag for her purse. She took something out of it and as she raised her hand, he saw that it was a credit card. But then he noticed something else on her other hand. She was no longer wearing a wedding ring.

24

The night had gone well for Beth up to now. Sally was such fun to be with and she always made her laugh. But she could tell as soon as they entered The Amber Room that Sally was getting itchy feet. While Beth tried to make conversation with her, Sally's eyes roamed all over the room, and it was obvious to Beth that she was eyeing up the men.

It didn't take Sally long till she'd polished off her drink and dashed to the bar for another. Beth was sitting with her back to the bar so she couldn't see what Sally was up to, but when she still wasn't back ten minutes later, Beth turned around to find out why. She wasn't surprised to see her friend deep in conversation with a good-looking young male.

Beth also couldn't help but notice the bar owner looking across at her. But much as she found him attractive, Beth didn't want to rush into anything at the moment. In fact, a relationship was the last thing she wanted. After everything she had been through, she knew it would be a while before she could trust a man again.

Beth sighed. Suddenly the night had turned sour. She took another sip of her cocktail, which only had a bit left in the bottom. Then she fiddled about with the paper umbrella, twisting it around in the glass. She'd give Sally a couple more minutes, but once she'd finished her drink she'd go and get another one herself.

She had just taken the last sip of her drink when she felt movement behind her. A moment later, a drink landed on the table in front of her. But the hand carrying it wasn't Sally's; it was a man's. She looked up to see the handsome face of the bar owner, Martin.

'I believe you're partial to Sex on the Beach,' he said.

It was a corny line that Beth had heard countless times before but somehow he made it sound sexy. 'I was just about to go and get one,' she said.

'Well, it looks like I've saved you the bother. This one's on the house.' Then he pulled out a chair. 'Do you mind if I join you? Only, I noticed that your friend seems busy, and I didn't like to see you sitting alone.'

Beth tutted. He was obviously on a full charm offensive. Before she had a chance to say anything, he had pulled out the chair and plonked himself on it. She noticed he had also brought over a drink for himself. Beth didn't complain. After all, it had to be better than sitting alone for God knows how long.

'How are you?' Martin asked. 'I hope you don't mind me saying, but things didn't seem so good last time I saw you in here.'

'What do you mean?' asked Beth.

'Well, you were a bit worse for wear for one thing, but I also noticed that your hubby didn't seem too friendly towards you that evening.'

'You notice a lot, don't you?' she asked, evading the question.

'I suppose so. But only because I was worried about you. You seem such a lovely girl and I didn't like to see you upset.'

She didn't quite know how to respond to that, so she said nothing. But then Martin spoke again. 'I noticed something else as well... you're not wearing your wedding ring anymore.'

Beth snatched her hand off the table and covered her ring finger with her other hand.

'I'm sorry, I didn't mean any offence,' he said. 'I just hope you're OK, that's all.'

His concern was too much. To Beth's embarrassment, she felt the sting of tears.

'Oh God, I really am sorry,' Martin said. 'I should learn to mind my own business. If it's any consolation, it does get better with time. And to be honest, I always felt you deserved better.'

'What... like you, do you mean?' she sniped.

'No, not at all. I wouldn't push myself on you knowing what you're going through. I'm just concerned, that's all. I hate to see you so upset.' He stood up. 'Anyway, I'll leave you alone, but if there's ever anything I can do.'

'No, there isn't. There isn't anything anyone can do,' she snapped. 'He's gone, and I've just got to manage as best I can.'

She heard the tremor in her voice and felt foolish for letting him see how upset she was.

'It might feel like that now, but things will turn around. Believe it or not, there'll come a day when you'll be glad you made the break, and you'll wonder why you stuck it out in the first place.'

'That's easy for you to say. You're not the one who's been left high and dry.'

'What do you mean?'

To Beth's surprise, she was glad when Martin sat down again. She didn't want to be alone at the moment. The breakup had left her vulnerable, and suddenly she felt herself wanting to confide in him. Maybe it was because he seemed concerned. Despite her initial reservations, he appeared to be a caring man; her mind shot back to the night she had vomited and the way he had taken care of her. But maybe it was because she was so eaten up with her worries that she found it difficult to talk about anything else. And with the amount of drink she had consumed, it was all too easy to offload all her problems to a virtual stranger.

'I'm out of work,' she said. 'I gave up my job because I was having a baby but then I lost the baby, and I haven't been able to find work since. And I'll soon be out of a home. And how the hell am I supposed to buy somewhere when I don't even have a job?'

'Will you not get any money from the divorce settlement?'

Beth found herself blushing. Although she was opening up to him, she still managed to exercise a degree of control, so she stopped short of telling him about Brady's blackmail. Instead, she stuck to her prepared story about Brady running up so many debts that there was little equity left in the house.

Before she knew it, she had confided in Martin about her problems, the words gushing out in a torrent of despair. Then, once she had finished, she became embarrassed.

'Now I'm the one that's sorry,' she said. 'I shouldn't have

put all that on you. It's just that, well, you caught me at a bad time.'

'That's alright,' he said, covering her hand with his in a gesture of reassurance. 'We all have our problems to deal with, and it always feels better to offload. I wish I could share mine with someone.'

He smiled wryly but Beth was so preoccupied with her own troubles and ignorant of his that she wasn't aware of the significance of his words.

'What work do you do?' asked Martin.

'I'm a PA.'

'Oh, right. Well, I can't offer you anything in that field, but if you want something to tide you over, we could use an extra pair of hands behind the bar.'

'But I've never worked behind a bar.'

'That's alright. There's not much to it. I'm sure you'll soon learn.'

'I… well… I don't know.'

Beth didn't really fancy the prospect of working behind a bar, but she couldn't think of a suitable excuse. To her relief, Martin seemed to pick up on her unease. 'It's OK, you don't have to feel obliged,' he said. 'I know you're probably a bit overqualified for it, but if you're worried about any trouble in the bar, I'd always look out for you.'

Then he removed his hand from hers and got up from his seat. 'It looks like your friend's on her way back so I'll leave you to it. But the offer's still there. If you change your mind, you know where to find me.'

25

Brady walked inside the city centre wine bar then scanned the room. He soon spotted Preston Watts of Sevran Cosmetics occupying a table across the other side and went over to meet him.

As Brady approached, Preston stood up and they shook hands. 'Nice to see you, Preston,' said Brady. 'Would you like a drink?'

Once he had got the drinks in, Brady went back to Preston, taking a seat opposite him.

'So, what's all this about?' asked Preston. 'You were a bit cloak and dagger on the phone.'

'That's because I don't want anyone to know yet, so please keep what I'm about to tell you under your hat.'

'Yeah, sure.'

'I'm setting up on my own. But, like I say, please keep it under your hat. Old Dodds doesn't know yet. At the moment, I'm at the stage where I'm making deals with suppliers and customers. Once I've got all that set up, I'll be ready to go. If word gets out to Repertoire via you then I'll make sure you don't sell anything else to either Repertoire or my new company.'

'Alright, I said I'd keep schtum, didn't I?' said Preston.

Brady didn't really trust him ever since the sales conference when he'd hinted to Beth about his infidelity. But he secretly knew that he needed Preston as much as Preston needed him. The Sevran products were top notch and demand for them was growing.

'OK, well make sure you do. Obviously, as one of our suppliers I'll be looking to cut a deal with you. I'm thinking pretty much the same prices as for Repertoire to start with, then we'll see how it goes.'

Preston sucked in air. 'Well, you know the deal we cut for Repertoire was based on volume. Do you think you'll be shifting the same amount?'

'Not to start with, but eventually, yes.'

'OK, what sort of numbers are we talking?'

'Probably about a quarter of what you're doing with Repertoire to start with but—'

'Then I can't let you have the same prices,' Preston cut in.

'Come off it, Preston. What difference does it make to you? I'll soon have the numbers up. In fact, I'll be chatting to a few of our customers tomorrow about my new company. I've got loads of brilliant plans. Internet advertising, the lot. Old Dodds won't stand a chance when he's up against me.'

'OK, well maybe we can renegotiate once the numbers improve, but for now, I can't do that. I'll email you a list of our prices and see what you think.'

Brady knew that Preston wasn't going to move on prices, and he was gutted. It really pissed him off when somebody had the upper hand over him, especially a little prat like Preston. But for now, he'd just have to suck it up. He was determined that things wouldn't stay that way though. And it wouldn't be long before Preston was begging him to take his products at a bargain price.

He'd always had ambitions of starting up on his own and when things had turned sour with Beth, it had given him the idea to go for it sooner rather than later. Why delay it when the money from the house would be more than enough to get him up and running?

The house was due to complete tomorrow and when it did, the money would be his. And once he had everything in place, there'd be no stopping him.

The day that Beth had been dreading had finally arrived. It was completion date on the house sale, and she had to move out.

The past couple of weeks had been challenging. Not only had she come face to face with Brady when he called to collect most of their belongings, but she had also been filled with trepidation about her future.

Despite her pleading, Brady had insisted on taking virtually everything with him, telling her it was part of their agreement. His manner towards her was uncaring, hostile even, and she wondered how she had ever fallen in love with a man like him. At least she wouldn't have to see him anymore, because from what she had learnt he was moving into a rental property out of the area.

The only advantage in having so few belongings was that she had no need to put them into storage. Her parents had agreed to keep them at their home for her. In fact, if it hadn't been for her parents and Sally, Beth didn't know how she would have coped.

Her parents were no longer at the house, as they'd left to take her things back to their home. They had been brilliant, even though she knew how upset they were about her divorce. At first they'd quizzed her about the reasons for Brady leaving and even though she'd stuck to the same story, she could tell they weren't convinced she was telling the truth. It made her feel such a let-down after they'd raised her so well.

Thankfully, Sally had offered her a place on her sofa and Beth opted for that in preference to staying with her parents. She felt too old to be living under their roof, and she didn't want to see in their faces the constant reminder of how much of a disappointment she had been. Besides, she was worried that their parents' intuition might finally penetrate through the lies she had fabricated.

Beth knew the situation with Sally wasn't ideal, but she regarded it as temporary. Sally only had one bedroom and Beth didn't want to invade her privacy by sharing that with her. Her friend had been a godsend. Not only had she helped Beth pack the few things she was taking with her, she'd also been a constant source of support whenever Beth was feeling overwhelmed.

While Sally was using the bathroom, Beth had a last look around the home she once shared with the man she had loved. It was difficult letting go. Despite how unfairly Brady had treated her, there was still some feeling there. She wished there weren't: he no longer deserved her love. But it was difficult to switch off when she had put so much into their lives together and had dreamt of their plans for the future.

Now the rooms looked bare. All the furniture they had

carefully chosen had gone, and the décor no longer appealed to her. With no furnishings to complement them, the rooms felt cold despite the heat of a summer's day. As she thought about how drastically things had changed in such a short space of time, her eyes welled with tears.

'Oh, sorry,' said Sally, peeping into the room. 'I'll give you a minute.'

But the moment was gone for Beth. There was no point dwelling on the past. She had the future to think of. And despite everything, at least she had somewhere to live for now. But she still hadn't found a job. Sally had been OK about it, insisting Beth should pay no more than she could afford. But Beth was conscious of putting pressure on their friendship. She wanted to pay her way; she just needed to find the means with which to do it.

Sally had asked her to go out with her that evening, but Beth had turned her down. Going out enjoying herself was the last thing she wanted when she was full of worry about the future and sorrow about the past. And besides, there was something she needed to do. She'd been having a long, hard think and had decided that it was the way forward, for now.

26

Martin was currently inside Virtuoso. He'd decided not to hang around inside The Amber Room every night in the hope that Beth would turn up. It was three weeks since he'd seen her, and despite him trying his best to offer support, she hadn't been in the bar since. And as for the job offer, he supposed she had since found something more suited to her talents.

He understood that she had a lot going on and, as she was still going through a divorce, there was no way she would want to go rushing into another relationship so soon. It was best for him if he got on with his life and put her out of his mind. And, the next time she came into the bar, he would play it cool.

It was while he was walking through the club that he caught sight of a familiar pretty face, only this one had a curtain of dark hair surrounding it and the girl was tiny, unlike Beth who was tall. She was standing in a group, which was a mix of young women and men. The rest of them seemed to be sharing banter and having a laugh, but she was disengaged from the conversation and peering around the room instead.

Because there were so many people between them, he

wasn't easy to spot, especially as she was only tiny and therefore had to peep between the taller people standing opposite her. Martin considered himself fortunate that he had seen Jodi first and had a chance to escape before she found him.

He left Virtuoso, telling one of his bouncers he'd be back another night. And soon he was inside The Amber Room chugging back brandies to try to drown out the memories.

Although it had been over five months since he'd previously seen Jodi, he'd recognise those petite elfin features anywhere. It had been such a momentous night that her features had remained in his mind along with those of her boyfriend.

He had tried so hard to put it behind him and had thought that it was over, that once the police couldn't prove anything there would be no further comeback. The last thing he had expected was to see Jodi. And seeing her brought it all rushing back, the scene playing over and over in his mind as he went back to questioning himself and wishing he'd have done things differently. Perhaps then the lad would still have been alive.

He couldn't understand why she would want to hang around in the last place her boyfriend had been seen before he was killed. Maybe that's why she'd been disengaged. Perhaps she'd gone along with peer pressure and ended up at Virtuoso against her better judgement.

Or perhaps she had gone there specifically for a reason. And of all the reasons why she might choose to hang around in Virtuoso, the most obvious one to him was that she might want revenge. And if that was the case, then he was seriously concerned.

***

Brady was in a city centre bar for the second night in a row. This time he was due to meet a customer. She was the last of three he had already seen that day and up to now it was going well. One of the customers had doubts about swapping her custom over to him from Repertoire, telling him that she didn't want to rely on a company that was still new.

The second client had been happy to oblige. Brady had built up a relationship with him over time and the man knew that Dodds wasn't getting any younger. It had therefore been easy for Brady to convince him that the new company would gradually access all the supply chains currently offered by Repertoire, as well as exploring new ones.

As the second customer was a much bigger prospect than the first, with several branches of hairdressers, Brady knew it was a win. This last customer had only two beauty salons, but Brady was nevertheless eager to secure a contract with them. He'd also earmarked several others to approach over the coming weeks as well as suppliers.

As the day progressed, Brady had been in constant touch with his solicitor, knowing it was the day of completion on the house. He'd left it to Beth to hand over keys to the estate agents. He had no interest in hanging around now that he'd cleared the place of all the best furniture.

His main interest lay in making sure he realised the equity tied up in the house. And as he and Beth had both owned their own property prior to buying their home in Marple, he was expecting a sizeable sum. As well as being in constant touch with his solicitor, he had also made regular checks of his bank account for the proceeds of the sale before he allowed the new owners to take possession.

At ten past four he was rewarded with the sight of a healthy bank balance, which had made his day. Things were going so well that he decided to do some celebrating once his client meeting was over. He might even be able to persuade her to join him. After all, the owner of Emmeline's Beauty Salons was a tasty lady, and he'd been aware for some time that she was interested in him. Why else would she agree to an out of hours business meeting?

By the time Beth walked into The Amber Room, Martin was bleary-eyed. He didn't often allow himself to get in such a state, but he had a lot on his mind. In fact, he was so preoccupied that he didn't even notice her until she was standing next to him at the bar.

'Oh, hi,' he said, surprising himself at still being able to speak coherently and noticing she was alone. 'Everything alright?'

He noticed even in his intoxicated state that she appeared nervous. 'It makes a change for you to be more drunk than me,' she said.

Suddenly Martin became embarrassed. He didn't like her seeing him like this; it made him feel vulnerable and not as much in control. But then he realised that she had probably said it to break the ice, and he tried to respond in the same vein. 'We all have our off days.'

He'd meant for it to be jovial but he couldn't hide the worry behind it.

'Sorry, are you having problems?' asked Beth.

Martin waved his hand dismissively. 'No, it's nothing. Just the usual business stress, nothing to worry about. What about you? How are things?' Then he waited for her to reply.

'Not so good. We completed on the house today.'

'Oh, sorry to hear that. It must have been hard. Did you manage to get sorted?'

Beth nodded. 'My friend Sally's putting me up for the time being.'

'And did you find work?'

She shook her head. 'No. I just can't seem to nail it. I don't think I'm coming over well at interviews. Probably because of all the stress.'

Martin could tell that Beth's nerves hadn't yet dissolved. Her words were tumbling out in a flurry. He placed his hand on top of hers and smiled sympathetically.

Then she came out with it. 'Actually, that's what I'm here for. I wondered if the job offer still stands.'

Martin smiled again. Since he'd made the offer, he'd taken on another member of staff at The Amber Room and was now full to capacity. But he knew he couldn't refuse her because if he did, he might never see her again.

'I'm sorry, there's no jobs here,' he said. Her expression clouded over, so he quickly added, 'There's a vacancy at my nightclub though. It's called Virtuoso.'

27

Beth was standing behind the bar in Virtuoso when another of the barmaids, Teresa, rushed in looking frazzled. Her plain blouse was hanging out of her jeans, and she tried to tuck it in then smoothed down her hair, which was sticking up on one side.

'Are you alright?' asked Beth.

Teresa shook her head, 'Toby's come down with something. He's running a temperature.'

'Aw, you should have taken the night off.'

'Can't afford to. Anyway, Carl's looking after him. I told him to ring me if he gets any worse.'

'I hope he'll be OK.'

'Me too,' said Teresa and Beth saw the worried look on her face.

'Anyway, how have things been here? Is the boss around?'

'No.'

'Good. That means I won't have my pay docked. You will cover for me, won't you?'

''Course I will.'

Beth meant what she said. Since she'd started working at Virtuoso a few weeks ago, Teresa had been brilliant. Beth was really nervous at the start. She'd never worked behind a bar and was uncertain what to expect. At first, she'd clung to Martin as he'd led her in and introduced her to all the staff. But she was disappointed when he hadn't stayed around long.

Initially she thought her clinginess was just because he was someone familiar in a strange environment, but she was gradually coming to realise that she enjoyed his company. Whenever she caught sight of him, her heart leapt in her chest. The man was gorgeous, but she tried to tell herself that it was just friendship, and she was foolish to consider a man like him in any other way.

To Beth's relief, before he departed for one of his other bars, Martin had asked Teresa to look after her. Thankfully, Beth hit it off with the other woman. Teresa was plain looking. Unlike most of the other barmaids who were glamorous, she wore the bare minimum of makeup and dressed conservatively. She was in her thirties and had three young children and a husband who worked days for minimum wage. Teresa did three nights a week at the club to supplement their income.

Beth could tell that Teresa thought the world of her family, and she had no doubt that she would spend all her time with them rather than working at Virtuoso given a choice. But Teresa had made it clear that she didn't have a choice because money was tight at home.

She often talked about her children and what they were up to. Beth had found that difficult at first because of her recent miscarriage, but once she became used to it, she found that she enjoyed their chats. Teresa painted a very rosy view of motherhood, making Beth hope that she would also become a mother one day. But for the moment she needed to get back on her feet, and her wages from Virtuoso were helping her to put a little money by.

Beth surprised herself with how much she enjoyed working at Virtuoso. It gave her a social outlet without the expense of going out. She supposed she had previously held a negative view of bar work and felt ashamed to admit to herself that some of Brady's snobbery must have rubbed off. That, and the role she had carved out for herself as a successful, married professional, like her parents.

But she found bar work interesting. She was interacting with people who she would never have associated with at one time. And she found that she had taken to people like Teresa, who was hardworking and caring. It gave Beth a wider view of the world and made her more rounded as a person. It was also good to be able to stand on her own two feet again despite the knockbacks she'd had.

'The boss never comes in much, does he?' she asked Teresa, referring to their earlier conversation.

'He used to. He doesn't anymore. But then, you never know with him. He has a lot of bars as well as this place and he likes to run a tight ship, so you never know when he might just turn up and check on things.'

Beth was fishing. She was secretly disappointed that she didn't see much of Martin in Virtuoso and was keen to find out more. 'He's alright to work for though, isn't he?'

'Oh, yeah. He's always fair. But it doesn't pay to get on the wrong side of him.'

'What do you mean?'

'Oh, he doesn't suffer fools. You'll find out what I mean if you stick around long enough.'

Teresa was then interrupted by a customer at the bar and

Beth didn't get a chance to ask her any more. She knew that once the club had been open for an hour or two it would become really busy, and all the bar staff would be run off their feet.

When Teresa finished serving her customer, she came over to Beth and nudged her. 'Eh, don't look now, but that guy coming over is trouble. He's a right lech. But don't worry, I'll sort him out. He knows better than to try it on with me.'

Just then Teresa's phone rang. She pulled it out of her pocket and looked at the screen. 'Shit, it's Carl,' Teresa said. 'Are you alright for a minute while I go and answer it?'

'Sure,' said Beth. 'I hope everything's OK with Toby.'

But Teresa didn't respond. She had already left the bar and gone to find a quiet area where she could take the call. Unfortunately for Beth, the troublesome customer took that moment to reach the bar, and Beth was the only barmaid available to serve him.

As she walked towards the counter, she was aware of him scrutinising her. Beth pulled back her shoulders and walked forward, determined not to stand for any nonsense.

'What would you like?' she asked.

'Ooh, that sounds like an enticing offer.'

Beth tutted. 'To drink.'

'Ooh, let me see. What bottled beers have you got?'

Beth turned around and looked at the bottles in the chiller then reeled off a list of them.

'What about the one at the bottom?'

Beth bent over and pointed to one of the bottles then read out the name.

'Yeah, I'll have that one.'

She grabbed the bottle and straightened up.

'No, I tell you what? Put that one back. What's the one next to it?'

Beth bent over again and pointed to the next bottle along. When he didn't reply, she looked up to see his eyes roaming over her body.

'No, not that one,' he said. 'How about the next one along. Let me see you bend again.'

Beth tutted. 'I'm not here for your entertainment, if you don't mind.'

'That's a pity 'cos you've got a nice arse.'

Beth approached the bar and hissed at him, 'Just tell me which beer you want and then clear off.'

'Well, that's a nice way to speak to a customer,' he said, but he must have spotted the look of annoyance on her face because he gave her his order.

When Beth put the bottle of beer on the bar he was fiddling with some cash in his wallet.

'That'll be four pounds eighty,' she said, holding out her hand for the money.

Instead of giving her the money, he grabbed hold of her hand. She tried to tug it away, but he held on tight.

'What the hell do you think you're doing?'

A sneer crossed his face. 'Just after a date, that's all. Agree to meet me and I'll let go of your hand.'

'No!' she snapped. 'I don't want to go on a date with you.'

'Why not? We'll have a great time. What do you fancy? A meal? Cinema? A few drinks?'

Beth continued to tug. 'None. Let go of my hand. You're hurting me.'

'Only if you agree to let me take you out. And if you stop struggling it won't hurt.'

Beth was busy trying to break free, her eyes fixed on their hands. Then she heard a voice and looked up to see Martin addressing the strange man.

'You heard what the lady said. She doesn't want to go on a date with you. Now, I suggest you do as she says and let go of her hand. Now!'

Beth's glance flitted from Martin to the man, and she could see the shock in his eyes, which mirrored the way she felt. This wasn't a tone of voice she was used to from Martin who had always been so kind to her.

28

Martin hadn't been inside Virtuoso much lately. He had been too nervous about another encounter with the girlfriend of the man he had killed. But on the rare occasions he had been, he hadn't caught sight of her.

Feeling more relaxed about the situation, he was gradually venturing inside, encouraged by Beth's presence. It frustrated him that he hadn't been able to keep an eye on her since she had started working at Virtuoso. What was the point in employing her if he never even got a chance to chat to her? Tonight, he was determined to spend a couple of hours sitting on a stool at the bar, watching his staff work, with one particular member in mind.

As he approached, he was almost blown away by her beauty. She had her hair up again and was wearing a fitted red top that suited her colouring. Martin kept his wits about him as he walked across the room, checking that Jodi wasn't around. Then his eyes flitted back to the bar, and Beth.

She seemed to be in conversation with a customer, but the look on her face told Martin it wasn't a happy conversation. He wondered for a moment if it was the ex and when he saw the man gripping her hand, he rushed to her rescue.

This man wasn't her husband; he was older, somewhere

in his mid-thirties, Martin guessed. His hair was greasy, and his appearance was unkempt with a shirt that was shiny at the edges of the collar from being ironed so many times. Martin drew close to the man, who turned and gave him a scathing glance.

'What the fuck do you think you're playing at?' demanded Martin.

'What's it to you?' asked the man, releasing Beth's hand and holding his own at his sides, his fists bunched.

Martin grabbed hold of the front of his shirt. 'I'll tell you what it's got to do with me...'

Before he could finish, the man rounded on him. 'Get the fuck off me!'

He pushed Martin in the chest with the flat of his hand but when Martin didn't budge, he yelled, 'You'd better get your fuckin' hands off me now if you know what's good for you.' He tried to loosen the grip of Martin's hand.

Keeping a solid hold of him, Martin began, 'Right, now you're going to listen to what I have to say.'

Before Martin had a chance to elaborate, he felt the man's fist in his face. It wasn't a hard punch, but it shocked Martin for a moment. He recovered quickly and began trading blows with the man, who soon ran out of steam and stood dazed from the weight of Martin's punches. Martin spun him around, pinned his arms behind his back and frogmarched him from the club.

But then Martin noticed Beth's anguished expression. She was obviously freaked out by violence. He felt bad for upsetting her, but it was something he'd had to do. He just hoped he hadn't blown it with her now she had seen that other side of him.

***

While Beth was still staring open-mouthed at the two men, Teresa joined her side and whispered in her ear, 'See what I mean about not getting on the wrong side of him?'

Beth tried to compose herself. 'Yes, I do.' Then she swiftly changed the subject. She didn't want Teresa to see how bothered she really was, otherwise she might guess why. 'How's Toby?'

'Oh, he's fine. Well, I mean, he's no worse. Carl just wanted to know where his favourite pyjamas were.'

'Aw, that's good then.'

For the rest of the night, she tried to take her mind off Martin, but she couldn't help thinking about him. To her amazement, she found that she actually liked what Martin had done in a way, because he'd done it to protect her. She also found his manliness a massive attraction. He was so unlike Brady who always seemed more concerned about himself than how she might be feeling, whereas Martin genuinely seemed to care about her.

Eventually it was time to head home. In the past few weeks, the shine of living with Sally had worn off. Beth had discovered that her friend was slovenly in her ways, and Beth was always the one who put out the rubbish or emptied the dishwasher. On top of that, Sally often hogged the bathroom, and she was prone to bringing back strange men after a night out. It put Beth in a difficult situation. But she had been reluctant to complain up to now because it was Sally's flat.

Beth had nearly spent all the money from the divorce settlement in the weeks when she had no work. The meagre amount Brady had paid her in maintenance hadn't been enough to live on. Therefore, at the moment, she couldn't afford to rent her own place as she would need to find a deposit as well as some money for furniture and other necessities.

Tonight, the situation at Sally's home was no different than usual, and as Beth walked into the living room, she was dismayed to find the place a tip. The first thing she noticed was the strong smell of cigarettes. Sally wasn't a smoker, so it was clear that a second person had been inside the room.

On the sofa, the cushions were dishevelled. Beth looked over to the coffee table to find two empty wine glasses and a bottle, which was lying on its side, its spout hanging over the edge. There was still some wine inside the bottle and a quick check of the carpet showed a sticky red puddle. Beth also noticed an ashtray with several dimps, and a cigarette packet left open with its contents spilling out.

She tutted and grabbed the pillow and duvet from the cupboard where they were kept. Then she straightened the cushions and lay down. She was too tired to shift the rest of the mess tonight. It would have to wait till the morning.

She didn't know how long she had been asleep when the sound of somebody in the room jolted her awake. Startled, she rubbed the sleep from her eyes and scanned the room. In the dimness of night, she spotted a naked man walking through the lounge towards her.

Beth shrieked and sat up, pulling the duvet around her. Unperturbed, the man stopped at the coffee table then bent and picked up the cigarettes.

'Sorry,' he said. 'Just came to get these.'

He was soon gone but Beth was still shaken. She wasn't used to being confronted by the sight of a naked stranger in the middle of the night. It took her an age to get back to sleep. She must have only slept for a couple of hours more when she was awoken again. It was the same man but this time he was dressed, and Sally was with him.

'Aw babe, we had the best night,' said Sally. 'James is a right laugh, and his mates are hilarious!'

Beth tutted at Sally, who then said, 'Oh sorry, babe. I thought you were awake. I was just going to get us a coffee before James goes.'

Beth was annoyed, and knowing that they didn't need to go through the living room to get to the kitchen made her even more irate. 'I was still asleep!' she fumed. 'I didn't get in from work till four and then I was awoken in the night when *he* decided to walk into the living room butt naked!'

'His name's James, actually, and he came for his cigarettes.'

'Eh, it's OK. I'm outta here,' said James in a mock American accent. 'I don't want you girls squabbling on my account.'

He left the room and Sally accompanied him to the front door. Beth tutted as she heard whispered conversations, then quietness for a few seconds, followed by Sally giggling before the door was slammed shut.

When Sally walked back into the room she appeared to be just as annoyed as Beth. 'You needn't have been so bad mannered!'

'Did you really expect me to welcome him with open arms when I'm trying to sleep? You know full well that I don't get in from work till late.'

'Well, that's not my bloody fault, is it?'

'No, but you could at least show some consideration when I'm trying to sleep.'

'I told you, I thought you were awake.'

'And what exactly gave you that impression? Was it my loud singing or the sound of my feet pattering around the room?' Beth asked.

'There's no need for sarcasm.'

Beth sat up, her anger now threatening to overwhelm her. 'There's every bloody need, especially when your latest squeeze had already woken me up once. Did you realise that he was starkers when he came in for his cigs?'

'Oh, grow up, Beth. It's not as if you're the virgin bloody Mary. You've seen it all before.'

'That's not the point, Sally. He gave me a fright. How the hell was I supposed to know who he was? I'm sick of all these strange men parading through the place.'

'Jesus! It sounds like sour grapes to me 'cos you're getting none.'

'How dare you! Not all of us jump into bed with the first man that gives us some attention, y'know. And another thing, look at the state of this bloody place. It's like a pigsty. I'm sick to death of clearing up after you.'

'Nobody asked you to clean up, Little Miss Perfect.'

'Well, if I didn't clean up, I'd have to sit looking at the mess because you never seem to do anything about it.'

'Well, if you don't like it then you know what you can do, don't you? I was only trying to help you out and that's all the fuckin' thanks I get!'

Sally's harsh words brought Beth to her senses, and she watched in awe as Sally fled from the room. After listening for a while, she heard no more movement and assumed that Sally must have gone back to bed.

Beth felt bad. She knew she'd come over as judgemental, which hadn't been her intention. As far as she was concerned, Sally could live her life any way she liked. The real problem for Beth was the lack of sleep. It was making her grumpy and unreasonable. She shouldn't have let her temper get the better of her. Why couldn't she have tackled the situation calmly? Then perhaps they might have reached some sort of a compromise.

Sally's attitude had told her all she needed to know. She was used to her own space and Beth was surplus to requirements. There would be a terrible atmosphere when Sally got up, and Beth didn't know if they could recover from this. The best solution all round would be for Beth to leave but as she couldn't afford it at the moment, she had no choice but to put up with things until she could.

29

Two weeks later, Martin was inside Virtuoso when he heard the sound of a bell ringing. It was coming from the back door, which was used by staff to enter the premises. Instinctively he checked his watch, wondering who it could be as it was still half an hour before the staff were due to start work. He was surprised to find Beth on the other side of the door.

'I thought you weren't in till Wednesday,' he said.

'I'm not. I've come to collect my brolly. I think I left it here last night.'

Martin thought it was strange to come all the way into Manchester to pick up a brolly and couldn't understand why it couldn't wait until she was in work three days later. But then a glow of satisfaction lit him up inside. It was obviously an excuse to come and see him.

Martin was now visiting Virtuoso regularly. He hadn't seen Jodi since that night, so he didn't see any reason to keep away. And he was glad he was spending time there because he and Beth were getting along well.

He had made a habit of sitting at the bar where she worked and chatting to her during the quiet times. The more he chatted to her, the more he liked her, and he could sense that she felt the same way. Why else would she confide in him about what was going on in her life? He knew the staff were tittle-tattling among themselves but let them talk. A bit of staff gossip and speculation about his love life was the least of his worries.

Martin had avoided rushing things, though, as it was still early days since Beth's divorce. But it was difficult when all he wanted to do was take her in his arms and comfort her. She had been through a difficult time from what she had told him. And whenever he listened to her pouring her heart out, his own problems were temporarily forgotten.

Tonight, he was happy to see her, and if she was so eager to spend time with him that she had made up a corny excuse, then he wasn't going to turn her away.

'Why don't you stop and have a drink while you're here?' he asked.

'Thanks,' said Beth, already pulling out a bar stool.

'What would you like?'

'Ooh, could I have a G&T, please?'

Martin prepared the drink and placed it in front of her while Beth dug inside her handbag for her purse. He waved his hand. 'On the house.'

'Thank you.'

'So, what are you up to on your night off?' he asked.

'Well, Sally's out, so I thought I'd take advantage and catch up with some TV.'

'You not going too?'

'No, she's off out with one of her man friends and, to be honest, it's a relief. The atmosphere's been terrible between us since we had that row a fortnight ago.'

'Why don't you leave if things are so bad? It can't be much fun sleeping on the sofa anyway.'

'I will be doing soon. I was hoping to buy somewhere but that would take too long, so I'm saving for a deposit on a rental place. It shouldn't be too much longer before I've got the cash together.'

'Good. I'm sure it will be for the best, and I bet you and Sally will become friends again once you're not under the same roof.'

'I hope so. We got on well before all this happened. I guess me and Sally are two different people. It doesn't stop us being friends, but it makes it a hell of a job living together.'

Beth smiled but he could tell it was forced. She was looking tired lately and it was obvious to him that she wasn't getting much sleep under her present circumstances. They talked for a while longer until he noticed Beth looking at her watch. Then the doorbell rang again, signalling the arrival of the first member of staff.

Martin went to open the door and as he walked back with one of his barmen, Beth passed them by, waving her brolly in front of them. 'I'd forget my head if it were loose. Thanks again for letting me come and collect it, Martin.'

He watched as she left the building. He might not have cared what the staff thought but it was obvious that Beth did.

Martin decided to stay around a while longer, and after chatting to the staff who worked the same bar as Beth, he had a walk around. He might as well check out the other bar and keep an eye out for any troublemakers or obvious drug dealers.

He was crossing the room when he ran into Jodi. This time there was no getting away from her and she spotted who he was before he could disappear. His breath caught in his throat as he locked eyes with her and saw her scowl.

'You fuckin' bastard!' she yelled. 'I knew I'd find you in here one day. You killed my boyfriend. You killed Lloyd.' Then she turned to the friends she was with and, pointing at Martin, shouted, 'It was him. He was the one who did it.'

Martin stepped towards her. He had noticed a crowd gathering and was anxious to calm her down.

'Let's go and talk about this somewhere quiet,' he said in a soothing voice.

'No fuckin' chance! I'm not having you dragging me out the back door and beating me to death like you did with Lloyd; you and your fuckin' bully boys.'

'Nobody beat anybody to death,' said Martin. 'We just took him out of the club because he was getting aggressive. His body was found elsewhere, and according to the police, he must have been jumped.'

'A likely story. The police might have bought it but I fuckin' haven't.'

Jodi was louder than ever, and Martin knew that his words alone weren't going to bring this situation under control. He searched around for Skippy, who he couldn't find, but two of his other bouncers stepped out of the crowd.

'Everything alright, boss?' asked one of them.

Martin took hold of Jodi's shoulder. 'She's trouble. Let's get her out.'

The bouncers moved in, and Martin left them to coax her

out of the club while she screamed abuse and accusations. He preferred not to be near her any longer than he had to. Instead, he made his way to the bar and ordered a double brandy.

The incident had left him shaken and was already playing havoc with his digestive system, causing the acid reflux he often had when he was stressed. He had hoped it was over when he hadn't seen her for a while. The police had finished asking questions, satisfied with the scenario that he and Billy conjured up. But it seemed that Jodi was still a problem. He just hoped it was a problem that would soon go away.

30

Martin was glad to see Beth when she turned up for work three nights later. Despite his confrontation with Jodi, he had decided not to carry on avoiding the club. Now that the dreaded encounter had finally happened, he hoped things would calm down. Maybe Jodi would stop coming to Virtuoso now she had got things off her chest.

Currently his concerns had turned to Beth. As the night drew on, he noticed how upset she seemed. Where she would usually be cheerful and chatty with everyone, she had hardly said a word.

Martin waited till it was her break. He watched her go and sit alone at the other end of the bar, so he got up and went to join her. 'Do you mind?' he asked, pulling out a stool. When Beth shrugged, he said, 'I couldn't help but notice that you're not your usual cheerful self today. Are things still bad between you and Sally?'

'You could say that. We're still hardly speaking and the least thing I say to her, she bites my head off. I can't blame her in a way; I was a bit harsh with her, but it was all the sleepless nights making me moody. And as if all that's not bad enough, I got my decree absolute today.'

As she said the words, he saw her eyes become misty, so he offered his sympathy. 'I'm sorry to hear that.'

Martin wasn't really sorry that she was now divorced. In his opinion, she was well shot of the guy. But it would have been insensitive of him to say so when he could see she was upset.

'I bet you're not really,' she said. 'He was an arse, wasn't he? You saw it, and everybody else could see it, except me. And I know it's for the best, but it still makes you wonder what if.'

'I know,' muttered Martin, placing his hand on her shoulder. 'I've been there, don't forget, although it was a long time ago. And you're still young, y'know. You've got your whole life ahead of you. Things might be bad now, but they will get better. And as for Sally, why don't you have a chat with her, maybe even apologise and see if you can work something out?'

She smiled and, as she did so, a tear slid from her eye and landed on her cheek. She wiped it with the back of her hand and then an uncomfortable silence descended on them until she said, 'Thank you.'

'For what?'

'For being there. You always seem to say the right things to make me feel better. And I know things will improve in time, but it's just that, well, at the moment I feel knackered all the time. It might be best to get a full-time PA role, but I haven't filled in any applications for ages. I'm too bloody tired.'

'I don't suppose it helps sleeping on the sofa, does it?'

'No, especially with Sally walking around all the time. It's not easy when I'm trying to sleep. I think she wants me out now, but until I've saved a deposit for my own place, I'm stuck with it.'

'Not necessarily,' said Martin. Suddenly he felt apprehensive. He was wary of messing things up between them, but he couldn't stand to see her this upset. 'You could always have a room at mine.'

He saw the shocked look on her face and for a moment he regretted saying anything.

'Oh,' was all she said.

'Don't worry, there'll be no funny business. I've got three bedrooms going to waste and it seems daft for me to be rattling around in the place while you're sleeping on a bloody sofa. You can take your choice of the bedrooms, apart from the one that's mine, of course. And if it makes you feel better, we can make things official. You can be my lodger.'

'Oh, I, er... That's very kind of you.'

Martin could see she was still taken aback, and he didn't want the situation to become awkward between them, so he stood up, tapped her on the arm and said, 'Anyway, I'll let you have a think about it. You can come back to me if you're interested.'

The past few weeks had been busy for Brady. Aside from setting up his business, he had moved into a rented flat three weeks prior. It wasn't as plush as the house he'd shared with Beth, and he would have preferred to buy a place, but it would do for now. With the furniture and furnishings he had brought it felt homely, and at least it gave him the room he needed.

There were two bedrooms: one he used for himself and the other he used as an office. The office was where he was currently going over his checklists while he sipped at a glass of shiraz.

As Brady went through his notes, he felt a tremendous buzz. He was thrilled with the progress he had made so far. He had plenty of customers to get him off to a good start until he could find a few more. The staff had been interviewed and were ready to start work. He also had some good suppliers in place and had managed to secure preferential rates with most of them. The only thing that remained was to take possession of a new building with offices for his staff and stockrooms.

Brady took another sip of his wine, feeling contented. He'd always known he could do it. After all, he had been the main driving force behind Repertoire, not doddery old Dodds. And once he was up and running, Dodds wouldn't stand a chance. But it served him right; incompetents like him didn't deserve success.

Brady was due to move into the business premises on the following Monday once the current occupants had moved out, and he couldn't wait. The sky was the limit as far as he was concerned. If Dodds could make a success of things, then he could only imagine how far *his* company would go with somebody competent at the helm.

As he sat there reflecting on how well it had gone so far, he also dreamt of the future and all that he would achieve once the money from his new business venture was rolling in. This flat could go for a kick-off. He might be happy to rent for now, but he belonged in his own home, and the house he would buy would be bigger and better than the one he had shared with Beth. Then the wife would follow. Hopefully this time he'd get someone who was able to carry a child, unlike Beth.

He had little regrets regarding Beth. Fair enough, she was a looker, but so were a lot of girls out there and he knew women found him attractive. As far as he was concerned, he was well rid, there was no room in his life for someone like her. He recalled the confession she had made and shuddered. Thank God he found out about her when he did. And at least that had worked in his favour. After all, if he hadn't had something on Beth then he wouldn't have been able to get the money together for his new company.

31

Beth checked the address she had entered into the notes on her phone, wanting to make sure she had got it right. To her surprise, she had, and she gazed at the house in awe.

It was in an older, stylish design, probably 1930s, she guessed. Wrought-iron gates opened onto a block-paved driveway, which was enormous, as was the lawn to one side of it. To the other side was a large flower border bursting with a profusion of colours and textures.

There was another smaller, neat border to the side of the lawn. At the end of the lawn, furthest from the house, were several small bushes, which provided some privacy. She stepped tentatively onto the driveway, at the end of which was an integral garage with the front door to one side and a large bay window further along.

As soon as she rang the doorbell, she was greeted by Martin's smiling face. It was as though he had eagerly been awaiting her arrival.

'Welcome!' he said, gazing down at her suitcase. 'Here, let me take that. I can't believe you've lugged it from the station. I told you I would have given you a lift.'

'No, it's OK. You've done enough for me as it is.' She

stepped inside and gazed around the huge and lavish hallway. 'You've got a beautiful home, Martin, and it's huge. Thank you so much for inviting me to live here.'

'Eh, you've seen nothing yet. Let me give you a tour,' he said, putting the suitcase down in the hall.

For several minutes she followed him like an eager puppy while he showed her around his lovely home. She was spellbound by the size of the rooms and the sheer opulence of the place. There was so much to take in, from the luxurious high-tech kitchen with its central island to the two comfy reception rooms, one of which had the most enormous TV she had ever seen.

Upstairs was just as impressive. The master bedroom had a separate dressing room and en suite with shower, loo and bidet. Inside the main bathroom was a whirlpool bath as well as a large shower unit, and the three other bedrooms were all doubles with a range of fitted furniture.

'Take your pick,' he said when he had shown her round the last one.

'Wow! I'm flabbergasted, Martin. Your home is gorgeous and it's huge.'

He grinned. 'Not what you were expecting from a wide boy like me, eh?'

'No, I didn't think that at all!' she said.

She hadn't meant it to sound so vehement and for a moment they both became a little uncomfortable. It was exactly what she had been thinking and she was embarrassed at having been caught out.

Martin broke the silence. 'I told you I was rattling around in the place. I thought it was a good idea at first but, well, it's better shared.'

'I see you're a keen gardener as well,' she said, wanting to change the subject.

'Oh no, not at all. That was all in place when I bought the house and I have a gardener to maintain it. I wouldn't know where to start, to be honest. Anyway, which bedroom would you like?'

'I erm, don't know. They're all wonderful.'

'I tell you what then, why don't you plump for the one nearest the bathroom? Would you like a coffee?'

'I'd like to unpack first, if that's OK.'

''Course it is. Tell you what,' he repeated, 'once you've got yourself sorted, why don't you come and join me downstairs? I'll even throw in a few biscuits just for you.'

Beth grinned. 'You really know how to spoil a girl, don't you?'

Once Martin had gone, Beth picked up her case and went through to one of the bedrooms. She liked this one. Not only was it nearest the main bathroom, but it was also decorated in warm, neutral shades with expensive-looking bedding and curtains to match. There was also a cosy armchair in the corner, where she could imagine herself sitting reading a book.

She couldn't believe her luck. If she was honest with herself, she hadn't expected him to have a home like this. She couldn't understand why she thought that way, though; after all, he must have been well able to afford it considering that he owned a nightclub and several bars. Maybe it was because the home exuded class, and she chided herself for thinking that way. Brady's snobbery must have rubbed off on her again.

It hadn't been easy for her to reach a decision about

moving into Martin's home. But at the end of the day, she hadn't had much choice. The situation with Sally was becoming unbearable and Beth knew Sally wanted rid of her. Her assumption was proved correct when her friend's face lit up at her announcement that she was leaving. So her options had been either to move in with Martin or go back home to her mother and father. And she knew that she couldn't face the latter.

Once she had made her decision, the prospect of living with Martin made her both nervous and excited. Nervous because after the way Brady had treated her, it was difficult to put her trust in a man again. And excited because that was the way Martin made her feel. He had a magnetism that drew her in, and the more she tried to resist, the more she was pulled towards him. She just hoped that she hadn't made a mistake in coming to live here.

After she had unpacked, Beth spent some time tidying herself up and applying a little makeup. She didn't normally wear makeup when she was at home, but she instinctively wanted to look good. When she got downstairs, she found Martin in the kitchen. Beth was glad she'd made the effort as she caught his reaction.

It was brief and he didn't say anything, but she saw the way he checked her out and a glimmer of satisfaction lit up his face. 'Here we go,' he said, nodding at the coffee percolator. 'I'll grab some cups. Would you like milk and sugar?'

'Milk, no sugar.'

'OK, I'll sort it. Why don't you go through to the living room and make yourself comfortable?'

Beth did as he instructed and was surprised to find the large coffee table decked out with two plates full of cakes and biscuits.

'You're so good to me,' she said when he came through with the coffees.

'You deserve it. I know these past few months can't have been easy for you.'

Beth found herself suddenly choked up with emotion, but she swallowed it down. She didn't want to make a fool of herself in front of him like she'd already done that night in The Amber Room. She supposed the last thing he wanted was an emotional wreck sharing his home.

'Now that you're here,' he said. 'I want you to make yourself comfortable. It's your home as much as mine, especially since you insisted on paying me rent,' he teased. 'I meant what I said about no funny business too. I respect you and wouldn't do anything to make you feel uncomfortable. As far as I'm concerned, I'm helping a mate out until you find your feet, and I'd do the same for any of my friends.'

She forced a smile. 'Thank you.'

But her smile hid the way she really felt. For some strange reason, she found herself wishing he was more than a friend. She couldn't help but notice that there was a vast contrast between the way he treated her and the way he was perceived in the outside world. And she mustn't forget that his violent behaviour, which she had witnessed first-hand, backed up the impression people had of him. Perhaps he was right; it was best to keep things on a strict friendship basis, and as soon as she was back on her feet she would move into a place of her own.

They continued to make general conversation about

his home, the club and various customers and employees as they drank coffee and munched cake and biscuits. Beth loved having the inside gossip on the workplace, but she promised to keep anything he told her to herself.

After a while he took the empty plates and cups through to the kitchen. Despite Beth insisting that she would help him clear up, he told her he was fine to sort it out himself. Left alone in the room, she was lost for what to do. Even though he'd told her to make herself comfortable, it wasn't quite home yet, and she wondered how to pass the time.

Beth walked to the window and looked out onto the street. She had chosen one of her days off to move as she worked most weekends. Therefore, it was a school day. She saw a few mothers walking down the road with young children and expensive-looking prams and felt a pang of regret. Beth noticed that they were all well-dressed. Checking the time, she assumed they were going to bring their older children home from school.

Beth was tempted to switch on the TV, but it seemed a bit intrusive. Maybe she should watch the TV in her bedroom instead and leave the living room for Martin to watch his choice of programmes. But, not wanting to disappear yet in case he came back into the room, she plonked herself down and took a newspaper from the rack at the side of the sofa.

It was a local rag and she flicked through, scanning articles about building developments, fundraisers and school triumphs. You could learn a lot about the area by reading the local news. She was about halfway through when something grabbed her interest, and the breath caught in her throat. She read through the item, surprising herself at how irate it made her feel.

Beth had read about two-thirds of the article when Martin walked back into the room, saying, 'Well, that's that lot in the dishwasher. What do you fancy for tea?'

She slapped the newspaper shut and pushed it back in the rack.

'Don't stop on my account,' he said.

'Oh, it's OK. I've seen enough anyway.'

'OK, no worries. So, what *would* you like for tea?'

'Oh, it's alright. I won't trouble you. I'll get something for myself later. I'm just going to go and have a rest. I'm feeling a bit done in. It must be all the excitement of the move,' she said, attempting to sound nonchalant but failing.

Then she rushed from the room. Beth just wanted to be alone now. She needed to process what she had just seen. And she knew she couldn't do that while Martin was there. He would soon see through her and suss that something was on her mind.

32

Martin didn't see Beth for the rest of that evening. When it was time to cook his evening meal, he knocked at her bedroom door and asked her if she wanted anything. But she still insisted on grabbing something later. Then, after he'd eaten and was parked in front of the TV, he heard her come downstairs and make her way to the kitchen.

He hoped she'd put in an appearance but, to his dismay, after spending around twenty minutes in the kitchen, she went back to her room. Whatever she had eaten couldn't have been very substantial if she had cooked and eaten it in that amount of time. Martin found himself disappointed but also concerned about her. What could have changed in such a short space of time?

Maybe she had taken a call while he had been loading the dishwasher from their afternoon snacks. Or perhaps it was something else. Then he remembered how she had shut the newspaper and shoved it back in the rack as soon as he had come into the room. Could it have something to do with that?

He plucked the newspaper out. It was still bunched up as she had put it away so quickly. Martin leafed through the pages, intent on discovering whatever had upset her. Then he saw it. A full-page article about a new business start-up with a photo of her sly ex-husband.

Martin read through the article. It was all about a company called Harris's Hair and Beauty Supplies Ltd. It was a new start-up, but according to the paper, it was run by a very competent MD, Brady Harris, who had years of experience in the industry. The item then went on to list some of his personal achievements during his career as well as detailing the future aims of the business. All of this was accompanied by several smug quotations from Brady Harris himself.

He put the paper down in disgust, muttering to himself, 'It's a fuckin' brag fest.'

Martin was surprised the newspaper publishers had allowed the dickhead to be so self-indulgent. But perhaps they were eager to hear about local success stories. It was a Cheshire-based publication and the article had pointed out that Brady was a local lad, hailing from Romiley originally and then Marple.

No wonder Beth was upset. It can't have been easy reading about her ex-husband's success when she was still struggling financially. Martin didn't like that she was taking it out on him though by keeping to her room. He hoped she wasn't still holding a candle for her ex. Or maybe it was just that she found it difficult to be sociable when she was filled with so much angst.

Martin mulled over the article for a while. What he couldn't understand was how Brady had got the cash together to set up in business. According to Beth there had been no equity left in their house because Brady had run up so many debts. Maybe that was it. Maybe he'd secured a massive loan from the bank. But what bank would want to lend money to a new start-up led by someone who'd never run a business before?

Unless he hadn't got a loan at all. Could there be something that Beth wasn't telling him?

He decided to leave it for now, even though he hated how it made Beth feel. By and large they were getting along well, and although he was respecting her space, he secretly hoped that eventually it would turn into something. He just needed to take it slowly and give her time to adjust. What he didn't want to do was to turn her against him by prying into her private affairs before she was ready to talk about them.

Martin decided that he would cheer her up instead. He'd propose a meal the following evening to celebrate her moving in, and he knew exactly the type of place he would take her. Somewhere upmarket in the city centre. Then perhaps they'd have a few drinks afterwards. It would be good to see her relax and let her hair down.

When Beth got up the next day, she felt awful. Martin had been so good. He'd opened up his home to her and how had she repaid him? By spending the night in her bedroom and completely ignoring him. She hadn't even popped her head into the living room to say good night. And all because of her rat of an ex-husband.

She was still annoyed at the fact that Brady had set himself up in business using the money that should have been half hers by rights. But she decided that she needed to put it out of her mind for now. Her first priority was to apologise to Martin.

Beth came across him in the kitchen and was shamefaced. She was just about to apologise to him when he asked, 'How would you like to come for a meal this evening? No ties. I just thought it would be a nice way to celebrate your move.'

'Aw, that's really nice of you, especially after how I was last night.'

Martin shrugged. 'Don't worry about it.'

'But I do. I shouldn't have been like that, but I came across something that upset me.' Martin cast her an inquisitive glance, so she continued, 'Brady has set himself up in business and from what I've found out it's going really well.'

'Take no notice of what he's doing. Concentrate on yourself now. With a bit of luck, he'll fall flat on his face anyway.'

His words made Beth giggle. Then she asked, 'Where are you thinking of going?'

'I've already booked it. I hope you don't think I'm overstepping the mark. It's *Tattu*. Have you heard of it?'

Beth's face dropped. She *had* heard of it. It was a high-end Chinese restaurant in Spinningfields, viewed by many as one of the best places to eat in Manchester. In fact, it was somewhere Brady had always promised they'd visit, as he liked a bit of luxury. But in her current circumstances she knew it was out of her reach financially.

'Yes, I have, but I'm sorry, I can't stretch to that at the moment.'

'No worries, my treat for being such a great house guest.'

He laughed and Beth knew he was teasing her for her moodiness the previous evening.

'Are you sure?' she asked.

''Course I am. I wouldn't ask if I wasn't, would I?'

Beth was bowled over when she saw the inside of the restaurant with its subtle lighting and polished wood floors. She noticed that the walls were a combination of wood panelling and padded leather in a diamond pattern. There were booths with circular leather seating to match the walls and other tables where the chairs had velour upholstery.

She'd taken care with her appearance, knowing that the place was upmarket, and as they walked through the restaurant she gazed around. She took in the faux trees tastefully adorned with beautiful red and pink flowers accentuated by feature lighting.

They were led to one of the booths and she noticed some familiar faces at the nearby tables. There was an actress she had seen on a soap opera, a local newsreader, and when they sat down Martin whispered to her that they had just passed one of Manchester City's star players.

'You certainly know how to cheer a girl up, don't you?' she commented.

Martin didn't say anything. Instead, he flashed an enigmatic smile, and passed her a menu.

Beth struggled on her choice of dishes. It was all so expensive, and she deliberated over how many courses to order. 'I'll just have a main course,' she said, trying not to take advantage.

'No, you don't have to do that. I'm having a starter so you might as well have one too. Otherwise, you'll just be sat twiddling your thumbs while you watch me stuff my face.' Then, as if picking up on how she felt, he added, 'Don't worry about the cost. I've told you; this is my treat. And if I want to treat a mate, I will, so have whatever you want.'

'OK,' said Beth, looking down at the menu again to hide her embarrassment.

It was the best meal she had eaten in a long time. They had three courses plus wine, and then Martin ordered a bottle of expensive champagne at the end of the meal and proposed a toast to her and the future.

'Wow!' she said, rubbing her tummy. 'That was delicious. Thank you so much for such a lovely meal.'

'You're very welcome.'

She was pensive for a while then, deciding to find out more about him, she asked, 'How did you get into the hospitality business?'

Martin cleared his throat before batting back his own question. 'You mean, how did I afford the nightclub and bars?'

'Well, yes, I suppose so.'

At first Martin wouldn't meet her eyes. He looked down at the table and began circling his forefinger round the rim of his glass. Eventually he looked up at her. 'Listen, I've done a lot of things in the past, things that I'm not proud of. You don't need to know the details. I've put all that behind me. Nowadays I like to keep everything above board.'

Beth could sense his discomfort and instinctively she replied, 'We've all done things we're not proud of.'

Martin grinned and shook his head, and for a moment she felt as though he was patronising her. He had no idea what she had been through, and it was tempting to put him straight. But there was no way she was about to confide. Like him, she preferred to keep some things to herself, for now.

33

After three weeks of having Beth as his house guest, Martin was feeling more relaxed about things. The meal had been a good idea. It had broken the ice between them after her reaction to the news of her ex-husband's new business venture.

Since that night they had often eaten together, chatted and watched TV. But Martin had never bothered trying to take things further. He knew she was still hurting after her divorce, and he didn't want to scare her off.

Tonight she was having a night off and had gone out with her friend Sally. As Martin made his way around Virtuoso, he thought about how gorgeous she looked when she got dressed up to go out. She was wearing a short, fitted dress which showed off her long, shapely legs. Her hair and makeup were perfect as always, and her perfume smelt wonderful. Like her, it was classic and seductive without being overpowering, and he found himself hoping she didn't attract the wrong sort of attention while she was out.

The night had drawn to a close and Martin locked up after watching the last of the customers and his staff leave the building. His head bouncer, Skippy, often did the job for him. He was so loyal and trustworthy that Martin had given him his own set of keys. But tonight he hadn't seen him for a while, and Martin presumed he had left the building without him noticing.

He opened the main door and went through to his own office, checking the door handle to make sure it was locked. It was one of several rooms up there. Some were used to store stock, and there was a second office used by a part-time bookkeeper during the day. She took care of the accounts and saved Martin a job, meaning he only had to check things over every now and again.

Martin was walking along the corridor, checking the locks on the other doors, when he heard the sound of movement coming from the bookkeeper's office. He tensed and approached the office stealthily. Then he put his ear to the door, to check he wasn't mistaken.

He had no doubt that there was movement coming from inside the room. It was difficult to tell just what the noise was though. There was a rhythmic rubbing sound and the occasional banging of something. Then he heard a groan, and Martin realised what the sound was.

Feeling less nervous but a bit irate, he pushed open the door to find Skippy bending over the desk with a girl hidden beneath him, his naked backside thrusting backwards and forwards. 'What the hell do you think you're playing at?' Martin demanded. 'Get you're fuckin' clothes on and get out, the pair of you!' he yelled.

Skippy turned around, his face a vivid shade of red, and stopped what he was doing. Martin could only see part of the girl's body from behind and he found himself wondering if she was one of his bar staff or a customer. He shut the door and walked up the corridor. It was enough for the couple to know that they had been caught in the act, and he didn't want to see any more. They might have been up to no good, but he'd allow them some dignity while they got themselves dressed.

He was amused in a way, knowing that he had done things just as bad in his younger days. He couldn't blame Skippy for taking advantage of his position, but he wasn't going to let him know that. It wasn't good to show any sign of weakness, and Skippy needed to be made aware that he'd overstepped the mark. Martin decided that he'd give them a couple of minutes before he returned and started laying the law down.

While he waited, he unlocked the door to his own office and sat behind his desk. After two minutes, when Martin had heard nothing further, he got up, determined to go and have it out with them. He walked out into the corridor and locked his office door.

Turning around, Martin caught Skippy leaving the office, his face a picture of embarrassment. Then the girl followed him. At first he couldn't see her face, as she was still hidden behind Skippy, who began to walk towards Martin on his way to the exit.

'Get her out of here and then come back up. I want a word,' said Martin, and Skippy nodded, shamefaced.

He passed Martin with his head hung low. Then Martin caught sight of Skippy's paramour and he stifled a gasp of shock. She met his eyes and plastered on a fake smile, then gave him a look that cut right through him.

Martin was dazed to discover that it was Jodi, the girlfriend of the lad he had killed. How the hell had she wormed her way around Skippy? He hadn't even seen her in the club. That in itself spoke volumes, telling Martin that she must have deliberately kept herself hidden from .him. Then there was the fact that she and Skippy were such an odd match: he was huge and very different in type from her previous boyfriend, whereas she was so petite.

There was no doubt in Martin's mind that she had engineered this. She had hooked up with Skippy for one reason only, and Martin knew that it was because she was on a revenge mission and she had chosen Skippy as a way to get to him. How exactly she would do that he wasn't quite sure, but he was dreading finding out.

There was something about her that unnerved him. Martin had never been frightened of much. He'd taken on bigger guys than him in his life. But this slip of a girl terrified him. Because she knew what he had done. And that knowledge had the power to destroy his life.

It was Friday night and Beth was having a great time. She was so pleased to have made up with Sally, and now that they were no longer living under the same roof, the pressure was off. Sally could boast about her conquests just like she used to without Beth feeling put out at the prospect of her parading a series of strange men through the flat.

Beth had always thought that what Sally did with her life was her own business. However, she had underestimated just how sexually active her friend was. She'd also naïvely assumed that it wouldn't affect her when they were living under the same roof.

Although Beth wasn't as forward as her friend, she was finally enjoying being single and carefree. There were certain advantages to being shot of her ex-husband, such as the ability to flirt outrageously without feeling guilty. And thanks to the dress she was wearing, together with her stunning good looks, she was commanding a lot of male attention tonight.

Currently they were in a taxi on the way to Manchester, having had a few drinks in the local bars of Bramhall before Sally decided there was a brilliant nightclub she wanted to show Beth. Up to now, Sally had been too busy soaking up the male attention to have a serious chat, but now that there were just the two of them in the back of the cab, she asked, 'So, how's it going with you and your dishy landlord?'

'What do you mean?'

Sally gave a forward jerk of her head. 'You know.'

Beth tutted. 'Sally! It's not like that. He just offered to put me up when I needed somewhere to live.'

'You sure?' asked Sally.

'Yeah, of course I'm sure.'

'Then why have you gone scarlet?'

'Alright,' Beth conceded. 'Maybe I do find him attractive. But he doesn't see me in that way.'

'Are you joking?' Sally scoffed. 'I've seen the way he looks at you. It's obvious that's why he asked you to live with him. He's got a thing for you, and he hopes that you'll get closer now you're under his roof.'

'No, Martin's not like that. Honestly, he's been so respectful, and he's insisted on keeping everything above board. He hasn't given any hint of anything like that. In fact, he's always telling me to let him know if he's overstepping the mark, like when he took me for that meal for instance.'

'But that's just the sort of man he is, isn't it? All enigmatic and composed. Fuckin' hell, Beth, that's such a turn on. And he probably doesn't want to come on too strong either. He knows what you've been going through, doesn't he? I bet you've even been mooning over bloody Brady in front of him, haven't you?'

'No! Well, only a bit.'

'There you go then. You're sending him the wrong vibes. All he needs is a bit of encouragement from you. Believe me, I know how men work.'

'Look, Sally, me and him wouldn't work. He more or less admitted to me that he's got a dodgy past, although he does seem to be a reformed character now.'

'It doesn't matter what he's done in the past, Beth. Especially if, like you say, he's a reformed character now. It's how he treats you that's important.'

'But it's not like that,' Beth repeated.

'Well, it could be if you'll let it. Bloody hell, Beth, if I had a hunk like that living under the same roof as me, I wouldn't be pussy footing around. And why shouldn't you and him get it on? You're not with Brady anymore, so you can do what the hell you like.'

Beth didn't say anything more, but she was pensive. Sally had pointed out what she already knew. There was a mutual attraction and Martin was being the perfect gentleman. But maybe, like Sally said, he was just waiting for a bit of encouragement from her.

34

The conversation with Skippy had been awkward for Martin, not only because Skippy's embarrassment at being caught in the act made him uncomfortable, but also because of Jodi. Skippy had apologised and promised he wouldn't take advantage again, but explained to Martin that he was quite taken by Jodi.

It had been difficult for Martin not to divulge who she really was. But he couldn't afford to do that. He wasn't sure how much Skippy knew about that night, and now that he was smitten with Jodi, Martin no longer knew where his loyalties lay. It was an unsettling feeling. What if Skippy, like Billy, was to take advantage of him?

By the time he got home, he wasn't in the best frame of mind and all these thoughts were spinning around in his head. The house was quiet, and he assumed Beth was already in bed as it was late. He locked the front door and made his way upstairs, taking care to tread quietly as he passed Beth's room.

When he opened his bedroom door, he was greeted by a trail of women's clothing on the bedroom floor. His eyes followed them to the bed, where he saw Beth. Her body was concealed by the duvet apart from her upper arms and shoulders. They were bare, and he assumed the rest of her must be naked too. It was his second shock of the night.

As he walked across the room, she opened her eyes and smiled at him. 'Hi. I was wondering when you'd get back. Me and Sally had a brill night. I wanted to come to Virtuoso to see you, but Sally insisted we went to this other club she keeps raving about.'

Martin could tell straightaway by her brazenness and the way she was rambling that she'd had far too much to drink. 'What are you doing?' he asked.

'Waiting for you, of course. I thought it would be a nice surprise for you.'

'Well, it isn't,' he said gruffly. Then, realising his tone was off, he added, 'Beth, I'm too tired for this, and you're drunk. I think you should go back to your room.'

She flung the duvet off to reveal her naked body. 'You sure?'

Martin took in the sight of her and for a moment he was tempted. But he didn't want it to happen like this. 'Beth don't, please. This isn't you.'

'What isn't me? One of us has got to make the first move. Why are you so bloody controlled? You're such a tease. But I like the way you're so cool. It's a massive turn on.'

'Beth, no. I don't want to take advantage of you when you've had too much to drink. Please go back to your room. We'll talk in the morning.'

She stood up and almost lost her footing. Her expression was one of a petulant child. 'I get it. You don't fancy me after all. Sorry for being an idiot. I must have misread the situation.'

'Beth, no! Don't be like that.'

But she had already passed him and stomped back to her room. Martin felt bad. He didn't want her to think he didn't fancy her. Of course he fancied her, he always had. But if he'd given in to his desires tonight, it might have created a bad situation between them. He respected her too much for that, and he didn't want her holding it against him in the morning when she had sobered up. Still, it was good to know that she felt the same way as him.

When Beth woke up, she recalled the previous evening and cringed with embarrassment. Did she really get into Martin's bed and throw herself at him? Worse still, she remembered how he had spurned her advances.

Deciding she needed to address the situation sooner rather than later, she dragged herself out of bed despite her throbbing head. She put on a dressing gown, one that covered her up as she didn't want to send out any more signals. Then she went downstairs.

She found Martin in the kitchen. 'Hi, want a coffee?' he asked.

Beth felt herself blush, but Martin didn't seem concerned, and she wondered if he was deliberately acting casual to spare her embarrassment. Even so, she knew she couldn't leave things unsaid.

She waited till he had his back to her while preparing the coffee before she began, 'I erm, I'm sorry about last night.'

She was just about to assure him that it wouldn't happen again when he turned around and said, 'No, I'm sorry. I think I was a bit harsh with you and I just wanted to let you know that, well, it wasn't because I'm not attracted to you, just the opposite in fact.

'I didn't want to take advantage of you when you were drunk, which was why I sent you back to your room.'

'I'm sorry, you must think I'm a right boozer. I mean, it's not the first time you've seen me in that state, is it? I don't normally get drunk and throw myself at men, but it's just that…'

'I know, you've been through a lot. Anyone would be forgiven for having a few crazy nights after what you've been through.'

'Thanks for being so understanding,' said Beth. 'And I want to let you know that it wasn't just because I was drunk. I'm attracted to you too.' She took a deep breath as she prepared to say her next words, 'But it's more than that. I think I'm developing feelings for you. You're so different to Brady. You're caring and considerate. I love the way you are with people, you're so fair with your staff, and you have a way of always making things seem better even when they feel like shit.'

Suddenly she felt self-conscious and was afraid she might have said too much, so she backtracked, saying, 'I'll understand if you don't feel the same though.'

'Beth, I do feel the same. I'm not just attracted to you. I adore you and I'd do anything for you. But you don't want to be with someone like me.'

'That's where you're wrong, Martin. I can't think of anyone I'd rather be with. And, you wouldn't have been taking advantage of me. It's what I want.'

She watched the shocked expression on Martin's face, then he walked over to her and took hold of her by the shoulders. 'I want you to think about what you're saying, Beth. Are you sure this is what you want? I mean, really sure?'

'Yes, I'm sure. I know how I feel.'

He didn't say anything more, but his lips found hers and they shared a long, passionate embrace. Her hangover was forgotten as she found herself craving the feel of him, then sighing with pleasure as he ran his hands along her body. Then he took her by the hand.

'Come on,' he said, leading her upstairs to his bedroom.

Once inside, he turned to her and kissed her again. Then he deftly loosened the belt on her dressing gown, slipped it from her shoulders and let it fall to the floor. When he began removing his own clothes, Beth helped him.

For a few moments they stood naked, kissing and caressing each other's bodies. Then they tumbled into bed together. By the time he entered her, all Beth's senses were tingling. She didn't think she'd ever wanted a man so much. It didn't take long till she climaxed, letting out an unrestrained gasp of exhilaration.

They stayed in bed for the rest of the morning, making love and chatting intermittently. He was a skilled lover, tender and giving, and for Beth it reflected the way he had treated her ever since she had met him. He made her feel special, and she knew that it didn't matter what he had done in the past, she wanted this man now more than ever, and there was no way she was ever going to let him go.

35

It was almost a week later. Since that first morning when they had slept together, Martin and Beth hadn't been able to keep their hands off each other. Sometimes they made love in his room, sometimes in hers, sometimes they didn't bother waiting till they got upstairs. Their intimate moments had brought them closer, as had their in-depth chats.

It was Saturday morning, and they were currently lying in Martin's sumptuous king-size bed, tired but satiated after a session of passionate lovemaking, when Beth stared into Martin's eyes and said, 'Who would have thought you and me would have ended up together.'

Her words took him by surprise and Martin stared back at her and smiled, 'Where I grew up there weren't any girls like you,' he said.

'Why, what were they like?'

Martin laughed. 'They were rough. Most of them could hold their own in a fight and they had mouths like sewers. I'm not saying they were all bad though. It's just that it was a tough estate, one of the toughest in Stockport. The lads were even worse.'

'Does that include you?' Beth teased.

Martin sighed. 'I did what the other kids did, getting up

to mischief, fighting, thieving. It was the done thing. You did what you had to do to survive. My parents never had any money, so it was the only way to get what I wanted. Sometimes we only had a piece of toast for tea depending on whether my dad had won at the bookies, so I either went thieving or went hungry.'

Beth stared at him with a look of astonishment, and Martin feared for a moment that he might have said too much. He quickly backpedalled, saying, 'I realise now how wrong it was but at the time I didn't know any different.'

But Beth's look of astonishment soon turned to one of sympathy. 'No, it's OK. I understand. Was your dad a gambler?'

'Yeah, big time. That's why we never had much, but we didn't realise it when we were kids. In fact, it was just the opposite. When he'd had a big win, he came home full of himself like the conquering hero. We'd get so excited about all the treats he planned to buy us that we'd forget all the times we'd been without.'

Beth stared intensely at him, and Martin suddenly felt embarrassed. 'Anyway, it's all in the past,' he added, trying to shrug it off. 'Look at me now.'

He waved his hand slowly around the bedroom, illustrating his achievements through his plush surroundings. He was aware that to Beth his upbringing would seem a world away from her respectable middle-class roots. Even though they grew up only a few miles apart, his background couldn't have been more different from hers, and he wanted to reassure her that he could now give her what she deserved.

Martin knew that Beth had hoped for better in life than working behind a bar in a nightclub. But at the moment there was no sign of her looking for a job elsewhere. She had been sucked into the excitement of the whole nightclub scene and was enjoying it. He couldn't help but feel that she was capable of greater things and that working for him was holding her back.

Although they were growing more intimate, they were still keeping to their arrangement of Beth paying him rent and helping out with the shopping. To Martin though, it didn't seem right now that they were a couple.

After thinking about it for a while, he said, 'I don't know why you don't move into my bedroom now. There's plenty of room in here for both of us.'

She looked pensive for a moment before she spoke. 'Is that what you'd like?'

'Yes. I want to feel like you're my partner rather than just the bloody lodger.'

She chuckled. 'OK, I'll do it, but you'll be sorry when I start nicking all your wardrobe space and leaving my makeup everywhere.'

He kissed her on the shoulder. 'No, I won't,' he said. 'Because it's all part of you. In fact, I'll bloody love it. And while we're on the subject, now that we're partners, you don't have to keep giving me rent every month.'

'No, I'll still pay you.'

'Why? It's not as if I need the money, is it?'

'I don't care. I don't want to take advantage of you. I want to pay my way.'

He smiled. 'OK, suit yourself.'

That was the end of the subject. Martin knew that she was independent and if that's the way she wanted to play things then he would respect her wishes.

***

It was Beth's own screams that woke her up in the early hours of the morning, and she sat up in bed clutching her racing heart. 'Oh my God! Oh my God,' she muttered, trying to clear her last vision of Rex from her mind.

It was the first time Martin had witnessed her nightmares and he also shot up in bed. 'What is it?' he asked.

Remembering how Brady used to react negatively to her nightmares, Beth tried to play it down, despite the fact that her heart was still pounding and she felt shaky. 'Oh, nothing. It was just a nightmare. I sometimes have them. It's OK. Go back to sleep.'

'But I heard you call someone's name. Rex, was it?' He touched her gently on the arm and asked, 'Who's Rex, Beth?'

She felt the sting of tears. 'He was my dog.'

'Really? What happened to him?'

Her voice dropped as she uttered, 'He died.'

'Oh, I'm sorry. What happened?'

The tears filled her eyes now and she said, 'I found him. In the woods. He... he was... he was dead and covered in blood.'

When her voice broke on a sob, Martin took her in his arms. 'Oh Beth, I'm so sorry. Why didn't you tell me?'

'I didn't like to. There's nothing you could do.'

'Do you think a fox might have had him?'

An image of the man holding the blood-soaked knife flashed through Beth's mind, but she tried to shake it away. 'No. He was cut.'

Martin seemed to realise that it was a difficult subject, so he didn't press her. Instead, after comforting her for some time, he said, 'You know, if I ever found out who had done it, I'd do for them.'

'Don't say that,' whispered Beth.

'I would, Beth. They're evil bastards and want sorting. I can't stand to see you upset. And if anybody ever hurts you in the future, they've got me to answer to.'

Beth pulled away from him and tried to go back to sleep. She didn't want to think any more about what he had said. But in her heart, she knew that Martin's love for her was so powerful that he would do anything to avenge her, no matter what it involved.

The next time Martin saw Jodi was the following night. He'd seen Skippy a couple of times since he'd caught him in the office with Jodi, so now it was business as usual between them. Martin was standing inside the club chatting to Skippy when she came over.

Martin tensed, worried for a moment about another outburst from her. He wondered whether she had yet voiced her suspicions to Skippy about the death of her former boyfriend. But instead of verbally attacking him, she stretched her neck up to Skippy, who stooped to meet her so that she could plant a kiss on his cheek. Martin noticed Skippy blush.

'Boss, this is Jodi. It's about time you two met properly,' Skippy said, slipping a proud hand around her waist and watching her gaze up at him.

Skippy was obviously still embarrassed about being caught on the job with her, but Jodi showed no such embarrassment. In fact, her reaction surprised him.

She smiled widely and said, 'Hi, pleased to *officially* meet you.'

She stressed the word 'officially' as though poking fun at the fact that they had last met under embarrassing conditions. Skippy giggled, relieved to break the tension in the atmosphere, and Martin responded likewise. It seemed the best thing to do under the circumstances.

Martin soon excused himself. He couldn't wait to break away and was left wondering what exactly Jodi was up to. It was clear to him that the persona she presented to Skippy was all sweetness and light, and far different to the version Martin had witnessed.

And why was she pretending she didn't know him? For some reason she didn't seem to want Skippy to know their history. Or perhaps he did know, and she had asked him to play along. Was this so that they could both catch him unawares?

He dismissed the notion. Martin couldn't see Skippy doing something like that. Normally Skippy was the sort of guy that would let him know if he had something to say. He wasn't the underhand type. Martin's paranoia stemmed from what Billy had done. He had thought he could trust him at one time, but the fact that he had let him down now cast doubts as to whether Skippy would too.

Skippy had never been so taken with a woman, from what Martin had seen, and Jodi obviously knew his feelings. Maybe she was playing for time, waiting till she had Skippy exactly where she wanted him so that he would then do her bidding. Martin was unsure how to deal with the whole situation. In the end he decided that all he could do was wait and see if Jodi made a move. He didn't have to wait long.

He was standing in the foyer, keeping an eye on things, when Jodi approached him. There were two of his doormen at front of house, but they were some distance away and would be unable to hear what was being said.

She gave him a look of disgust then hissed, 'Don't think you've got away with things. You haven't. And I'm still gonna make sure you pay for what you did.'

'I didn't do anything.'

'Don't even bother trying to lie. We both know what you did.'

Her gaze was intense while she waited for his reaction, as if daring him to deny it again. But Martin kept quiet.

'Do you realise how easy it would be for me to tell Skippy what you did?' she asked.

Feeling that he had to say something more in his defence, Martin spoke up. 'Tell him what you want. We both know you're lying.'

Then he walked away before she had a chance to fire any more accusations in his direction. What she had said confirmed for Martin that Skippy wasn't yet aware of anything. Perhaps she didn't think he'd believe her. Or perhaps, as Martin had previously surmised, she was biding her time, waiting until Skippy was so taken with her that he'd believe anything.

Or maybe that wasn't part of the plan. But if Jodi wasn't hoping to get Skippy on board in her quest to get revenge, then he had to ask himself, where did Skippy come into her plans? Because, as far as Martin was concerned, she was with Skippy for a reason, and that had to somehow involve him.

36

For more than three months, Martin had been on edge. Whenever he was in the club, he felt tense, expecting Jodi to walk in at any moment. She wasn't always there, but when she was, she often gave him that knowing look – which unnerved him – or glowered at him when nobody else could see. It left him feeling that it was just a matter of time before she did something drastic.

Martin had hoped she might have given up when the police hadn't been able to prove anything against him. But her attitude told him that she was as determined as ever to keep hounding him.

Tonight, as always, he was aware of her presence in the club, and noticing how she hung around Skippy, he kept his distance. As with any night when Jodi was around, Martin couldn't settle. He decided to plonk himself at the bar and get a drink. Beth was working tonight, and he snatched brief conversations with her between customers.

All the staff were now aware of their relationship and seemed to have accepted it. In fact, from what Beth had told him, they were mainly happy for them, although Teresa had warned her to be careful. Martin didn't hold it against the older woman; he knew the reputation he'd gained over the years and Teresa couldn't be expected to know how he felt towards Beth. Fortunately for him, Beth did, and she made light of Teresa's words.

As he sat at the bar, Martin kept casting wary glances in the direction of Skippy and Jodi. They were several metres away so he couldn't hear what was being said, but he noticed the way Jodi seemed to be clinging to Skippy. Martin was just glad that she was keeping away from him.

Then he noticed a shift in Jodi's body language. She stepped away from Skippy and was waving her arms about with her chest thrust forward and chin tilted up. It was evident to Martin that they were arguing, particularly when she stepped forward again so that she was invading Skippy's personal space with her finger pointing in his face.

As the club owner, Martin would normally have walked over to diffuse the situation. It sent out the wrong messages if a member of his staff was seen having a prolonged confrontation, and Martin didn't want the club to be known as a trouble spot.

But he was reluctant to get involved in something involving Jodi. He looked around and spotted one of his other bouncers not too far away. Martin called him over.

'Eh, have you seen what's going on over there with Skippy? I think that girl's trouble. Go over and make sure everything's alright, will you?'

As the bouncer walked over, Martin could hear Jodi screeching and he knew that the situation had escalated. To Martin's relief, two other bouncers joined the one he had sent over. As he watched, Jodi threw a punch at Skippy, who grabbed her in a bear hug. Her arms were flailing about, and Martin could hear Skippy shouting at her now, telling her to calm down or he'd have to have her thrown out.

This seemed to make her even more angry, so Skippy handed her over to the other bouncers who between them removed her from the club. As they carried her away, she continued waving her fists at Skippy and hurling abuse. Martin couldn't catch everything she said, but it was something about Skippy being a dirty womanising bastard.

Heaving a sigh of relief that it wasn't about him, Martin walked over to Skippy to find out what had happened. 'You alright?' he asked.

Skippy shifted uneasily. 'Yeah, sorry about that, boss. I wasn't expecting her to kick off like that.'

'What's the problem?' Martin demanded.

He could tell Skippy was uncomfortable; he kept squinting and wouldn't make eye contact, and he folded his arms across his body as though shielding himself. When he spoke, his words were rushed.

'I dunno, she's off her fuckin' head, boss. I knew she was jealous but it's worse than I thought. She's always going on about all the girls in the club and making out I'm giving someone the eye. She can't stand it if I'm friendly with the customers. But you know how it is, girls come up to us all the time. There's one who Jodi thinks fancies me. She's always coming over for a chat and when Jodi saw her looking over tonight, she just went apeshit. I can't get through to her that she's the only one I'm interested in. I fuckin' love the girl. Things would be sound if it wasn't for her jealousy.'

'I think it might be an idea to keep her away from the club,' said Martin. 'It doesn't give a very good impression when my bouncers are involved in personal scrapes.'

Even as he said it, Martin was worried. What if Skippy were to tell her that she wasn't welcome in the club anymore? How would she retaliate if she knew Skippy was acting on Martin's instructions? 'I'm not saying she's banned,' he added. 'But it might be an idea if she doesn't come in so much.'

Skippy's response surprised him. 'Oh, don't worry, boss, it's over.'

'Really?'

'Yeah. Don't get me wrong, I'm really into her. She's a great girl in a lot of ways. But all this jealousy is doing my head in. I can't even do my job properly when she's around 'cos she's always obsessing about other girls.'

The word 'obsessing' caught Martin's attention. It was worrying because he knew she was also obsessed about getting revenge on him, but at the same time, he was glad Skippy had ended the relationship. His hope was that if she were no longer seeing Skippy then perhaps she wouldn't hang around the club so much. With a bit of luck, she'd find another mug and move on.

'To be honest, I think you've made the right decision,' he said. 'I can see the situation's making you unhappy. And of course, it doesn't do a lot of good for the comfort of the customers.'

'I know, boss. I'm sorry,' said Skippy, hanging his head sheepishly.

For a moment Martin was tempted to tell him about her beef with him. He wouldn't tell him everything, of course, just that she kept claiming he'd killed her ex. But then he thought better of it. If he focused on what had happened, it might make Skippy suspicious. And although Skippy had always been loyal, Martin was no longer sure who he could trust.

37

Beth was sitting in the lounge of Martin's home. While he was taking a shower, she was surfing the net on the laptop he had bought her. She loved Sunday mornings when they would laze around after a late night at the club, then either cook Sunday dinner together or go out to a carvery.

As her relationship with Martin progressed, Beth found that she was happier than she had ever been. Despite his reputation, she found him to be a good man. She, like many others, had adversely judged him, but it was only by getting to know him that she had learnt what he was really like.

Unlike Brady, Martin didn't prejudge people. He gave everybody a fair chance, donated to charity and wasn't always trying to get one up on the competition. He was liked and well-respected by staff and friends alike. He was also very charismatic and charming, which was what had drawn her to him in the first place. And as for the lovemaking – wow!

Beth couldn't help but draw comparisons between Martin and Brady, and she was beginning to wonder what she had ever seen in her ex-husband. Although he was good-looking, his personality was lacking. He was a total snob, and when she looked back, she realised just how much he talked down to people. Brady was also very materialistic, in fact, in Beth's view, money was almost like a god to him.

Despite how well she was getting on with Martin, she couldn't help but feel that he had never fully opened up to her. That was part of the attraction; as Sally had said, he was very enigmatic. But there was something that she couldn't quite put her finger on. For the first three months that they had been a couple he seemed constantly on edge, especially when he was in Virtuoso.

Fortunately, he'd been a lot more relaxed for the last couple of weeks. Beth knew it had something to do with the club. She'd noticed that the change in Martin seemed to have taken place since the night Skippy had a row with his girlfriend and split up with her. There was something about the girl Beth didn't like. She'd seen the hateful way she looked at people, including Martin and herself.

Beth hoped that everything was alright with Martin and that he wasn't involved in anything shady. She didn't have the nerve to ask him though; after he had told her he'd moved on from his past, it would have seemed like she was doubting his word.

Despite that one niggle, Beth knew that Martin was a better man than Brady. She just wished that she could move on from what her ex had done to her. It sickened her to see Brady doing so well knowing that he had funded his business by blackmailing her.

Martin walked into the lounge to find Beth on her laptop, but she quickly shut it as soon as she saw him. Her glance towards him was only a cursory one and when she spoke, she didn't maintain eye contact.

'I think I'll grab *my* shower now.'

She leapt up and was soon out through the door, calling over her shoulder, 'Do you fancy binging on Netflix later?'

'Yeah, sure,' said Martin.

His response was half-hearted as his mind was on the laptop. Martin had seen her using it a lot lately. She never discussed what she was looking at, but he often noticed a look of concentration on her face and sometimes a frown. When he'd asked, she'd just said she was looking at her friends' posts on social media.

Martin knew it was more than that, and curiosity made him pick up the laptop and open the lid. It had shut down and was password protected but he knew the password. He shouldn't have done but he'd been so troubled by her obsessive use of the laptop that he'd made a point of watching her key it in previously.

As he tapped the letters in and saw the screen ping to life, Martin felt bad. But he had to know what Beth was up to. He loved her more than he had ever loved any woman and he couldn't bear to think that she was keeping secrets from him.

Listening out for Beth in case she should come back downstairs, he went straight to the Internet search engine and called up Beth's search history. There were various websites listed, one of which was for Harris's Hair and Beauty. Martin knew it was Brady's company because of the newspaper article he had previously spotted. So that's what she was up to?

Curious, he called up the website and spent a few minutes

surfing through pages relating to the business and its staff, including a glowing profile of Brady. Then he looked at details and prices of the various products and customer testimonials. There was nothing there that Martin wouldn't have expected.

He came out of the website and tried a couple more of those listed in Beth's search history. There was a beauty-based forum in which consumers were raving about this new company that supplied great products they couldn't source elsewhere. That company was, of course, Harris's Hair and Beauty. Then there was the website of another company called Sevran Cosmetics, but Martin wasn't quite sure how that fitted into the picture.

The next few websites he looked at were news sites with articles all about the new company. Many were similar to the newspaper article Martin had read, as they gave details of the new company and the achievements to date of the managing director. But then Martin read a piece by an industry insider who predicted that Brady's company would do great things and would probably even take the prize for the best up-and-coming company at the next industry awards.

Martin slammed the laptop shut and put it back where Beth had left it. He felt sickened by what he had seen. He could understand Beth being interested in what her ex-husband was up to, but the amount of time she had spent on the laptop and the number of sites she had visited appeared excessive.

He sat and pondered over the situation, realising that he wasn't only sickened, he was hurt. As they had become closer, Beth had told him repeatedly how much she loved him and how she felt that he was more of a man than Brady would ever be. But if she really felt that way, then why would she still be obsessed with her ex-husband?

Martin was tempted to speak to her about the situation but that would have meant admitting that he had been spying on her. There must be a better way to tackle it, he thought. But at the moment he couldn't think how, so he decided to keep schtum for now while he had a good think about things.

38

It was the following day and Beth was waiting for Martin to go out. He had told her he needed to check on a few of his bars while they were open, which would be late morning. Once he was gone, she had a bit of business to attend to herself, but she preferred him not to know about it.

Alighting from the train at Piccadilly, Beth followed the map on her phone till it led her to an office block in the city centre. She looked at the nameplate outside the entrance and was happy to find that the company she was looking for was listed. Then she checked the time on her phone. Ten to twelve. All she had to do now was take a seat in the coffee shop opposite and wait for the staff to take their lunch break.

In the end, Beth waited for over an hour till she spotted the man she was looking for. She tried not to be too disconsolate as she'd known it was a gamble. After all, she was lucky to see him at all; he might have been out on business for all she knew. But he wasn't: he was here.

Beth left her cup half empty; she was tiring of the stuff anyway. Pulling her coat on, she fled from the coffee shop and looked around. At first she couldn't see him, but then she noticed someone she hoped was him in the distance and rushed to catch up.

As Beth got closer, she felt confident that the small man she was following was the one she was looking for. She drew alongside him and glanced his way. Yes, it was definitely him. The confident swagger had given him away but now that she saw his moderately attractive features, she knew she'd got her man.

'Preston! I thought it was you,' she announced. 'How are you?'

Preston Watts did a double take.. Suddenly, a look of recognition lit up his features. 'It's the lovely Mrs Harris. How are you?'

'I'm fine, thank you, but I'm afraid I'm not Mrs Harris anymore.'

'Oh, sorry. I did hear something through the grapevine, but it just escaped my mind for a moment. Anyway, if you ask me, you're well shot. You were far too good for him.'

'Do you not deal with him anymore, then?'

'Well yeah, I do, but just because I do business with him doesn't mean I have to like the guy, does it?'

He flashed an ingratiating smile and Beth couldn't help but smile back. 'Well, as it happens,' she said, 'I'm glad I've bumped into you because there's something I'd like to discuss.'

Preston asked, 'What's that?'

'I'll tell you over lunch,' said Beth.

'Lunch? Really?'

'Oh yes. You'll be glad you came.'

'Will I now, and why's that?'

'You'll have to trust me on it, but I promise, you'll like it.'

***

Martin returned home earlier than expected. It hadn't taken him long to inspect a couple of his bars. The staff there seemed to have everything under control so there was no point in him hanging around. Besides, he much preferred to spend some time with Beth.

But when he got home, he was disconcerted to find that she was out again. She'd had a few mystery outings lately and always told him that she had either gone shopping or gone for a walk. But he was suspicious. She never used to go out alone so much, and because of the amount of time she was spending on the laptop, he wondered whether it could have anything to do with her ex-husband.

He saw that she had left her laptop in the lounge again, and although he hated himself for it, he couldn't resist another peek. This time he started with her social media accounts. He wanted to check whether she had been arranging to meet anybody. He cringed as he scrolled through her private messages, especially when he read one from Sally teasing her about her love life. But there was nothing incriminating.

Convinced there was something she was hiding, he went through her search history again. As with the previous time he had checked, there were various websites relating to the beauty industry, although not so many linked to her ex-husband's company this time. Instead, her latest search related to the company called Sevran Cosmetics, which he'd already come across last time he looked at her laptop. He saw that she had scrolled through a few pages, including the contacts, but the page that struck him was one containing the staff profile of a man called Preston Watts.

Martin studied the photograph on screen and read the brief details. The guy wasn't bad looking. Martin didn't recognise him from anywhere but perhaps he was somebody Beth had known in the past. Somebody associated with her ex-husband. The only reasons he could think of for Beth to be meeting this man were either in connection with her ex or because she was having an affair with him.

Is that what this was all about? Was she seeing this other guy? But why the obsession with the ex? Unless she was deliberately seeing this other guy to get at Brady. Martin was perplexed. Why would she do that? She was supposed to be in love with him.

His confusion soon turned to anger. Whatever she was up to, it wasn't good. But he was through with sneaking around. He wasn't the sort of man to be messed about by anyone, not even Beth. He needed to have it out with her, and he decided that as soon as she got back home that was what he would do no matter how painful the consequences might be.

Preston hadn't been able to believe his luck when Brady Harris's ex-wife approached him in the street. He knew straightaway that he'd seen her before – after all, he wouldn't forget a woman like her – but he couldn't remember where at first. Then she had spoken, and he'd realised who it was.

He remembered meeting her at the Repertoire Christmas party over a year ago where he'd gone as Brady's guest. Preston had been surprised at Brady's nerve in inviting him to a company do where his wife would be. Brady had known full well that he had witnessed his behaviour only a few weeks prior when he'd bedded another woman at a trade show.

At the time, Preston had been struck by how good-looking Beth was. He couldn't understand guys like Brady. Why mess around with other women when you had a wife like that at home? He'd immediately taken a fancy to Beth, although he knew he had no chance, not when she was married to someone else. But she was no longer married to Brady. And here she was, asking him to go for lunch with her.

When they got inside the restaurant, Preston could tell Beth was flirting with him. As she sat opposite him, tucking into a sandwich, she kept giggling girlishly at his jokes and flicking her hair back. But to Preston's consternation, once she had finished eating, she brought the conversation round to her ex-husband and Preston surmised that she must still have a thing for him.

'So you still deal with Brady?' she asked.

'Yeah, that's right.'

'Would you mind if I asked what sort of prices you charge?'

'Huh, nowhere near enough.'

'Why's that?' she asked.

Preston saw an opportunity to put her in the picture about what sort of a man her ex-husband was and, at the same time, portray himself in a good light. 'Well, at one time he was willing to pay whatever it took for me to keep his dirty little secret.'

Beth sat up with an inquisitive look on her face. 'Really? What was that?'

'Well, I don't mind telling you, but I don't want to hurt your feelings.'

'Believe me, I'm over Brady. Anything you tell me about him won't surprise me anymore.'

'OK. Well, we were at a trade show. It was a few weeks before I met you at the Repertoire party. And I'm sorry to tell you this but...' Preston paused for effect then cleared his throat as though it pained him to utter his next words, 'he was with another woman.'

To his astonishment, Beth grinned and shook her head. 'That doesn't surprise me one bit. And I suppose you took advantage of that situation by charging him top price, did you?'

'No! Well, yes, in a way. But it wasn't my idea, I swear. He practically threw money at me so that I wouldn't tell.'

'Sure,' said Beth, grinning again. 'And now that you don't have a hold over him anymore, you're having to settle for bottom dollar, is that right?'

'In a way, I suppose. But it's not my doing. Your ex is a very manipulative man. Repertoire are struggling since he left them so we're not getting anywhere near as many orders from them. Plus, once Brady left them, the guy who took over from him renegotiated the deal, so we don't get as high a price from them for our products.

'Brady knew all that. He knew we needed the business from his new company. At first, I was selling to him at a good price but once he knew how things were going, he renegotiated. The cheeky bastard told me I could either suck it up or lose his business.'

'Sounds about right,' said Beth, grinning again.

Preston wasn't sure whether he'd convinced her that he was the innocent party in all this. But he got the feeling she was laughing at him. The flirting had stopped too, and he was beginning to wonder where all this was going.

Deciding there was only one way to find out, he said, 'Anyway, you still haven't told me what it was you wanted to discuss.'

When she arrived home Beth was feeling upbeat. The meeting with Preston had gone better than she had thought. Her head was so full of plans for the future that she didn't pick up on the negative vibes from Martin when she saw him sitting in the lounge watching TV.

'Hi, love,' she said, walking over to him and giving him a hug and a kiss.

His eyes switched from the screen to her, and it was then that she noticed the fierce expression on his face as he asked, 'How was shopping?'

'Oh, great,' she said.

'And where are your shopping bags?'

Beth felt a rush of guilt. She normally returned with some shopping, even if it wasn't much, so that her cover story would be convincing. But she had been so preoccupied with everything she and Preston had discussed that she'd forgotten to swing by the shops.

'I erm, I didn't see anything that took my fancy.'

Then she noticed the anger in Martin's eyes. 'Don't lie to me, Beth. I think it's about time you told me what the fuck has been going on!'

39

For a moment Beth didn't say anything. Martin wasn't stupid. She could tell by his face that he knew something, so there was no point insulting his intelligence by continuing to lie to him.

'I-I was meeting someone,' she said.

'Yes, I know that. Some guy called Preston Watts from a firm called Sevran Cosmetics. But what I want to know is why. Why were you meeting him, Beth?'

His voice was almost pleading now, and Beth wondered how he knew. 'Have you been following me?' she asked.

'No, I haven't.'

'Well, how do you know who I was meeting then?'

'It wasn't difficult,' he said, and she noticed his eyes flick to the laptop.

She wasn't sure whether he'd wanted to give it away or whether it was a subconscious reaction, but either way, she was livid. 'You've been fuckin' spying on me, haven't you? You've been going through my laptop!'

'Yes, and with good reason.'

'You sly bastard! How could you? That's private. You've no reason to go sneaking into my business.'

'If you hadn't been sneaking around, I wouldn't have

needed to. I knew even before I looked at the laptop that there was summat going on. You're fuckin' obsessed with your ex-husband. I saw it that day when you'd been reading a newspaper article about him. But why, Beth? Why fuckin' tell me you're in love with me when all the time you're hankering after him?'

'I'm not fuckin' hankering after him!'

'Well why are you obsessed with what he's doing then? Or is it this other guy you're sleeping with?'

Beth laughed. 'Have you heard yourself? You sound like a possessive prat! I'm not sleeping with anyone!'

'Well, if you're not, then what the hell is going on? Why are you so obsessed with your ex-husband? I thought you were over him.'

'I am! I am over him,' she cried but she could tell by the look on Martin's face that he wasn't convinced.

She realised that in her eagerness to get back at Brady for what he had done to her, she had driven a wedge between herself and the man she really loved.

'Have you just been using me all this time for somewhere cosy to live while you pursue your ex?' Martin asked. 'And then I suppose you were just planning to up sticks and move back with him, is that it?'

Beth couldn't bear the way this was going. 'No! No!' she yelled. 'I don't want to be with him. That's the last thing I fuckin' want. And as for Preston, why would I want to sleep with that little wimp? He's just someone I'm getting information from.'

'What the hell are you talking about, Beth? What information?'

Beth sighed, then slowly began to explain. 'He's one of the

suppliers to Brady's company. I knew him from previously, but I also knew he had a bit of a thing for me.'

She tried to ignore Martin's angry expression as she continued. 'I used that to my advantage. I'm not proud of it, but I needed to get some information about his dealings with Brady. And Preston was only too happy to oblige. It seems that Preston isn't a big fan of Brady, so he told me everything I needed to know.

'You see, I'm planning to go into business as Brady's competitor. I've found out from Preston how much he charges Brady for his products. Brady pays him so little that it won't be difficult to match. In fact, I've offered to pay slightly more to make sure I get Preston on side. He's even going to send me details of the products and quantities that Brady's company buys.

'I already know several of Brady's old customers and suppliers so I'm planning to approach them as well, although they probably won't be as eager to help me as Preston was. I know a fair bit about the industry too because Brady was always going on about it. If he wasn't slagging his customers off, he was bragging about how he'd got one over on them.'

Beth realised she had been getting carried away, so she drew her monologue to a close by adding, 'That should give me a starting point. The rest I can learn as I go along.'

'But why?' Martin demanded. 'Why would you want to go into the same industry as your ex? There are plenty of other things you could do. Why are you so obsessed with that bastard?'

'Because I want to fuckin' destroy him!' she yelled, her voice tinged with emotion.

'For God's sake, Beth! You're divorced from the man. Move on! If you really want to go into business, there are plenty of other opportunities out there. I'll even help you get started.'

'I knew you'd react like that!' she said. 'That's why I kept it from you.'

'But you would have had to tell me at some point, unless you really were planning on upping sticks.'

'No, I was never going to leave you. It was just difficult to explain why I wanted to do this. Besides, I wasn't sure I could pull it off at first but now that I've seen a few people, I think I can.'

Beth realised that she still hadn't explained why she was set on going up against Brady. She had to tell Martin, otherwise he would assume that a part of her was still in love with her ex. And she couldn't have him think that. 'There's a reason I want to bring him down,' she said. 'You see, we didn't lose money on the house because of his debts. There was plenty of money. He used it all to set up in business.'

'Beth, you're not making sense. How the fuck would he cop for everything and leave you with nothing? You're legally entitled to half.'

She could feel the tremor in her voice as she answered his question. 'Because he blackmailed me.'

Martin looked shocked and it was a moment before he spoke. His next questions were predictable but nonetheless difficult to answer.

'How? How did he blackmail you?' he asked. 'What did you do?'

40

Beth sat down, afraid her legs might give way if she remained standing up.

'OK,' she said. 'This isn't going to be easy, but I'll start at the beginning.' She took a deep breath then said, 'Do you remember when I told you about my dog?'

'Yeah.'

'It was before I met Brady. I used to live alone. And, well, what happened to Rex – it was bad, worse than I told you. That's why I have nightmares. I've been having them ever since it happened, but I don't think I've had any since that night I told you about Rex.'

'Yes, you have.' Beth looked surprised at this observation. 'I've only noticed a couple, but you called out your dog's name, Rex. Both times you went straight back to sleep, so I didn't disturb you. I figured you wouldn't want reminding.'

Beth watched as Martin crossed the room and sat beside her. He took hold of her hand, and she was grateful for this comforting gesture. She would need all the comfort she could get. Looking into his face, Beth forced a smile until she felt her lips tremble, recalling Brady's reaction when she had told him the same sorry tale.

She took another deep breath and prepared to tell Martin

those parts of her life story that only Brady knew. The prospect was terrifying. What if Martin should react the same way? But it was a chance she was prepared to take, not only because she felt she owed him an explanation for her plan to ruin Brady, but also because she had to know if she could trust him with her secret.

When I found Rex, he was in a terrible state. His throat had been slit and his fur was covered in blood. But I didn't spot him at first. There… there was a man. He was holding a knife full of blood. It was only when I saw Rex later that I realised where the blood had come from.

The man pounced on me. He was so quick. He dragged me behind the bushes. It was then that I saw Rex. The shock hit me, and it must have thrown me off guard for a minute because the next thing I knew the man had pushed me to the ground. Then he was on top of me. He still had the knife. It was full of blood. Rex's blood.

She paused for a moment, feeling overwhelmed with grief. Martin tightened his grip on her hand and gazed intently at her. The warmth in his eyes gave Beth the strength to carry on.

It was all happening at once. I was petrified but I think I must have been angry too. The man was trying to pull my jeans down. But seeing Rex like that, I was determined he wouldn't beat me.

At first, I tried to push him off. But he was too strong. Then I reached around for something. Anything. I could feel a rock. It was big. Big enough to cover most of my hand. I grabbed at it then smacked him over the head.

He looked stunned and his head bounced back. I could see the astonishment on his face, but before he had a chance to recover, I hit him again. His hands went to his head, and as he tried to prise the rock from me, the knife fell loose from his hand.

I grabbed it quick and thrust it up into his throat. He screamed. It was awful, gut-wrenching. But I knew I had to carry on. I couldn't give him a chance to get back at me. While he was still in shock, I pushed him off me. Then I got up quick.

And then I... well... I stabbed him. In the face. In his hands. In his throat again. Anywhere that was exposed. I couldn't seem to help it. I just kept stabbing. And stabbing.

Her voice broke, and she noticed her whole body was shaking. She paused to gather herself then saw Martin pull away. Her sorrow was surpassed by a feeling of dread as she awaited his reaction.

'So, you killed him?'

Beth nodded solemnly in response.

'What did you do with the body?' he asked.

'What?'

'The man's body. What did you do with it?'

'I–I buried it. I had to. I didn't want anyone to know so I went back to the woods late that night. I was terrified after what had happened, I was even more terrified that someone might find him. I buried Rex too but in a separate grave. I didn't want him in the same...'

Then her voice caught as she recalled the scene again. It had been so eerie in the woods, and she had been freaked out and weeping the whole time as she dug the two graves. It had taken her ages to dig a hole big enough to conceal the man. And then she'd returned home still trembling and swigged a brandy to calm her before running a bath and trying to wash away the feel of death.

Martin was up out of his seat now. 'Did Brady know everything?' he demanded.

She nodded again, then watched while Martin paced the room with angry footsteps. She could see he was deep in thought and dreaded what he would do next.

'Is that why he blackmailed you?' he asked. 'Because you killed a man for attacking you?'

'Yes,' whispered Beth.

Then Martin shocked her when he shouted, 'The dirty, low down, stinking bastard! What a way to treat you after what you'd been through. Didn't he think you'd already suffered enough?'

She could sense his anger spiralling as he cursed Brady. 'The gutless little tosser to take advantage of you and leave you penniless. I can't believe it. I should fuckin' kill him for this! I will, I'll kill him, I'll fuckin' kill him.'

Beth cried out in anguish, 'No, please don't, Martin! Please don't do anything stupid.'

'Why not? Give me one good reason why I shouldn't get rid of the little bastard. He's scum! He doesn't deserve to fuckin' live.'

Beth was still sobbing, and it took a while for her to get her words out. 'Because I–I don't want to lose you. If you do something stupid, you'll get locked away then I'll have to live without you. Can't you see, all I want is for us to be together? That's why it took a lot for me to tell you all of this. I was scared that I'd lose your respect and that, well... that you'd walk away.'

Seeing her upset, Martin seemed to calm down a little and he came to sit beside her again. Then he took her in his arms and drew her head to his shoulder. 'I'd never hold it against you, Beth. You did what you had to do. Nobody could blame you for that. At least, nobody that cares enough.'

She pulled her head up and looked into his eyes. 'You sure you won't hold it against me? Can you bear to live with a woman who's a killer?'

'Shush,' he said, putting his finger to her lips. 'We've all done things we regret, some more than others. As far as I'm concerned, you didn't have much choice. I didn't always have many options in life either and I've done some bad things. But I don't want to talk about all that. I want to put it all behind us. It's not about what either of us has done in the past. What matters more than anything to me is us being together.'

Beth was relieved. 'Oh Martin, I'm so glad you won't hold it against me. But I need you to promise me something. Please, promise me that you won't do anything to Brady? I couldn't bear it if you got into trouble because of all this.'

Martin nodded, then left the room without offering her any assurances.

41

After what he had just heard, Martin was finding it hard to calm down. He'd always thought the guy Beth was married to was a bit of a worm. But now he realised; he wasn't a worm, he was a fuckin' snake. And from that moment he hated the guy just as much as Beth now did.

After a couple of minutes, Martin came back downstairs. He didn't want Beth to come looking for him. He didn't feel like talking to her right now, not because of what she'd done but because he was still angry about the ex.

Martin was finding this situation hard to process. He couldn't believe Beth was a killer. All this time he had been troubled by what he had done, never realising that Beth had done the same. Not only was that shocking in itself, but it also brought home to him his own crimes.

But he still couldn't tell her. She was distraught enough over her own situation without him adding to it. And the circumstances were different. Beth hadn't had much choice, but he had, certainly when it came to Billy.

Sticking his head through the living room door, Martin could see Beth had been crying. He couldn't handle it. Just seeing her like that made him even angrier. He had to get out.

'Beth, there's something else I need to attend to so I'm off out. I won't be long. See you later.'

Without giving her a chance to respond, he dashed from the house and got into his car, a top of the range four-by-four. He drove for some time, eventually stopping in Marple in a quiet area close to the canal. Martin parked the car and went for a walk. He needed to clear his head.

But he kept going over everything. No wonder she was obsessed with checking how Brady was doing. The cheeky bastard had gained his success through her misery. How he hated blackmailers! He had enough experience of them to know how much the evil twats could fuck with your head. He was furious and kept asking himself what sort of man could treat his wife like that.

Martin wanted to kill him in that instinctive way when you feel protective of the one you love. But he didn't want to do the killing. He couldn't bear to replicate that moment when a person switches from life to death, and that harrowing feeling of being a cold-blooded killer.

As he trudged along the canal embankment, another thought occurred to him. Brady was a blackmailer, clearly, so what was to stop him coming back for more? Beth might not have much to give now but if she made a success of her business then she would have. And if her success was at the detriment of Brady's own business then he was bound to retaliate.

Martin made his way back to the car. He'd reached a decision and knew exactly how he would handle this situation. He might not be able to face killing Brady, but he could hire somebody else to do the job; that way he didn't have to come face to face with the act of murder.

Bob Latchley was a man who made a living out of taking people out. It was well-known in criminal circles that if you wanted someone rid of and you wanted a professional job then Bob was your man. He was so good at it that he had never been caught, even though he'd been doing it for decades. And he always made sure that nothing could be traced back to the person who'd ordered the hit.

Martin clicked the key fob and got inside his four-by-four, then he made a couple of calls trying to obtain Bob's number. His contact wouldn't release it till he had an assurance that Martin would dispose of his phone once the business was taken care of. But Martin was no fool, he'd always had a throwaway phone to hand. It went back to the days when he was involved in some shady dealings.

Once he'd got the number, Martin made the call. He was sweating and his sodden hands were gripping the phone tightly.

'Hi, Bob,' he said. 'Martin Bradshaw here. I need you to take care of a bit of business for me.'

He listened while Bob outlined a few instructions, including the cost, how to deliver the money and the requirement to dispose of the phone. Then he asked for the target's name.

Martin tensed. He could have backed out at this point. But he didn't. It was the best way. He would be rid of Brady with no comeback. And then he would put it out of his head and carry on as normal. He tried to convince himself that it wouldn't be as bad as doing the job himself.

He took a sharp breath then said, 'His name's Brady Harris. No, no address, but he runs a company called Harris's Hair and Beauty Supplies.'

Once he'd received Bob's OK, Martin terminated the call.

When Martin arrived home, he was much calmer. He walked through to the kitchen where he found Beth preparing a meal and he walked straight over to her, hugging her from behind while she peered over her shoulder.

'It's a bit early for tea, isn't it?' he asked.

'Not really. I wanted to do something special for us, so it'll take a while.'

'Great. What is it?'

'A surprise,' she said.

Martin noticed that there were still tear stains on her cheeks. He wondered whether the special meal was out of guilt because of her revelation or whether it was a way to make them both feel better. His heart went out to her.

'Beth, could you stop what you're doing for a minute? I need to talk to you.'

She put down the knife she had been using to chop veg and turned around, a worried look on her face.

'It's OK,' he said. 'Nothing to worry about. It's just that while I was out, I was thinking about your plan to start up in business. You do know Brady won't take it lying down if you start doing better than him, don't you?'

'Yes,' she said hesitantly.

'So what's to stop him blackmailing you again or doing something else spiteful? You need to keep a low profile so that word doesn't get back to Brady about what you're doing. Make sure the people you're speaking to can be trusted.'

'Don't worry,' she said. 'I've covered my back. Preston won't say anything, and I'll make sure the others won't either. From what Preston told me, Brady doesn't have many friends in the industry and there are plenty who'd like to see him fall off his perch.'

'There's another way you can protect yourself,' he continued. 'You could put the business in my name. That way he won't trace it back to you. I can even help you to run it if you like, although obviously I'll make sure that you take the bulk of the profit.'

He knew it was chancy. She might not like having the business in his name. But his main reason for the suggestion was to cover his back and make sure she didn't suspect him of anything. After all, if he had just ordered a hit on Brady, then there was no way he'd be planning contingencies based on Brady being alive and well.

42

Martin was trying not to think about what would happen later, but the gurgling of his stomach and the burning sensation in his chest and throat kept reminding him of the stress he was under. He knew that ordering a hit was a drastic measure, but he swore to himself that he would put it out of his mind once the job was done and he and Beth could get on with their lives in peace.

When he returned home that evening after spending some time attending to his businesses, he found Beth in the office. She was working on her laptop, surrounded by bits of paper, some of which seemed to be lists of tasks.

'What do you want to do for tea?' he asked.

'What time is it?'

Martin checked his watch and stifled a shudder when he noticed the time. It wouldn't be long before the hit was carried out, if it hadn't been done already. Bob had been in contact and told him that the job would definitely be completed by the end of tonight.

But, of course, Martin didn't mention any of that. Instead, he said, 'Nearly seven.'

She looked surprised. 'Oh, I'm sorry, Martin. I completely lost track of the time, so I haven't cooked anything. Would you mind if we had a takeout? I've been so busy with everything. But it's been brilliant.'

She picked up one of the printed lists from the desk. 'These are suppliers that I've already approached and,' nodding at another of her lists, she added, 'that one is customers. I remembered the names from when Brady used to talk about them. Most of them have been brilliant. And something I found out was that very few of them like Brady. Apparently, he drives too hard a bargain but a lot of them stick with him because there's no better alternative.

'Do you know, Brady used to look down his nose at you but you're a thousand times the man he'll ever be. But don't worry, he'll get his comeuppance once I'm up and running. He thinks he's smart, but I'll outsmart him. It shouldn't be too difficult as I'll have the suppliers and customers on my side. I just wish I knew more of the people he deals with but I'm sure there'll be a way of finding out eventually.

'I've got loads of ideas for the business too,' she gushed.

As she outlined a lot of her exciting plans, she radiated enthusiasm. Martin had never seen her so alive, neither when she had worked as a PA nor when she was behind the bar in Virtuoso. He only took in half of what she said as his mind was on other things, but then she said something that caught his attention.

'Brady won't know what's hit him once I get to work, and I'm really going to hit him where it hurts, in his wallet. And call me vindictive, Martin, but I'm not going to stop until I put Brady out of business.'

Her words made Martin realise how much she wanted this. It was something she had to do for her own satisfaction after everything Brady had put her through. And now, with what Martin had planned, he was about to deny her that chance.

Bob Latchley was currently sitting in a Ford Focus outside the apartment block where Brady Harris lived. He'd done all his prep that week and managed to trace his target's address. Bob was wearing a disguise, a dark brown wig adorning his bald head and a matching beard concealing most of his face.

He had also taken advantage of the cold weather and was heavily padded, making him appear much more rotund than his usual slim physique. The car had been recently stolen to order and would be ditched as soon as the job was done. And lastly, he was carrying a handgun with a silencer.

After parking the car, he looked up at the apartment occupied by Brady Harris, checking to see whether there were any lights on. At the front there was only one, which he already knew was the lounge, as he'd done his research. He also knew how easy it was to get into the building. He would merely wait until somebody else was entering then sneak up behind them, pretending he had forgotten his key. It was surprising how many people simply took you on trust and left the door open for you.

Before stepping out of the car, he switched his phone to vibrate. He didn't want to alert any of Brady's neighbours to his presence before he'd had a chance to knock on Brady's door and force his way inside.

Bob shut the car door gently using the key; it was quieter than using the key fob and had no flashing lights to draw attention to himself. Then he stepped stealthily across the road and made his way to a vantage point where he could hide in the shadows while he waited for someone to approach the main door.

As he waited, Bob felt the rapid beat of his heart as the adrenaline rushed around his body. His senses were on high alert; every sound and vision magnified. He felt energised at the thought of his mission and the prospect of a handsome monetary reward. For him, there was no better high.

He hadn't been there long when he felt the phone vibrate. He tutted quietly and ignored it. But the caller persisted. Bob snatched the phone from his pocket and checked the caller ID. Martin Bradshaw. Why the fuck was he ringing at this time when he knew the hit was about to take place?

Martin was currently in the kitchen of his home on the pretence of digging out the takeaway menus and then placing their order. Seeing Beth's enthusiasm had made him think again. He could tell how desperately she wanted to destroy her ex-husband. And he didn't blame her. He would want to do the same in her position. So why was he snatching that opportunity away from her?

She needed this, not just because she was bright and resourceful and well up to the challenge of running her own business, but also because of her desire to incapacitate her ex-husband. Take the latter away from her and she would have no reason to succeed.

He understood where she was coming from. When Brady had blackmailed her, he hadn't just left her destitute, he had trashed her good character. Instead of showing empathy for what she had been through, Brady used her actions as a stick to beat her with. And now she needed to prove that she wasn't lower than him. What better way to do that than to triumph over him at the very thing he was good at?

But there were other matters to consider, things he had missed in his eagerness to get at the man who had hurt the woman he loved. If he went ahead with the hit, Beth would be the first person the police suspected. And if they found out she was living with him, then they would be looking into his movements too.

He had suggested they put the business in his name so Brady wouldn't know it was Beth. But he'd also done it to disguise his part in Brady's murder. Would Beth still suspect him, though, especially as he'd already threatened to kill Brady? What if that were to drive a wedge between them? He couldn't bear the thought of that. His love for Beth was so powerful that, as he'd once told her, he'd do almost anything for her. And that meant he'd do things her way, because he wanted to give Beth the satisfaction of bringing Brady down.

As soon as he was in the kitchen and far enough away from Beth, Martin took out the burner phone that he'd kept hold of, not wishing to dispose of it until his current business with Bob Latchley was concluded. He gave him a call.

Bob didn't answer straightaway, and Martin stood there sweating. He couldn't do this any longer, not only for Beth's sake, but suddenly the prospect of another death at his hands repulsed him. He might not be the person carrying out the act, but he would be the one responsible. And Beth had shown him that there was a better way.

Cursing Bob for not taking the call, he rang repeatedly,

his heart hammering in his chest. He hoped to God Beth wouldn't wonder where he had got to and come searching for him.

Eventually, he was rewarded by the whispered sound of Bob's voice. "For fuck's sake,' he hissed. 'Why are you ringing me *now*? I'm just about to carry out the hit.'

'I know,' Martin whispered back. 'That's why I'm ringing you. Change of plan. The job's off.'

'No, you can't do that, not at this stage. I've put in a lot of research, a lot of man hours.'

'Don't worry, you'll still get paid.'

'Everything?'

'Yeah, everything.'

Having pacified Bob, Martin cut the call, then quickly grabbed the takeaway menu and placed his order. Once that was done, he dashed back to the office where he found Beth still tapping away at her keyboard.

'Bloody hell, it took me ages to get through,' he said, but he needn't have spoken. She probably hadn't even noticed how long he had been; she was that engrossed. 'It'll be twenty minutes. Are you going to wind it up now?'

She looked up. 'What? Oh yeah, sorry. I was just in the middle of something.'

Martin grinned. 'You're really keen on this idea, aren't you?'

He was rewarded by her ebullient smile. 'Oh yeah, I'm determined to make it succeed.'

'Well, I can understand where you're coming from. After what Brady did, it's no wonder you want to get back at him. And don't worry, you've got my backing. I'll help you in any way I can.'

As she smiled at him again, Martin's imagination had already switched up a gear. He was thinking of ways he could help Beth to succeed. His methods sometimes operated on the fringes of the law, but they were effective, and he felt a glow inside at the thought of what he and Beth could achieve. He was content in the certainty that there was no way a pathetic little office wimp like Brady could possibly compete.

43

Martin was sitting inside a city centre bar waiting for a contact he had arranged to meet. He had deliberately chosen not to use one of his own bars; the fewer people that knew about this the better.

He was glad he'd made the decision not to use Bob. Since that day almost two weeks ago, he and Beth had discussed her business plans at length. In fact, they were no longer just her plans but his too, and he was feeling almost as enthusiastic about their budding business as she was.

They had agreed that she would take his financial backing to help grow the business more quickly and then, when the business grew so large that she could no longer run it alone, Martin would step in to provide managerial help. He was happy with this. It made sense because Beth could use his help, but also from a personal perspective as he'd been growing tired of the hospitality industry for a while.

There was far too much trouble with drug dealers and rival firms, and the older he got the more he realised that he would love to move away from that line of business. The nightclub would be the first to go as that was the riskiest, but he'd probably shed a couple of the bars too, apart from the ones where he had reliable and trustworthy managers in place and there wasn't too much hassle.

He'd been impressed with Beth's outlook too. She was already thinking about Brady's staff who might lose their jobs once his business went downhill, and she had vowed to interview them all for positions within her company. He felt thankful as he thought about how lucky he was to be with someone like Beth.

Martin was jolted out of his reverie when a man entered the bar. He fit the description Martin had been given by one of his old contacts who had put Martin in touch with the man. He was young, about early thirties, and casually dressed, and he obviously knew who Martin was as he looked straight at him. Their eyes locked and the man walked over. At close range, Martin could see that he was a good-looking guy, but there was something slightly dishevelled about his appearance. Like a lot of computer geeks, he had no idea when it came to dress sense.

'Martin Bradshaw?' he asked in a low tone.

Martin nodded and offered to get him a drink. Once he was back at the table they got down to business. Chris Bloxham was an IT specialist with a drug problem, from what Martin had been told. Despite his addiction, he was very good at what he did, and loved a challenge. He put his immense talents to good use in accessing other sources of income outside his normal working pattern. It helped to fund his habit.

'Did you bring it?' asked Martin.

Chris nodded and opened the backpack he had set out on the seat beside him. He pulled out a wad of printed sheets and passed them over to Martin, who leafed through them, checking the details.

'It's all there,' said Chris. 'I spent hours cracking the system.'

Martin put the papers inside the briefcase he had brought with him. Then he reached for his wallet and pulled out a wad of notes. He counted them out discreetly under the table then handed Chris the agreed amount.

Chris didn't bother to check the money. He whispered his thanks, then downed his drink in one and bid Martin goodbye. Martin watched, amused, as the guy sped out of the bar, presumably on his way to score his next fix.

Beth was hard at work in Martin's office again, but she was content. She hadn't realised before just how satisfying it could be to be your own boss. Martin left her to it for the main part as he was busy running his bars and nightclub. But he was always there as a sounding board, and she knew that when the time came for him to join the business they would work together fine.

When Martin returned home and walked through to the office, she looked up, saying, 'I suppose you knew exactly where to find me without bothering to search the rest of the house.'

He walked over and pecked her on the cheek. 'How's it going?'

'Fine. I've managed to source some more customers but I've no idea whether they already buy from Brady, and I don't know how to find the other suppliers he deals with.'

Martin lifted his briefcase and opened it. Then he slapped the printout onto her desk. 'Will that help?'

Beth picked up the printout and scanned through the list of names. 'Oh my God! Is this what I think it is?'

'A list of all Brady's customers, yes. And if you carry on reading through to the end, you'll find the names and addresses of all his suppliers too.'

'Oh my God!' she repeated. 'How the hell did you get this information?'

He tapped the side of his nose. 'Never mind that. Can you use it?'

Beth shut the list and placed it on one side of her desk. 'No, I can't. I won't! Martin, how on earth did you get hold of this information? You've not done anything illegal, have you?'

'Not me personally, no, but obviously that list is hot property now.'

'Well then, I can't use it. Please get rid of it.'

She pushed the list away and it tumbled from her desk, landing in a tangled heap on the floor.

'Beth, listen to me. If you want to beat Brady at his own game, then you're gonna need all the help you can get. Don't forget, he's worked in the industry for years; he's already one step ahead of us.'

'I don't care. I'm not using information that's been obtained illegally.'

'Then you won't beat him.'

Martin watched her reaction. He could see the creases of frustration criss-cross her face and sensed that her resolve was about to crumble.

'Once you've gone through the list, we'll destroy it.

Nobody needs to be any the wiser. If anybody asks, then you just tell them you contacted these firms in the normal run of business; some you remembered and others you found through the Internet. Who's to know any different? You could even add a few that Brady doesn't deal with just to make it look convincing.'

'But what if Brady or even the police trace it back to me through you?'

'I promise you, Beth, they won't. There'll be no comeback, believe me. And even if there was, there's no way I'd let you take the rap for it. I'd say I added all these businesses to our books.'

Once he'd said his piece, Martin walked out of the office, leaving Beth to her work and the list on the floor. He had no doubt that she wouldn't be able to resist the temptation to pick it up and go through it as soon as she was alone.

44

Brady worked in a corner section of the main office where his staff worked. It was divided from the main office by fabricated walls, which had large windows enabling Brady to easily watch what his staff were up to. There was also a door that he mainly left open unless he wanted a private meeting, in which case he would shut the door and pull the window blinds down. The open door also made it easy to summon his staff whenever he needed, as he did now.

'Lesley!' he called through to the main office.

A woman in her forties came scuttling through his door. 'Yes?'

'Did you get that order off to The Pembrook?'

'Yes,' said Lesley. 'It's all been organised. It should be with them by the end of the week.'

'Good. Did they say whether they'll be ordering for their new Liverpool hotel too?'

'No, they didn't say anything.'

How strange, thought Brady.

He'd seen the owner of The Pembrook a few weeks prior and he had more or less assured Brady that they'd be ordering from Harris's Hair and Beauty Supplies for the new hotel. Brady knew the Liverpool hotel was already up and running because he'd been checking the news announcements. Then it occurred to him that they might have been placing all the orders through the hotel in Manchester.

'Did they order more than usual?' he asked Lesley.

'No, about half.'

'What do you mean, about half?'

'About half of what they usually order,' said Lesley, who then gave him the figures.

'What the hell is going on? Why wasn't I told about this?'

Lesley shrugged. 'I thought you might know.'

'How the hell was I supposed to know about it when they placed the order through you?'

'Dunno. I thought maybe you might have discussed it with them beforehand or you might have seen it on the system.'

Brady scowled. 'That's assuming you've entered the latest figures onto it, which isn't always the case,' he said sarcastically. 'Go and check whether there's another order for them. It might be for the Liverpool hotel. Has anyone set up a separate account for the Liverpool branch of The Pembrook that you know of?'

Lesley shrugged again.

'Right, well go and check, will you? And make it snappy.'

Two minutes later and Lesley was back. When Brady heard her tentative knock on his office door, he sensed that it wasn't good news. He looked up and beckoned her to take a seat.

'Well?'

'No, nothing.'

'Shit!' he cursed while Lesley remained seated and looked nervously across at him. 'You can go,' he said loudly.

But Lesley didn't move. 'Erm, I thought you might want to know, well, that is, if you don't know already. Another two of our customers have reduced their orders as well.'

Brady tutted. 'Go on, hit me with it.'

Lesley gave him the two names and Brady was perturbed to note that they were both big clients. One was a hotel with a dozen branches, the other a chain of beauty parlours with eighteen shops.

'Have you entered them on the system?'

'Not yet, no.'

'Then go and get me the figures!' he ordered.

Again, it wasn't long before Lesley came back to his office, leaving a handwritten note of the figures on his desk while he was on the phone. Then she dashed off before he could quiz her about them.

As soon as he had finished his call, Brady picked up the handwritten note. He couldn't believe his eyes. The hotel chain had reduced their order by a third and the beauty salons by about 20 per cent. Instinctively he knew there was something amiss.

Determined to get to the bottom of it, he rang his contact at The Pembrook. He had always had a good business relationship with Simon Chorley, so he figured it was worthwhile sounding him out.

Adopting his most ingratiating tone, Brady gave Simon an enthusiastic greeting. 'Simon, I just wanted to touch base with you. I've just received your latest order and wanted to check whether you're happy with everything.'

'Erm yes, everything's fine.'

His reply floored Brady, and for a moment he was stuck for what to say but he quickly regained his composure. 'I noticed you haven't ordered any of our anti-aging products this time. Was everything to your liking with the last order?'

'Oh yeah, no problems but, sorry mate, I've managed to obtain the same products cheaper.'

Brady was shocked. He'd sourced the new supplier of these particular products from overseas and got them at low cost. Therefore, he found it difficult to believe that anybody else had got hold of the same products so soon let alone that they could beat him on price.

'Do you mind if I ask where you obtained them from?' asked Brady.

'No, not at all, it was that new company, Babette.'

'And could you tell me how much they're charging?'

'Yeah sure. Wait a minute.'

Brady could hear Simon tapping away at his keyboard, and it was a few seconds before he came back on the line and reeled off a list of prices. Brady jotted them down.

'Cheers, Simon. I'll see what we can come up with.'

He put down the phone and called up The Pembrook's account on screen. Then he frantically began comparing his prices with those that the new company was charging. He was dismayed to find that they were charging far less than him. What's more, there was no way he could compete with their charges and still make a healthy profit.

'You do realise that we're only just turning a profit for those three customers, don't you?' Martin asked Beth.

She nodded. 'Yeah, but don't worry, it'll be worth it.'

'I suppose they're customers of Brady's, are they?' Martin asked.

'Yeah, but I'm not going to do that with all the customers. They're what I call loss leaders. I've got plenty of others where I'm turning a profit.'

'Are the others Brady's customers as well?'

'Some of them, yeah. Funnily enough, I've had a few who have said they're happy to pay the same as they pay Brady. They just want to be shot of him. Apparently, he's not as switched on as he claims. Some of them said he's never available and a lot of his staff are next to useless.'

'Erm, I wonder why that is?'

'Probably pays them peanuts.'

Martin laughed. 'Probably, and you know what they say about paying peanuts, don't you?'

'Yeah, well from what I've heard, he's definitely got a load of monkeys working for him.'

'Have you finished with that list yet?'

'Yeah, it's shredded.'

'Good. So have we taken on all the customers we're going to for now?'

'No, there's still some names, but I typed up a separate list of them and shoved in a few I'd found on the Internet. That way it won't look suspicious if anyone comes across it.'

'Brilliant. Then there's no way anyone can prove those names came from Brady's accounts.'

'No, thank God!'

'You're not going to keep on undercutting him are you, I mean, to our detriment?' asked Martin.

'No, like I say, there are only those three clients where I've done it, basically because I know they're big customers of Brady's. All his turnover figures were on that list too. So

I know how much losing those three will unsettle him. But apart from that list, I've got other plans that'll help us get more business than him and we won't have to drop our prices at all.'

45

'You see all of those?' Beth asked Martin as she pointed to a list of search results on the computer screen.

'Yeah.'

'Right. Now look at the ones at the top of the list that have "Ad" next to them.'

'Oh, yeah.'

'Well, there's a reason they have "Ad" next to them and why they appear at the top of the screen. It's because they've paid to advertise online using a thing called pay-per-click. That means you pay so much every time somebody clicks on that search term.'

Martin looked confused so Beth went on to explain further. 'OK, let's put the words, "solicitors, Manchester" into the search engine.'

As she spoke, she typed the words and then hit enter. 'Right. Now, all these are solicitors in Manchester with the most relevant ones listed at the top. Those that have advertised will appear at the very top of the screen unless their advertising budget is low. Then they might appear at the bottom.'

'But isn't that an expensive way to advertise?' he asked.

'It can be, but it depends. You see, the more specific the search term, the lower the cost per click because there's less demand for it. So, for example, "criminal solicitors Manchester" will be less in demand than "solicitors Manchester".'

Martin nodded. 'Alright.'

'So if it's a beauty brand sold by very few companies then there won't be much demand for it.'

To illustrate her point Beth put the name of one of the brands they had started stocking. It was from a relatively new company and was being sold by Brady's company but very few others, as far as she knew. She followed the name of the brand with the words 'beauty products Manchester'.

As Martin looked at the screen, she said, 'As you can see, there are only Brady's company and one other advertising these products, probably because few other companies are selling them yet. That means it shouldn't cost us too much to advertise.'

'Sounds good. How much will it cost to get to the number one spot?'

'That all depends on how many search terms you use, what the cost per click is and how much other businesses want to pay.'

She saw the enthusiasm on Martin's face and knew he was thinking the same as her. They wanted to knock Brady off as many number one spots as possible.

'You can set your own budget,' said Beth. 'And I don't think Brady's will be very high. He's probably cut back on his advertising spend since he lost so much business.'

'Bloody hell, Beth. How do you know about this stuff?'

Beth could tell he was impressed with how savvy she was. 'We used to use pay-per-click advertising at work and it was very effective. When I mentioned it to Brady, he said that he would use it when he eventually set up on his own. He always had that dream of his own company in the back of his mind, you see. And, looking at the results on screen, it looks like he took out the pay-per-click advertising.'

She saw Martin deep in thought for a moment. Then he said, 'OK, let me know how much and we'll go for it.'

Beth grinned. 'Great.'

Martin couldn't have been happier when he turned up at work that night. Beth rarely worked in Virtuoso nowadays as she was so busy with the beauty business and although he missed chatting to her at the bar, Martin didn't mind. Things were going so well with the beauty business, and as well as welcoming the opportunity to diversify, he also realised how happy it was making Beth.

It was he who had suggested the name of the business to her. He wanted something that represented her but not so obvious that Brady would guess. He'd therefore done a search of her full name, Elizabeth, on the Internet, looking for variations and had come up with the name Babette. And Beth had been thrilled with it.

As they had gained more suppliers and customers, Beth was no longer able to work fully from home, although she still couldn't resist carrying out research on the laptop every chance she got. Martin had recently sourced some cheap offices with storage on an industrial estate near Stockport through a contact of his.

As the house had become full to bursting with beauty products, they had spent the last few days transporting them to the new premises. Beth had also been conducting interviews from the new offices for an admin assistant and various other staff as she'd already reached the stage where the volume of work was too much to deal with single-handedly. Martin helped out as much as he could and was always on hand to offer advice, but he still had to spend time at his own businesses.

All these thoughts were still going around in his head as he walked through the club. Martin was so preoccupied that at first he didn't notice who Skippy was talking to. He did notice how happy Skippy seemed, though, as he chatted to two young women who had their backs to Martin.

He headed towards Skippy, intent on checking how things were going in the club and thinking that perhaps he would also share a bit of banter with Skippy and the two girls. He often had a laugh with the customers, but he never took it further than that, knowing that to do so would be disloyal to Beth.

To his surprise, Skippy's appearance changed as he drew near to him. He still looked happy but now his smile seemed forced and there was something else about him that felt awkward. Martin couldn't put his finger on whether it was in his face or his stance but something about Skippy was uneasy. Then one of the girls turned around and Martin realised why; it was Jodi.

She scowled at Martin. His eyes flitted from her then back to Skippy, whose expression was quizzical. While she and her friend were still facing Martin, Skippy shrugged, and then came that fake smile again. He didn't need to speak; Martin could tell exactly what was going on from Skippy's reaction. He felt uncomfortable.

Martin also felt awkward now. His impulse was to turn around and walk away, but how could he? It was quite obvious that he had been heading in Skippy's direction, so he kept walking towards him.

Ignoring Jodi and the other girl, Martin asked Skippy, 'Everything alright?'

Before Skippy had a chance to respond, Jodi spoke. Her tone was ingratiating, her face pleasant, and Martin could tell that it was for the benefit of Skippy and her friend. 'Hi, Martin, how are you? Bet you didn't think you'd see me in here again.'

Ignoring her second sentence, Martin replied, 'I'm good, thanks.'

He shot Skippy another look, but Skippy remained tight-lipped.

'Me and Skippy are back together, you'll be pleased to know.'

'That's up to you,' said Martin. 'If it's what you both want then I'm sure you'll work your differences out.'

Again, Skippy stayed silent. He just stood there looking uneasy. Jodi spoke for them both, 'Oh, 'course we will. We're gonna be fine.' Then, looking up at Skippy, she added, 'Aren't we, babe?'

Skippy nodded and, his voice almost a whisper, he replied, 'Sure.'

Martin couldn't wait to get away, so he made his excuses and walked to the bar. He couldn't believe it! How could Skippy take her back after everything he'd told him about her jealousy and obsession? It seemed she must have found the big man's weak spot and was making the most of it.

But this didn't just mean bad news for Skippy, who was

bound to have more problems with her further down the line: it also spelt disaster for Martin. After feeling so good about everything he was suddenly thrown into turmoil. What if she hadn't backed off and was still out to get him? His question was soon answered when, a few minutes later, Jodi appeared at the bar next to him.

'I'll have a double gin and tonic,' she said to Martin, 'and you're paying.'

Not wanting to upset her, Martin did as she demanded, at the same time hating himself for succumbing to her manipulation. 'What do you want, Jodi?' he asked.

She grinned. 'I bet you thought you'd got rid of me, didn't you?' Martin stared at her as he waited for her to finish what she had to say. Her venom surprised him when she hissed, 'Not a fuckin' chance. It just took me a while to get things back on track with Skippy. And there was no way I was going to leave things the way they were. After all, I've not had my revenge yet.'

Then she held her glass up, saying, 'Cheers,' and sauntered away, leaving Martin angry but also very uneasy.

46

'What the fuck!' yelled Brady, staring at his computer screen and hammering at the keyboard.

He was going through the search terms that he had used in his pay-per-click advertising to see where his company appeared in the results. To his dismay, he wasn't occupying the number one spot for any of his search terms.

It had been like this for weeks. He could understand it for the more generic terms. He'd had to cut the budget for them as he was losing so much business. But he still would have thought he was in with a chance with the more specific words and phrases, especially for the products that weren't sold by many companies.

At first, he had thought it was a general increase in the cost of pay-per-click advertising due to a surge in demand. Now, however, he was beginning to realise that most of the damage was due to this one company: Babette Beauty Ltd. And not only did they occupy the number one spot on the Internet for the more specific terms, but they occupied the number one spot for a lot of the more generic terms too.

Brady had a feeling that this was personal, especially as it was the same company that was taking away a lot of his existing custom. But how could it be? He hadn't made any enemies to his knowledge. Well, he supposed he'd had a few disagreements, but that was just business. He didn't think he had upset anybody enough to make them want revenge. And this was beginning to look like some kind of vendetta against him.

He decided to check out this rival firm, entering the name in the search engine and reading all he could about it. As far as he could see, it was a brand-new company, which hadn't filed any accounts yet, so it was difficult to tell how big the business was. For all he knew, they might have a huge advertising budget, which would make it impossible for him to compete on spend.

Although he couldn't access any business accounts, the name of Babette's director was listed as M E Bradshaw. Brady couldn't think of anybody in the industry by that name. He had a vague recollection of the name, but he couldn't think why. He picked up the phone and checked with a few of his contacts, the ones he knew he could trust, but they hadn't heard of anyone called M E Bradshaw either.

At first, he thought it might have been a subsidiary company of one of the main players, but if that were the case, then surely he would know the name of the director. He concluded that it was perhaps a member of staff who had left his employer and started up on his own; somebody a bit like himself.

Feeling disturbed, Brady examined his own company's accounts, same as he'd done every day for the past three months, but no matter how much he checked them, it didn't seem to make any difference. He was losing money rapidly and couldn't see any way of clawing it back.

In the three months since he had found out about this

new company, Brady had lost 40 per cent of his business. That was in addition to the loss of potential business that he might have otherwise gained through Internet advertising. He had sounded out people in the industry, wondering whether he might have gained a bad reputation for some reason. But no, nobody had heard anything, and his online reviews remained relatively good.

Things had become so bad that he'd had to lay off staff. This in turn meant that he didn't have the manpower to fulfil any major orders. He found himself being sucked into a downward spiral. There didn't seem to be a damn thing he could do about it, and he was becoming seriously worried.

His one saving grace, he thought, was that at least he had cornered the market for natural aloe vera products. He couldn't see anybody competing with him on those because they weren't sourced through the Internet but directly from the manufacturer. A small overseas business had made a living selling the products to passing tourists until he had stepped in and offered to place regular bulk orders with them.

His customers loved the aloe vera products because not only were they effective, but they also offered something you couldn't obtain elsewhere in the UK. They were more organic than the mass market aloe vera products sold by big businesses and contained less additives. Thankfully, none of his competitors had managed to figure out the source of his products yet.

'Are you alright love?' asked Beth after Martin had tumbled out of bed that morning and come to see her in the office.

'Yeah, sure. Why?'

'Oh, it's just that you seem troubled lately and I heard you muttering in your sleep last night after you'd come home from the club.'

'Really?' asked Martin. 'What was I saying?'

She noticed his tone was defensive and hoped to God that he wasn't involved in anything he shouldn't be. Although she had grown to love Martin for the man he was, she was also aware of his unsavoury past and it bothered her occasionally.

'I don't know,' she replied. 'I couldn't pick out the words.'

She made a mental note to listen more carefully next time. She knew Martin operated on the fringes of the law. The list of Brady's customers and suppliers was one example of that, but she also knew that nothing she said would change the way he was. On the balance of things, the way he treated her more than made up for his minor transgressions.

Besides, at the moment her mind was too engrossed with Babette to pay much heed. She had been waiting for Martin to get up so she could tell him all about her latest idea. It was something she was very excited about.

Martin was shocked to discover that he had been talking in his sleep. There was an agonising moment when it felt like time stood still while he waited for Beth to face him with her suspicions.

Lately Jodi was on his mind constantly. Whenever she was in the club, he felt uneasy seeing her drape herself all over Skippy who was obviously smitten. Once Skippy was out of view, she would give Martin scornful looks or make threatening remarks.

Martin was worried that if Beth heard him utter Jodi's name, she might jump to the wrong conclusion that he was having an affair. Then he would have to tell a lie because he couldn't risk having her know what had happened.

With all this going on in his head, he had to concentrate really hard to take in what Beth was saying. 'So, what do you think?' she asked.

'What?'

'Martin! Have you been listening to a word I've said?'

'What? Yeah, course I have. About selling aloe vera products.'

Beth tutted and started again. 'When I was with Brady, we went on holiday to the Canary Islands and found a shop that sold natural aloe vera products. They had a brilliant selection, much better than anything you can buy in the UK. I remember Brady saying at the time that if he ever had his own beauty business, he would import them from these producers.

'I've noticed that he sells a lot of aloe vera products and I can't get anything like them on the Internet so I'm assuming that he gets them from the same place we visited on holiday. So I'm thinking of taking a trip there to source some products myself.'

When Beth finished speaking, she had a huge smile on her face. This time he had taken in what she said, and he responded by saying, 'Yeah, it sounds like a great idea. Wish I could come with you but I'm far too busy keeping an eye on things here.'

'It's OK,' she replied. 'I'll be fine.'

He couldn't blame her for feeling wounded by what Brady had done and it seemed to him that she wouldn't settle until she saw him in the gutter. But he had to admit to himself that it would give their business the edge. He had noticed himself just how many aloe vera products Brady's company sold so he knew it was a good market to get into.

But there was another reason he was happy for Beth to go and source the products. It was because she would be out of the way while all this was going on with Jodi so at least he could relax when he was at home without fear of giving anything away.

47

Martin looked over to where Skippy was standing and noticed that, yet again, Jodi was with him. As he watched them discreetly, it was apparent that they were sharing some banter with Jodi's friend and one of the other bouncers. Jodi was laughing raucously and much too loudly. It seemed to Martin as if she were doing it deliberately.

Her sidelong glances told him that all this was for his benefit. Maybe it was her way of showing him that she had Skippy wrapped around her little finger. He shouldn't let her get to him, but he couldn't help it, knowing that she was justified in tormenting him. After all, he was the man who had killed her former boyfriend. It left him with an uneasy feeling that she was plotting something against him and that it would only be a matter of time before she struck.

Despite her falseness, Skippy and Jodi seemed to be getting on well whenever they were together. After they reunited, Skippy had abashedly told him that he loved Jodi and had agreed to give her one last chance. Martin concluded that this was the reason she was on her best behaviour. It obviously suited her purposes to stay well in with Skippy.

Martin would have loved to have thrown her out of the

club when she made one of her sly comments to him. But how could he when he knew it would only upset Skippy, who already knew too many of his secrets.

He had toyed with the idea of coming clean to Skippy about the situation with Jodi. But how did he know he could trust him with something like that? Skippy's judgement was evidently flawed enough to take Jodi back after complaining about her jealousy and paranoia. And for all Martin knew, Skippy might have already been aware of her suspicions about him.

Beth had been away for a day now, and although she had phoned him to update him about her trip, Martin was already missing her. While she wasn't there, he had done a lot of thinking and vowed to himself that he would try to be more relaxed around her once she was back.

Beth was having a great time. She'd been a little nervous about going abroad on her own at first, but she hadn't had much choice. She needed her staff to run Babette in her absence and Martin was too busy with his own businesses to spend more than a little time helping out.

Once she'd got used to it, she felt fine. Beth had booked a four-star hotel near the sea front in Fuerteventura, all paid for through her business expenses. She had opted for half board, choosing to eat at the hotel in the evenings rather than wander around unfamiliar streets on her own at night. But in the daytime, in between carrying out her business research, she intended to eat at the bars that lined the sea front.

To her delight, once the hotel staff had discovered that she was alone, they did their best to make her feel as welcome as possible. By and large they couldn't do enough for her. And currently, she was sitting in the hotel bar sipping cocktails and reflecting on the success of day one.

Although she was missing Martin, it was proving a very productive trip so far. The first place she visited that day was the shop that she had last seen while holidaying with Brady. She tried to put all thoughts of him out of her head. All that was in the past; she was here on business now.

The first thing that hit her when she entered the shop was the refreshing fragrance of aloe vera. It was so enticing, and the selection of products was great. There was something about the appeal of the shop that made Beth want to spend ages milling around. There wasn't anything like that selection in the UK and she was more reassured than ever that the products would be a big seller for her.

Despite all that, Beth didn't place any orders at the shop. She wanted to price up the products first, sound out the owner, and then have a think about things. The owner was very cooperative and advised her that they would sell in bulk for approximately 20 per cent below the retail price.

The problem was that their bulk offerings didn't stretch to the quantities Beth wanted to stock. She felt sure there must be a bigger business somewhere which could offer her more quantity at lower prices. As it was lunchtime and she was hungry, she went to a nearby bar to have something to eat while she mulled things over.

Beth took a seat and viewed the menu, looking up to catch the waiter's eye once she had decided what she wanted to eat. But the first person she noticed wasn't the waiter; it was a lady who she recognised as a customer from the shop.

She was sitting on a neighbouring table and looking over at Beth.

'Hi,' said Beth, smiling.

'Hi, did you find anything you liked? It's a lovely shop, isn't it?'

Beth agreed and wondered for a moment how much to tell her. In the end she decided there was no harm in sharing things, so she told the woman her predicament.

Fortunately, she was very helpful. 'There is a much bigger stockist on the other side of the island,' she advised. 'I've never been because I've heard that they don't sell to the general public, just to businesses. But if you're looking to buy in bulk, that's probably the best place to try.'

Beth was amazed at the woman's knowledge. 'Have you been here before?' she asked.

'I live here, have done for five years. I run that English bookshop on the corner. Pop in whenever you like; you could even tell me how you get on.'

'Thanks, I will,' Beth replied, and she then asked for the name and address of the stockist.

48

It was day three of Beth's trip and Martin was missing her more than ever. He was in the club again this evening watching Jodi and Skippy as usual but as he looked across at them, he could tell that the vibe between them was completely different from two nights ago.

Skippy looked angry, which was unusual for him. Although he was capable of inflicting damage on anyone who dared to cross him, he was usually laid back. Martin had always assumed it was because he didn't feel the need to prove himself; his height and physical presence were enough to intimidate people.

Although Jodi was normally the hot-headed one, she seemed to be on the defensive rather than the attack. That also seemed strange to Martin, and it struck him that she must have done something bad to upset Skippy.

Eventually she walked away and, feeling curious, Martin went over to Skippy to find out what was happening. 'Hi, mate,' he said, patting him amicably on the back. 'Are you OK?'

Skippy shrugged. 'Yeah, I suppose.'

'Right, well, I don't mean to butt into your private affairs, but I noticed you and Jodi having a set to. It's not going to cause any problems in the club, is it?'

'No, 'course not.'

'OK, as long as you're sure. Where is she now? Has she gone home?'

'Nah, I doubt it. She'll be back over later, trying to worm her way round me.'

Martin decided not to press him any further. It was obviously a personal matter. Maybe the shoe was on the other foot tonight and Jodi had done something to make Skippy jealous. Well, as long as they kept it between themselves and didn't cause a scene in the club, he was happy to let things lie. He also hoped that while Jodi's problems with Skippy were on her mind, she might leave him alone for a while.

Today had been a nice, relaxing day for Beth following on from her business dealings. The previous day she had visited the stockist recommended by the bookshop owner and had been very impressed. It was a factory outlet where they produced and sold their own products. They had an even bigger range of aloe vera items than the smaller shop, and when she'd struck up a conversation with the owner, he had been delighted at her interest in his products.

Apparently, the factory sold mostly to the Spanish mainland and had plans to venture further into Europe. The owner was therefore delighted to hear the amount of products Beth wanted to order and she had, in turn, been delighted at the low prices. She knew that Brady must have sourced his merchandise from the smaller shop, and it would therefore be easy to beat him on both price and range.

Now that her business had been concluded, Beth decided to enjoy her last day prior to catching her flight home the following morning. She'd spent most of it relaxing by the pool, reading a novel she had bought from her new friend's shop and taking in the hot rays of the sun while sipping cool drinks and watching the holidaymakers having fun.

There was nothing quite like the friendly atmosphere of a holiday resort to lift your spirits, and she had even more reason to feel upbeat. She was now content in the knowledge that her order would arrive in the UK within the next fortnight.

By the time evening arrived she was in the hotel bar knocking back cocktails. Beth was sitting with three British couples who were on holiday. They were very friendly and had welcomed her into their company. While the guys talked football and politics, the girls were happy to chat to Beth. She knew she'd had a bit too much to drink but she didn't care, she was enjoying having a drink and a laugh with the holidaymakers.

Beth had kept Martin up to date by phone regarding her successful trip. Because he had been busy, she hadn't been able to go into detail, so she couldn't wait to return home the following day and tell him everything. She'd tried to ring him again this evening but was perturbed when there was no reply. Telling herself that there could be any number of reasons why he wasn't answering his phone, Beth had put it out of her head and carried on enjoying herself.

It was three hours later when she excused herself from the small crowd for the second time and went to the ladies' where she checked her phone for missed calls. There were no calls from Martin, but she was surprised to see a missed call from Teresa.

Beth didn't hear much from Teresa these days. She was more of a work acquaintance than a close friend, and since Beth had been running her business, she no longer worked behind the bar in Virtuoso. She still visited occasionally when Martin was working there but that was the only time she saw Teresa. The fact that Teresa had rung her while she was abroad was strange, unless Martin hadn't told her Beth was in the Canaries.

Curious, she returned the call and Teresa answered straightaway. It was obvious from the background noise that Teresa was in Virtuoso, and it occurred to Beth that she must have been listening out for her call to hear the phone ring over the racket of the nightclub.

'Teresa! Hi, what's wrong?' she asked, her instincts telling her that something must be.

'It's Martin,' Teresa replied. 'He's been arrested.'

'Arrested? What on earth for?' As Beth asked the question, she could feel her heart racing.

'Drugs. They found a stash of them in his office.'

'Jesus!' said Beth. 'No. It can't be. Martin wouldn't do that.'

'I know,' Teresa cajoled. 'I didn't think it was his bag. He's always been so against them in the past, and if he gets so much as a sniff of someone dealing in the club, he chucks them out.'

But despite her own and Teresa's words, Beth was beginning to doubt everything Martin had ever told her. He'd sworn vehemently to her that he was against drugs. But what if he'd been lying? Maybe it had all been just a front.

49

Feeling dejected, Beth retired to her room, no longer wanting to be in the company of others. Her first impulse was to get a flight home as soon as possible, but then she didn't see the point. It was already late, and she'd be home early the next day anyway. Besides, there wasn't much she could do if Martin was in custody. Presumably he'd already rung his solicitor.

Aside from all that, she was still feeling tipsy, and she knew that it wouldn't be sensible to book a flight and make her way home in that state, assuming she could get an earlier flight at such short notice.

Her thoughts turned to Martin's situation as she tried to make sense of things. She couldn't understand it. Although he'd admitted to her that he had been involved in some nefarious activities in the past, he'd always drawn the line when it came to drugs. She remembered him telling her he was strongly against them as a close friend of his had died of a drug overdose some years ago. So why the hell did he have them in his office?

There was only one reason she could think of, though she didn't want to believe it, and it appalled her. She'd forgiven Martin's past transgressions, knowing that deep down he was a decent man who treated her like a princess. She could understand why he'd followed the wrong route because he was a victim of circumstance growing up on a rough estate with few other opportunities open to him.

But if he'd been involved in the supply of drugs then that was something she would find hard to overlook.

The police cell offered little comfort. It had stark white walls, a floor covered in plain grey vinyl, no windows and a thick metal door that kept Martin firmly locked in. The only furniture was a bed, which was made of stone and built into the side wall. On it was a thin mattress, the type more suited for sitting than sleeping. There was a toilet tucked behind the wall to the left of the door so that when he was on it the officers had a limited view of him through the spyhole.

Despite the lack of home luxuries, Martin was glad when the police finally led him to the cell because it gave him a break from their relentless questioning. It had lasted for hours with the police going over the same points again and again in the hope of catching him out.

When the police led him to the cell, they had passed him a single paltry blanket and he tried to settle down to sleep. It was the early hours of the morning and Martin knew he needed to grab some shut-eye while he could because he had no doubt that the questioning would continue again early the next day.

But he was unable to drift off. The rock-hard bed and the dim light that seemed to bounce off the pale walls made it impossible. So he was left to dwell on what had brought him to this situation.

Martin knew he was innocent. Despite everything he'd done in the past, a lot of which he wasn't proud of, he'd been vehemently anti-drugs for most of his life. He'd dabbled a bit when he was young and foolish but had soon come to his senses when he found out the devastation they could cause. And nowadays it sickened him to see scrotes profiting from the misery of others.

He was convinced that the drugs had been planted. His number one suspect without a doubt was Jodi. Because of her connection to Skippy, who had keys to all the rooms at the club, she could have found a way to gain access to the office, and the police said they'd received an anonymous tip-off from someone about the drugs. Furthermore, this witness claimed to have seen him taking a mysterious package into his office and had also seen him snorting coke on a couple of occasions.

But the other reason he suspected Jodi was because she had motive. He had been on edge for weeks knowing she was after revenge. And now it seemed she had finally thought of a way to exact it.

His mind drifted back to how she and Skippy had seemed that night and he wondered what Skippy's involvement was in this. He wondered whether the row between Skippy and Jodi might have had something to do with him. Maybe she had bad-mouthed him and Skippy had jumped to his defence, then she had planted the drugs to get her own back.

He even wondered whether Skippy might also have been involved. Maybe that was why he had refused to confide in him about the row with Jodi. But if he were involved then why would they be rowing about him? Perhaps the row was a personal matter completely unconnected to him.

And then he thought about Beth. How would she ever believe that he was innocent in all of this? And if she suspected that he had put the drugs there himself, how would it affect their relationship? He couldn't stand the thought of her walking away. She was the sort of woman he had wanted to meet all his life and he knew that life without her would be meaningless.

Then there were his businesses. If he were found guilty, he'd be locked inside for a long time and he'd have to find someone to look after them for him. But if Beth walked, then he wasn't sure there was anyone else he could trust. And that meant that if he lost Beth, he could end up losing everything.

50

When Beth arrived home from the Canaries, Martin wasn't there. She rang his solicitor, but his phone went to voicemail. Assuming that Martin's solicitor was probably with him at the police station, she rang the solicitor's office and spoke to his secretary who confirmed that that was the case.

Frantic with worry, Beth asked her for the phone number of the police station that Martin had been taken to and rang it. She made the call out of desperation, and she didn't know what she expected to achieve from it. A blunt response telling her he was being held for questioning was exactly what she had anticipated. The next person she spoke to was Teresa, but she wasn't able to tell her much more than she had the previous day.

'Any idea how the police knew about the drugs?' demanded Beth.

'No idea. All I know is that one minute I was serving a customer and the next minute the police were storming the place. I thought it was a raid, that maybe they were looking for a known drug dealer who was touting his drugs in the club. I had no idea it was Martin.'

'Hey, steady on!' snapped Beth. 'We don't know that he's guilty.'

'Sorry, I didn't mean that. I just meant that I had no idea the police were going to arrest Martin.'

Beth cut the call. She was feeling annoyed, but although she had directed her anger at Teresa, it was the situation that angered her. Why? Why did this have to happen when things had been going so well?

The rest of the day dragged. For a while she feigned normality, grabbing herself something to eat and drink, then putting away a few valued items from her suitcase and changing into more comfortable clothing. But she couldn't settle. She was restless and worried, so she decided to make some more calls.

It was evening when Martin arrived home and Beth rushed into the hallway as soon as she heard his key in the door. His clothes looked dishevelled, and he had stubble on his chin. His whole manner was dejected as he walked over and wrapped his arms around her, clinging on as if she were a life raft. Then he held her away from him and, looking into her eyes, announced, 'They've released me under investigation. I'll have to go to court. But I swear, Beth, I'm innocent.'

Later that night, Martin slipped his shoes on. 'You're not going out now, are you?' Beth asked.

'Yes, I'm off to the club. It might help to take my mind off things.'

He desperately hoped she wouldn't offer to come with him. But she didn't. Maybe, like him, she thought it would be better if they weren't together at the moment, even though they had already been apart for three days.

Since he'd been home, the atmosphere between them had been fraught. She looked as worried as he was, and he felt terrible that she had to go through this even though it wasn't his fault. He didn't know how to deal with her concerns other than to keep reassuring her of his innocence.

But there was another reason why he needed to go to the club. He needed to find out what the hell was going on and his best chance of doing that would be to have a word with Skippy. He'd have to tread carefully though, as he didn't know how involved Skippy was.

When Martin arrived at Virtuoso, he could sense the tense atmosphere among the staff. He also noticed the strange looks he was getting from the customers and the way some of them turned away from him and whispered amongst themselves. Deciding to deal with the situation head on, he called together his two bar managers and Skippy and took them up to his office for a chat.

Once they were seated, he began. 'OK, I know you're all probably wondering about last night, so I just want to set the record straight. The police found a stash of cocaine in my office after somebody had reported it. I didn't put the drugs there and I think I've been set up. I don't know who by, at the moment, but I intend to find out, so if any of you hear anything, can you please let me know?'

They all muttered their assent, so Martin continued. 'Right, now I know there'll be plenty of rumours circulating so I want you to make sure you squash them right away. No matter what people might be saying, I haven't been found guilty of anything so please make sure the staff are aware of that.'

When they all agreed again, he said, 'Oh, and if you or any of the staff hear any mumblings from the customers, can you please make them aware too? The last thing we need is for the club to come into disrepute because that would leave us all in the shit.'

Having said his piece, Martin dismissed them from his office. Then he took a few moments for himself. He hadn't mentioned the witness who had come forward. He decided it was best not to because, although Jodi was his prime suspect, it could be any one of the staff.

They all had reason to go into the upstairs rooms from time to time. It was where they stored their personal possessions and there were also stockrooms up there. But Skippy was the only one of his staff who had a key to all the offices.

Although Martin had told Beth about the witness, he hadn't given any specific details, because he was afraid that if he did then he'd have to tell her everything about Jodi. And he didn't want to do that. Things were bad enough without giving Beth even more problems to deal with.

He didn't spend long in his office as he didn't want people to think he was hiding away. Besides, Martin wanted to keep an eye on the situation between Skippy and Jodi. He was curious about what was going on between them, and he wouldn't find any answers while he was ensconced upstairs.

He was interested to see that Jodi wasn't in the club tonight and he wandered over to where Skippy was standing. He'd noticed earlier in the office that Skippy seemed out of sorts, and this was confirmed when he drew level with him. Skippy's expression was downcast, his body tense.

'Hi Skippy, how are things?'

'Alright, everything's good. How about you? It must have been shit spending the night in the cells.'

'How did you know I was there all night?' Martin probed, studying Skippy's face for a reaction.

But Skippy wasn't giving anything away. He remained impassive as he said, 'Well, it was late when they arrested you. I didn't think they were gonna send you home straightaway without giving you a good grilling. So how was it?'

'It *was* shit! They kept asking me the same things over and over and kept at it till I was absolutely knackered.'

Again, he didn't divulge anything more about the police witness. Skippy's mention of his night in the cells had done nothing to allay Martin's suspicions. Instead, he shifted the conversation.

'No Jodi tonight?'

This time he did notice a change in Skippy's demeanour. His expression darkened, but Martin couldn't tell whether it was because of hurt, annoyance or even guilt.

'I've given her the brushoff,' he said.

His tone was sombre and didn't invite a response, nevertheless Martin persisted. 'Why? What's happened?'

'You don't wanna know. Let's just say I won't be taking her back this time.'

Martin didn't know how to react, so for a moment he dithered before doing what would have been expected by tapping Skippy lightly on the back and saying, 'Never mind, mate. You've probably done the right thing, if it's any consolation. At least you won't be getting grief every time a girl comes chatting to you.'

At the same time, Martin was fishing. If it were Jodi's jealousy and paranoia that had caused them to split, then surely Skippy would say. But he still wasn't giving anything away. His response was nonverbal, just a shrug of the shoulders before his eyes wandered around the club, telling Martin he was focusing on his job rather than discussing his disastrous love life.

Martin took the hint. 'See you later,' he said, walking away.

51

Three weeks after Martin's arrest things had changed for him and Beth. Although she believed in his innocence, she was troubled. What if he didn't manage to clear his name? How would they both cope if he had to spend years behind bars? The police had been round on two further occasions to question him, and he'd been told his case was going to trial. Apparently, they'd had an anonymous tip-off about drugs in his office. Martin had told her he thought he'd been set up and Beth couldn't help but feel anxious about it. How could she relax when Martin had this hanging over him?

The police had also questioned Beth. She hadn't been able to help them much as she had been away at the time of Martin's arrest, but they'd still persisted, quizzing her about his lifestyle and whether she had ever known him to be involved in drugs. Although she had answered in the negative, it upset her to have to defend him like that.

Martin's arrest was putting a strain on their relationship. He was often down and no matter how much she tried to reassure him, she couldn't cheer him up. Beth knew that they would only find peace of mind once the trial was out of the way. Hopefully, Martin would then get the chance to prove his innocence in court.

To take her mind off things, Beth poured herself into work. In that aspect of her life, at least, things were going well. Martin had barely set foot inside the offices of Babette since his arrest, probably because he was under too much strain to take on anything else.

Despite her other problems, Beth couldn't help but be delighted at the way Babette was shaping up. As she had envisaged, both old and new customers alike loved her range of aloe vera products.

In the last five weeks alone, her takings had gone up by 30 per cent once word of the product range had got around. Not only were customers interested in the aloe vera products, but they were increasing their orders for other items too. She knew that was probably due to upselling by the efficient team of staff she had working for her.

Beth was now so busy that she worked late most evenings. It meant spending time away from Martin, but he was aware of how much work she had to get through. In fact, she was now toying with the idea of adding to her senior management team. It was something she wanted to avoid, if possible, as to her it would mean a certain loss of control. Nevertheless, she knew it was something she had to consider.

One thing that delighted her was the number of customers who had come from Brady's company. She had also held interviews for two additional members of staff in the last week, and she wasn't surprised that some of the interviewees were Brady's ex-employees.

All of this told her that he must really be feeling the pinch at the moment, and she felt a sense of triumph picturing his moody expression as he dealt with the damage to his company. Beth didn't like this side of herself, but she couldn't help it. When she pictured Brady nowadays, she didn't see the face of the man who she had fallen in love with.

Instead, she saw the man who had denigrated her for confiding in him about the worst experience of her life. She had wanted support and reassurance but rather than help her, Brady had sought to destroy her by leaving her penniless. Because of that, she would always loathe him. And she wouldn't settle until she had destroyed him in return.

Brady was sitting inside a strange pub in the city centre nursing a pint of lager with a whisky chaser. He was already embarrassingly drunk, having started on the red wine over lunch, but he didn't care. It helped him get away from all his problems and that was what he wanted right now. Oblivion.

The lunch had been with an old industry contact. It was a last-ditch attempt by Brady to regain some of the custom he had been losing over the past few months. The custom that he had, in fact, been losing ever since this new company Babette had come into existence.

Brady had now reached the stage where his company was operating with a skeleton staff and the decline of his business had gone from gradual to rapid. Not only was he losing out to Babette, but he was losing out to other companies too as word got around the industry about his failing company, and customers raced to abandon the shrivelling wreckage that Harris's Hair and Beauty had become.

Lunch had gone well. Brady had been at his charming best, regaling his contact with anecdotes and witty one-liners in an attempt to win him round. Then he had come to the reason for the meeting: to try to persuade the man to give him some business. And that was when things had changed.

'Sorry, mate. I thought we were having a nice lunch for old time's sake. I didn't realise you wanted to discuss business. Anyway, there's no openings I'm afraid. You're too expensive. And, if you want me to be honest with you, Brady, your level of service isn't up to scratch either.'

His callous dismissal had ignited Brady's anger and where he would normally have swallowed it down, he now saw no reason to do that. This had been Brady's only hope of saving his company. And now that he'd lost that hope, he had nothing left to lose.

'You cheeky bastard!' he yelled. 'You've got the fuckin' bare-faced cheek to sit there stuffing your face and guzzling drink that I'm fuckin' paying for and then you go and tell me there's nothing doing. Why else do you think I'm buying you fuckin' lunch?'

He was practically screaming at the man by now, who quickly excused himself and left the restaurant. A waiter dashed over and asked Brady if everything was alright. Brady, not wanting the humiliation of being thrown out, assured the waiter that it was.

He took a while to calm himself down before returning to work to do the job he had been putting off for as long as possible. He had to tell the staff that this was the end of Harris's Hair and Beauty. And it broke his heart to have to admit it even to himself.

He knew he'd have to lay staff off, but he was also confident that they would all get jobs elsewhere. In fact, most of the staff who he had previously laid off had already succeeded in gaining alternative employment from what he'd heard. His biggest sympathy was for himself because the business had been more than just a job to him: it had been everything he'd worked for.

The last straw had been when he lost the aloe vera business. He'd always been confident that that was the one thing that would save him. But when Babette started offering not only a more extensive range of products but also at lower prices, he knew the end was near.

And there wasn't even any point in advertising the aloe vera range because he knew that once he did that, it wouldn't be long till Babette would do the same, except they'd have a far bigger advertising budget. And now he finally had to concede that everything he'd worked for was going down the pan.

He hadn't even succeeded yet in buying that luxury home he'd dreamt of having once the business took off, as his focus had been on the business. He was still living in a crumby rented apartment, and now that the business had failed, he had nothing left. He was finished.

52

For weeks Martin had been on edge. He couldn't relax at all. It was so stressful waiting to see how the court case went. What if he was found guilty?

It was obvious to Martin that the police thought he was. Everything was stacked against him. The drugs had been found in his office and the police had a witness who swore they'd seen him with the drugs and seen him taking drugs on other occasions. Then there was the fact that he was already known to the police because of his shady past.

Martin was worried. And there was no escape from it because work was a constant reminder of his problems. Although the whispered conversations between customers had stopped, he felt as though the staff suspected him. At times he felt like grabbing the DJ's mike and screaming at the top of his voice that he'd been stitched up.

Looking back at his life, and he was doing a lot of that lately, it had never bothered him too much previously when he had been in trouble with the law. Prison had just been an inconvenience that paused his nefarious activities until he reached his release date when he could return to them. He had never feared it because the other prisoners had been the type of men he was used to dealing with every day of his life.

But most of his spells inside had been when he was younger, before he'd learnt how to evade the law. And he'd had nothing to lose then. Now it was different. Before this happened, he'd finally got what he had wanted for a long time: a life on the right side of the law with a decent woman who he loved unconditionally and who loved him in return. And he was terrified of losing it.

Martin was sitting at the bar knocking back shorts, something else that he was doing a lot of lately. He was pretending to show an interest in what was going on around him, if only to reassure the staff of his presence. But his mind was too preoccupied to take much in.

Then his attention was diverted when he became aware of someone climbing onto the stool beside him. He glanced across to see that it was Skippy, who looked awkward and out of place on the barstool. His body language was uncomfortable too, and Martin could see tension in his shoulders, which were bunched up so high they almost touched his ears.

'Hi boss, are you OK?' Without waiting for a reply, Skippy then asked, 'Do you mind if we both stay a bit later tonight? There's something I need to talk to you about.'

Martin nodded his agreement but as he watched Skippy walk away, he was already dreading the encounter.

It was late when Beth returned home from work, and Martin was already out. She presumed he'd gone to the club, but she didn't ring him to find out. Although she could have done with his company tonight, she preferred to stay at home rather than go to Virtuoso where there was an atmosphere of suspicion.

For a while she toyed with the idea of ringing Sally and seeing if she was up for a night out, with it being Friday. But she decided against it. She was tired. Beth had worked late every night this week and she was looking forward to a lie in tomorrow, although she'd probably pop into the office for a couple of hours even though it was Saturday.

Deciding she owed it to herself, she grabbed a bottle of red from the wine rack that was built into the central island and housed thirty bottles. Then she popped it open. As she filled a large glass, she gazed around the kitchen, taking in the size of it, the granite work surfaces, the large central island and all the fancy gadgets. It had been almost a year since Beth had moved into Martin's home, initially as a lodger, but she was still dazzled by its luxury. It was a shame that they were both too troubled now to enjoy it.

It felt to Beth as though she was putting on a façade, pretending that everything was alright when deep down she knew it wasn't. And it would never be alright until Martin's name was cleared.

But tonight, she had other issues that were bothering her. While she had been in work that day, she received a call from reception advising her that a man had rung in and started asking questions about the company. Who were the directors? Did they have a general manager? Who was in charge of day-to-day operations? That sort of thing.

Beth had a strong feeling that it had been Brady making the call. She was familiar with how he operated. He would be well aware by now that Babette was taking his business, and he'd be curious as to who was behind the company. Fortunately, she'd anticipated that eventuality and left instructions with the reception staff that they weren't to divulge any such information.

But now, as she took her seat on the living room sofa, she felt uneasy. Instinctively, she got up and checked that all the doors and windows were locked. Then she sat back down, gulping her wine while she flicked through the TV channels. But all the while she was listening out for any sounds outside.

Beth didn't regret what she'd done to Brady though. She'd been pushed to it by the vile way he had treated her, and her actions had been fed by anger and upset. Her only regret was that Martin might not be here with her for much longer. As long as Martin was with her, she had no need to be afraid of anything Brady could do.

By the end of the night, the club was empty. The last of the staff had now gone home and Martin was sitting at the bar waiting for Skippy to finish locking up. During the night he'd tried to take his mind off the imminent conversation with Skippy by walking around the club doing repeated checks and stopping at the bar intermittently for another whisky.

He was now feeling slightly more relaxed than earlier, but probably due to the handful of whiskies he had consumed. Martin had taken care not to drink more than he could handle though. He wanted to have his wits about him for this meeting.

Martin saw Skippy approach and flash a smile, but it was a tentative one laced with apprehension. He returned the smile and invited Skippy to grab himself a drink from behind the bar. Then he waited till Skippy was ready to join him, noticing that the big man's body language was still tense.

Outwardly Martin was ice cool, a trait he had perfected over many years whenever he came up against a potential enemy. It was his way of hiding his fear. But inside, the whisky he had consumed was bubbling up through his digestive tract like molten lava, searing his throat and leaving a sour taste on his tongue.

Skippy didn't bother with small talk. Once he had sat down and taken a sip of his whisky, he said, 'Jodi came to see me last night. She was off her fuckin' head, high as a kite.'

Martin nodded. Certain that Skippy hadn't called this meeting just to confide in him about his love life, he waited for him to carry on.

'She wanted us to get back together but I was having none of it.' Martin nodded, encouraging Skippy to continue. 'She was spouting the same crap as last time.'

Then he seemed to check himself as if he had said something he shouldn't.

'What crap was that?' asked Martin.

'Sorry I didn't tell you, boss, but I didn't know what to think until last night. She was coming out with summat about you killing Lloyd. I knew it was a load of bullshit. I told her that the first time she said it. That was why I finished it. She's fuckin' paranoid. Everyone knows you were cleared of that.'

So that was what the row was about a few weeks ago, thought Martin. But he was curious as to why Skippy hadn't told him at the time. 'So why was last night any different?' he asked.

'Well, like I said, she was coming out with all the same bullshit at first. I told her where to go. I said if you think that's gonna persuade me to take you back then you've got another think coming. Then she went apeshit, going on about how I believed you over her.' Skippy chuckled nervously before adding, 'She called you a murdering bastard. Then she said that's why she did what she did.

'I didn't know what she was on about at first but then she said you needed to be punished, which was why she'd seen to it that you'd serve time. Well, the fuckin' penny dropped then, didn't it? It was her that had fuckin' stitched you up! I should have known. That coke's done her fuckin' head in. I swear, she's fuckin' paranoid.'

'She's on coke?' said Martin.

'Yeah, that's summat else we used to fall out about. She kept promising me she'd ditch the stuff, but she never did.'

'But if she's a cokehead then why didn't you suspect her before?'

'Well, I did, kind of, but... well... I wasn't sure.'

Skippy was becoming hesitant now and Martin could tell he felt embarrassed. 'I get it,' he said. 'You weren't sure whether it was her or whether I'd actually done it.'

Skippy shrugged uncomfortably. 'Well, it could have been someone else.'

'No it couldn't, Skippy. Me and you are the only people with keys to the office. You knew it was either her or me.'

Skippy shrugged again. 'I'm sorry, boss. I didn't know

who to believe. I fuckin' loved the girl. But I know now what a bitch she really is.'

Martin was furious. It was all apparent to him now. Skippy had come to the conclusion that he had been stashing drugs in his office even though he knew that his girlfriend was the cokehead! If Martin had only known that about her then he might have been able to clear his name. He felt sure the police would have viewed things in a different light if they had known that their only witness was a cokehead.

He could have gone ballistic with Skippy. To think that he'd been through hell these last few weeks just because Skippy hadn't called her out on it. And the fact that Skippy even suspected that he might have been guilty of stashing the drugs made him even angrier.

But he didn't go ballistic. He was thankful that he hadn't had too much to drink and was still capable of rational thought. At the end of the day, he hadn't been entirely straight with Skippy either, choosing not to tell him that he had actually killed Jodi's ex. And after what he had just heard, there was no way he was about to do so.

But at least Skippy had come good in the end. He hadn't needed to share that information with him tonight. He could have kept it to himself if he had wanted to. But he'd had the decency to tell him. So Martin would keep a lid on his temper rather than risk upsetting Skippy now.

Besides, he needed him on side. Because Skippy was the only one who could help him clear his name.

53

Martin was upstairs when Beth heard a knock on the door. After the strange call to her business three days ago, she was still feeling wary. She shouted up the stairs to Martin but didn't get a reply. Beth was just debating whether to go upstairs and ask him to get the door when there was another knock. This time it was much louder and made her jump.

The heavy knocking persisted, putting her on edge but also making her curious. Whoever it was sounded impatient. Curiosity won out over caution and Beth made a quick decision to answer it, knowing that the caller might have gone by the time she located Martin.

It was the police again and Beth's mood soon shifted to one of dismay. Why couldn't they leave Martin alone? It was bad enough that he was up in court, without the police continually pestering him.

This time they weren't detectives. It was two uniformed officers, one a man who seemed to be in his early twenties and had a gullible look about him. The other was a woman who wasn't much older but had a confident air about her that suggested she was experienced in these matters.

'Is Martin in?' asked the female PC.

Beth frowned as she held the door open for them. 'You'd better come in.'

Once she'd led them through to the lounge and asked them to take a seat, she said, 'I'll just go and get him.'

Beth didn't bother offering them a drink; she didn't want them to stay. Instead, once Martin had come downstairs, she asked, 'Do you want me to leave the room?'

'No, I think you should hear this,' he said.

Beth noticed that instead of looking hacked off that the police were here once again, his manner seemed indifferent, although he was rubbing his chest as though in discomfort. As they both sat down, she looked at him curiously wondering if he knew something she didn't. Then her gaze shifted to the female PC who didn't waste any time in explaining the reason for their visit.

'Mr Bradshaw, we're here to inform you that you are no longer under investigation.'

Beth felt a surge of relief at the same time as she saw it wash over Martin. She hadn't realised how tense he was until his muscles sagged as he relaxed back in the chair and blew out a puff of air. Then he took hold of her hand and gave it a squeeze. Rather than ask the officer why, he waited while she spoke again.

'We've arrested someone who we believe responsible following information from a witness. She's admitted .planting the drugs and we've now charged her. It's a Miss Jodi Bacon who claims she planted the drugs as revenge against you for killing her boyfriend.'

Beth felt Martin grow tense again as he sat up, his body now rigid. 'I've already been through this,' he snapped. 'I was cleared of the killing ages ago.'

'Yes, yes, we know,' the officer rushed to assure him. 'We just wanted to give you some context. It appears that she has a drug problem.'

'Yes, she's a fuckin' paranoid cokehead,' Martin snapped.

Beth's mouth gaped open at his aggressive use of bad language in front of the officers but before she could say anything to calm him down the female PC said, 'Yes, we're aware of that too.' Then she got up and the younger officer followed her cue. 'Anyway, we're sorry for what you've been through, and we won't take up any more of your time.'

Beth could tell the officers were eager to get away now that they had done what they set out to do, especially after Martin's display of temper. She stood up too and led them out of the door. When she turned back, Martin was already standing in the hall. She rushed to him and enveloped him in her arms, burying her head in his chest so deeply she could hear his heart pounding.

'Oh, Martin, I'm so glad that's over,' she said.

Martin clung on to Beth and didn't want to let her go. It was so good to have her in his arms, to smell the scent of her and feel the softness of her touch. He said a silent thank you to a God he didn't believe in for finally regaining Skippy's loyalty. Following their chat a couple of nights ago, Skippy had promised to go to the police with what he knew, and Martin was glad he'd kept to his word.

Beth was the first to pull away from the embrace.

He wasn't surprised when she asked. 'What was all that rubbish about you killing someone's boyfriend?'

The question made him realise that it wasn't over yet.

But Martin was ready with his reply. 'A while back a guy was jumped after we'd thrown him out of Virtuoso. It was ages ago, long before you started working there.'

'Right,' said Beth, nodding her head for him to continue.

'Well, this Jodi was his girlfriend. She's had it in for me since her boyfriend died because I threw him out of the club on the night he was attacked. Like I said to the cops, she's a paranoid coke addict and she got it into her head that I'd killed him even though the police found him a long way from the club after he'd been jumped.'

Martin waited for Beth's reaction. The fact that she had stuck by him since his arrest made him hopeful that she would believe him.

'How long has this been going on?' she asked.

'Ages, like I said. But I didn't want to trouble you with it. You've had enough problems of your own to deal with.'

She looked pleased with his apparent consideration, and he was relieved that she had swallowed the story. It was fortunate that Beth had never been around when Jodi had been sniping at him in the club. But she'd known there was something wrong even before he had been arrested for the drugs. It had been difficult to hide the strain he had been under.

If he were going to confide in Beth about everything then now would have been the time to do it. But he'd already decided that the secret of Jodi's boyfriend's death was one that he couldn't share with anyone, not even Beth. Especially not Beth! Nothing could be gained from baring his soul to her, tempting as it was.

He loved Beth so much that his instinct *was* to tell her everything, as she had done with him. But he was only just regaining her trust. And he didn't want to risk losing it again.

Beth's view of the world was very different to his. She had a strong sense of right and wrong, and even though she would have tried to accept what he had done, she would have found it difficult.

It was important to Martin that Beth thought well of him. Despite what he had done, he wanted to do the right thing and put his past behind him. But he knew that if he told Beth everything, it would always stand between them. And it might end up destroying what they had.

So he'd keep his mouth shut and try to move on. The most important thing for him now was to look towards the future.

54

To celebrate clearing his name, Martin suggested a Saturday night meal at their favourite restaurant, *Tattu*, the first place he had ever taken Beth for a meal. There was also another reason Martin wanted to take her there. He had some news he wanted to share with her, and he hoped it would be cause for a double celebration.

On Saturday evening, Martin felt a buzz of excitement as he waited in the living room while Beth got ready upstairs. His excitement intensified when she appeared inside the room dressed to go out. She was wearing a beautiful red wrap dress, low at the front with the neckline edged in subtle frills. It was calf length with a curved hemline that came tantalisingly higher at the front, and the fitted waistline emphasised her perfect figure.

He stepped forward and touched her gently on the waist, planting a kiss on her cheek. 'I haven't seen that dress before. You look gorgeous in it.'

As he kissed her, he could smell her perfume. It was his favourite, the one he had bought for her. The one she knew he liked. He was grateful that she was making an effort to please him, and he wondered whether she wished for the same finale to the evening as he did. Because of all the stress they had been under, they had stopped being intimate. In fact, it had been so long since they had made love that it took all his self-control not to lift her up and carry her to the bedroom there and then.

She smiled. 'It's a new one. I bought it today.'

Summoning all his restraint, he said, 'Come on. Let's get going before our table gets taken.'

Towards the end of the meal while they were finishing a bottle of Châteauneuf-du-Pape, he decided to share his news. 'I've got something I want to tell you.'

'Well should we do it over another bottle of this lovely wine?' she asked, raising her glass and giggling before she took a slurp.

They were in good spirits and Martin hoped he hadn't waited too long to tell her. Maybe he should have broken the news before she became too tipsy. But she seemed to sense his seriousness and her face straightened.

'What is it, Martin?' she asked, concerned.

'Oh, nothing to worry about. It's just that, after everything that's happened, I've decided to put Virtuoso up for sale. This drugs business was the final straw for me.'

'Really? You're really selling up?'

'Yeah, really. I think it's about time I moved away from that lifestyle. There are too many problems and I'm a bit long in the tooth to be getting into brawls and all the other hassle that comes with running a nightclub in the city.'

'But what about the bars? Are you selling them too?'

'Not yet. I'll keep hold of them for now, but I'll take a hands-off approach. I've got good managers running most of them, so I don't need to get as involved as I do with Virtuoso.'

'Wow, Martin, I'm shocked! What will you do with all your spare time?' she teased.

'Well, that's the other thing I wanted to speak to you about. I wondered if you might need any help running Babette from someone with good credentials who's used to dealing with wholesalers and the public.'

Beth's response was automatic. 'Yes! That would be brilliant. We've always worked well together when you've had time to get involved with Babette. And to be honest, I could really do with the help right now.'

'I was hoping you'd say that. Well, that settles it then. This calls for a celebration.' Then he waved at the waiter who came across to their table and Martin ordered a bottle of Bollinger champagne.

His news, together with the flow of champagne, lightened the mood between them even more. Martin felt elated, sensing that it was just like it had been before all this business with Jodi had come between them. Carried away in the moment, he had temporarily pushed all thoughts of their other problem aside: Brady. But maybe that was because, up to now, he hadn't really seen him as a major threat.

Almost two weeks ago, Brady had broken the news to his staff that Harris's Hair and Beauty Supplies was finished. Since then, he had been going through the process of shutting the place down. There was a lot to deal with: getting rid of the remaining stock, staff issues, serving his notice on the business premises and countless other matters.

But apart from the physical aspects of shutting down his company, Brady had begun to reassess things. Losing the business was a bitter blow, and one that he hadn't taken lightly. And now, as he sat in his rental apartment swigging wine, he became pensive. It occurred to him that just because the company was finished, it didn't necessarily mean he was.

Could he perhaps set up another company? But what if the same thing were to happen again? There must be another way. He knew there was. But he hadn't figured it out yet. He would do though, once he'd finished with the business of shutting the company down. He just needed a little more time.

Beth and Martin were still in good spirits when they returned home from the restaurant. While Martin was paying the taxi driver, Beth rushed into the house, kicking off her shoes in the hallway. She heard Martin walking in behind her and was about to speak to him, her head in a half turn when she felt his hands settle on her shoulders.

He whispered into her ear, 'Do you know what I'd like to do right now?'

His touch set Beth's senses on fire. She was facing forward now, her head cocked back slightly while she revelled in the feel of him. Without waiting for a reply, he nuzzled the back of her neck. Martin knew what that did to her.

'I can guess,' she laughed.

Martin carried on whispering into her ear. 'I'm gonna make mad love to you all night. You're driving me crazy. I've hardly been able to think of anything else all through the meal.'

He eased his hands down her arms and Beth turned round and looked at him. 'You should have said. I would have come home earlier. To hell with your good news.'

As she gazed into his eyes, his lips met hers. The kiss was deep and passionate, and Beth could feel herself becoming more aroused. When he broke away it was so that he could slip one hand under her arms and the other under her knees. Then he lifted her off the floor and carried her upstairs, not stopping till they were inside the bedroom.

Martin set her down and kissed her again hungrily, his hands searching for the fastenings on her dress. She felt it loosen and shivered as it dropped to the floor, followed by her underwear. With a penetrating gaze he caught hold of her hand and led her to the bed.

'Turn around,' he instructed.

Beth complied and relaxed as he bent her over the bed, his hands stroking her body up and down as she purred with pleasure. Then he took her from behind, gently at first but then increasing in ferocity as waves of ecstasy swept over her body. They built to a crescendo and she yelled out in a frenzy of enjoyment.

When it was over, Martin took her in his arms. 'I love you so much,' he whispered into her hair.'

'I love you too,' she murmured.

They lay there silently for several minutes until Martin began to run his fingers down her body, settling on her breasts and teasing her nipples until she became aroused again. She knew it wasn't over yet and that their lovemaking would continue for as long as she wanted. She smiled and gave in to her desire.

Two hours later, Martin was asleep beside her. Beth's eyes travelled over his taut, muscular physique, settling on his handsome face. She was still on a high. The evening had been perfect and had ended the best way possible. How she had missed their lovemaking sessions, and she was so glad that their lives were back to normal in every way.

She still couldn't sleep as her mind kept replaying the wonderful things that had happened recently. Not only were things going well with Martin at last, but she was also beating Brady. She'd heard on the grapevine that his company was shutting down and had even sent one of her buyers to acquire some of his leftover stock at a reduced price.

She sighed with contentment. After all she had been through, everything was finally coming together. The business was thriving, she had a gorgeous man who loved her to bits and her revenge on Brady was almost complete. At that present moment she couldn't have been happier.

55

A few months later, things were going from strength to strength between Beth and Martin in terms of both their personal and professional lives. Martin now spent most of his time in the offices of Babette, making occasional visits to his bars to check that things were running smoothly.

He had found a buyer for Virtuoso and was currently in the process of transferring the business to the new owner. Beth had been concerned that he would miss the nightclub, which had been a part of his life for several years. However, since finally freeing himself of the burden of Virtuoso, she could see how relaxed he was becoming.

Despite their success, in the few months that he had helped Beth run Babette, things hadn't always run smoothly between them. It was easy sometimes for Beth to overlook the fact that there were two of them running the company now. And Martin was the sort of man who commanded respect.

She remembered the decision she had made to start delivering their own products rather than use transport companies. Her thinking had been that they would save a fortune not having to pay other companies for delivery. But Martin hadn't agreed, arguing that there would be a big initial outlay in terms of buying vehicles and employing staff, and he thought that the company wasn't developed enough yet to take such a major step.

But Beth had gone ahead and done it anyway. She had been so confident that her idea would work and now she was happy to see that it was finally paying off. Martin had been furious at her going behind his back and it had taken a while until he accepted what she had done.

But on the whole, she much preferred to work with Martin because he had proved to be an asset to the company. After several discussions they agreed that the way forward was for each of them to have their own areas of concentration. One of his responsibilities was staff matters utilising his years of experience in employing people. *Her* focus was on the product side of things, and she had already gained a wealth of knowledge since running Babette.

Beth knew that Martin wouldn't be happy with the latest decision she had made. Not only did it encroach on his areas of responsibility, but it was also a contentious move. Despite all that, it was something she felt compelled to do. She had got round things by making the arrangements without Martin's knowledge. It was all set to go, but before that she had a customer visit to attend.

When Beth returned to the office after the meeting with her customer, one of her staff rushed across to see her. It was Katie, the office junior who had only been with the company for a few weeks. 'Beth, I'm so sorry,' she said. 'I told Martin.'

'Told Martin what?' asked Beth, alarmed.

'Y'know,' the girl muttered nervously, 'about what's happening later.'

'Oh no! Why?' demanded Beth.

'I didn't mean to. It just slipped out.'

'Jesus! That's all I need. Where is he now?'

'He said he had to go out of the office on business but that he'd have a word with you when he got back.'

Beth dismissed the girl and then slumped into her office seat. She hoped Martin wouldn't return too soon because she knew he'd try to scupper her plans. If he would just stay away for another hour, it would all be done. Unfortunately for her, however, he walked into her office a few minutes later.

Beth could tell by his body language that he wasn't happy. His broad shoulders were tense and his features were strained as he yelled, 'Just what the hell are you up to, Beth?'

Brady had reached the lowest of lows over the last few months. Having to shut down his business had almost destroyed him. But he didn't stay down for long. In the end, his natural resilience and self-assurance had come to the fore once again. The cosmetics industry was his life. And he was damned if he would be beaten by it.

He knew that the main reason for his downfall was Babette, and he was still convinced that whoever was behind Babette had run a personal vendetta against him. But after some thought he'd come to the conclusion that he couldn't beat them through his own business. So he'd come up with a plan. The best thing would be to join an established company and progress from inside.

After all, there weren't many people in the industry who

were as good as him. He knew that for a fact. It wouldn't be difficult to convince any company of his talents. He already had an interview lined up, which was due to take place today. And he'd chosen the company very carefully.

For days he'd been rehearsing for this opportunity. He wanted to make sure he said all the right things so that by the end of the interview, the company would realise that they couldn't do without him.

Brady was being interviewed for a senior sales role, but he knew it wouldn't be long until he was promoted, and he had his sights set on eventually occupying a seat on the board of directors. Ultimately, he wanted to be in charge of the business. Then he would give everyone in the cosmetics industry something to think about, and he'd find a way to exact his revenge on those who had wronged him.

It was this dream that had got him through the last few dismal months. His unshakeable self-belief always won out eventually because, at the end of the day, he was prepared to do whatever it took to prosper. He never went so far as to break the law. No, he was no criminal, and he frowned on those that were. But he was ruthless. He didn't care about hurting people's feelings; all that mattered to Brady was success.

He arrived at the company's offices wearing an Armani suit, retained from a period when he was far more affluent. As he looked around at the modern décor and sleek furniture, and took in the overall air of professionalism, he felt that he would fit in well within this environment. *Yes, I could really thrive in a place like this*, he thought.

Then he strutted over to the reception area and introduced himself. Brady could see the two receptionists eyeing him appreciatively as they took in his swarthy good looks and affected charm. Their obvious interest boosted his already heightened feelings of self-worth.

'Hi, I'm Brady Harris,' he announced to the younger of the two receptionists. 'I'm here to see Mrs Marks.'

The girl looked confused for a moment till the older receptionist nodded at her and said, 'Top floor. She's expecting him. It's for the sales job.'

Brady responded confidently, 'Yes, I'm here for the position of senior sales executive.'

'OK, I'll take you up. I'm having a break now anyway,' said the girl.

Brady was amused by the girl's eagerness to please and he followed her to the elevators. 'Did you have a good journey here?' she asked in an effort to engage him in conversation as the elevator shot up to the top floor.

Brady obliged her by making all the appropriate responses, but really he had no interest in the silly girl. She wasn't his type. He preferred someone a bit older and far more intelligent.

They got out of the lift, and she walked him through the department till they reached an office with a closed door. He could hear the sound of raised voices coming from within and the girl smiled awkwardly at him.

'If you want to take a seat, I'll just tell her you've arrived.'

'Why, Beth? Why would you do that?' Martin demanded. 'Things have been going so well for us and this could wreck everything.'

'No, it won't,' she said.

'Don't lie to me, Beth. You know yourself the trouble this is going to cause. I think you should cancel.'

'No! No way. I'm not cancelling. Anyway, it's too late to cancel now.'

Martin looked at his watch and frowned. 'What time have you arranged it for?'

'Three.'

As it was already two fifty-five, he said, 'OK, have it your way. Let it go ahead. But I want to sit in on it with you.'

'No, Martin. I need to do this on my own.'

'Do you really think I'd risk that? Not a chance, Beth. I'm staying and that's that.'

The receptionist pointed to a vacant chair, and Brady sat down and waited. When the girl went inside the office, the shouting stopped. Instead, he could hear a murmur of conversation. He strained to catch what was being said, but he was sitting too far away to decipher the words.

The girl walked out a few seconds later and said, 'Right, she's ready to see you now. Good luck.'

Brady stood up, squared his shoulders, beamed at the girl and approached the office, ready to give the performance of his life.

When Brady walked inside, he was on a full charm offensive. The smile he had bestowed on the receptionist was still plastered on his face. He was glad he would be interviewed by a woman. It would be so much easier to win her round. In fact, he felt sure that by the end of the interview he would have her eating out of his hand.

But as he walked inside the room, his jaw fell slack

because there, sitting behind the desk, was Beth. She had obviously used the fake name of Mrs Marks to dupe him. Next to her was a man. But not just any man. It was the lowlife scummy owner of the bar where he used to take Beth, The Amber Room.

He had known the name Bradshaw rang a bell! And now he knew why. It was this bastard who was the director of Babette!

56

'What the hell?' demanded Brady, with a look of confusion. 'Beth? What are *you* doing here?'

Beth smirked. 'I run the company. Well, me and my partner, Martin.'

She turned and looked at the guy, smiling at him. But the smile held a warmth that was now a distant memory for Brady. It became immediately apparent to him that Beth and Martin were more than just business partners. And the thought sickened him. Despite his rejection of Beth, Brady had some regrets. But he'd buried his feelings, telling himself she didn't deserve him. Not after what she had done. He could never stay with a woman like her. A killer.

He stood for a while, speechless, while inside his head myriad thoughts ran riot. Jealousy. Humiliation. Repulsion. And fury! How could she? How could she do this to him? And with a man like Martin Bradshaw! A glorified fuckin' gangster.

He knew of the man's tough-guy reputation, but Brady was too angry to exercise caution. 'You fuckin' bitch!' he yelled. 'You planned this all along, didn't you? You destroyed my business. And now you have the nerve to rub my fuckin' face in it. And with this thug! How could you even consider being with a man like him?'

Martin got up from his seat and stepped to one side of the desk, his large frame imposing in the limited space of the office. 'That's enough!' he growled.

But Brady was undeterred. He thrust himself forward across the desk, pointing in Beth's face. 'You fuckin' lowlife, murdering bitch. No wonder you've saddled yourself with a bastard like him. You fuckin' deserve each other!' Then he addressed Martin, who was now heading towards him. 'Did she tell you what she did? She fuckin' killed a man.'

He felt the force of Martin's powerful hands as he hauled him towards the office door. As Martin dragged him away, Brady looked back over his shoulder at Beth and continued bawling, 'Don't think you're fuckin' getting away with this!'

Beth remained seated, displaying a cool reserve that made Brady even angrier as she calmly said, 'I think you'll find that I just did.'

She was no longer recognisable as the submissive wife who he had manipulated with ease. And Brady realised with startling clarity that her personality had transformed for the better since they had split. She was now a self-assured businesswoman who refused to be intimidated.

'Did you manage to get rid of him?' asked Beth, looking up from her computer when Martin walked back into the office.

'Yes, but it wasn't easy. He was cursing and shouting all the way to the door. I had to bolt it to keep him outside. Jesus! I tell you what, Beth, your ex has got some bottle.'

'Not really. He usually only picks on people weaker than himself. He probably knew you wouldn't hit him with witnesses around.'

'I shouldn't have been put in that position,' said Martin, raising his voice. 'Jesus, Beth, what the hell were you thinking?'

Martin rarely spoke to her in that tone, and Beth realised how much she had annoyed him. For a moment, she stared at him dumbstruck as a sense of shame washed over her.

'You know this won't stop here, don't you?' Martin continued. 'He's probably calling the police right now and telling them all about you killing that guy.'

'No, no he wouldn't do that,' protested Beth, her words belying the tremor of fear that shot through her.

'Why? Give me one good reason why? You've just brought a load of trouble on yourself, Beth. And for what? So you could twist the knife and sit there while you watched him grovel?'

Martin's words hit her with the force of a bullet, and she suddenly felt foolish. But she tried in vain to defend herself. 'Are you forgetting what he did to me, Martin? He took everything from me. If it hadn't been for you, I wouldn't have had a home, a job, a business. Nothing! I'd have had nothing. So yes, I wanted to see him punished. Is that so wrong?'

But even as she asked the question, Beth knew it was. She had set out to teach Brady a lesson. To show him that she was now the one in control. She had wanted to see him broken.

It hadn't given her the satisfaction she had expected though. Because, in punishing Brady, she had brought herself down to his level. And the first stirrings of shame and regret were beginning to take hold. Martin had made her realise that her behaviour had been reckless and immature.

'He won't go to the police,' she said, her voice merely a whisper.

'Why not?'

'Because he knows that everything would come out. How he blackmailed me. And how he kept it quiet instead of reporting it to the police at the time. He'd be in as much trouble as I would.'

'Not quite,' said Martin, and she felt the force of his disapproval.

'So I suppose you're going to disown me too now, are you?' she asked, feeling embarrassed as a fat tear rolled off her face, smudging the papers in front of her.

'No, not at all!' Martin replied.

She knew he'd noticed her tears, but he didn't step over to comfort her as he normally would. Instead, he turned to the window and stared out. His shoulders appeared tense and for several moments he seemed deep in thought.

Finally, he turned around and spoke, 'OK, maybe you're right. Maybe he won't go to the police. But I'm warning you now, Beth. Your ex is a very vindictive man. I saw what he was like when I threw him out, and I heard the poison that was spewing out of his mouth. He hates you with a passion, Beth. He hates me too, and I'm sorry to have to tell you this, love, but we haven't heard the last of him. We've just got to make sure we're ready for him when he strikes back.'

57

The comfort she had been craving from Martin came the following day when he stepped behind her and wrapped her in his big arms, telling her that whatever happened they would face it together and he would always defend her. It was a relief to know she had his full support. He had just needed time to calm down and process what she had done.

Nevertheless, for the next few weeks Beth couldn't settle. Martin's words on the day of Brady's bogus interview had really hit home and she was jumpy every time the phone or doorbell rang, expecting a call from the police any minute. Thankfully, that hadn't happened. But she wished she hadn't acted so foolishly. It was too late now though and all she could do was sit and wait, wondering what Brady's next move would be.

Since the day of the interview, she had been desperately searching for information about what Brady was up to, convinced that he would find a way to hit back at her, probably through her business. She had asked her contacts about any business start-ups in the industry or new appointments in senior sales roles but had found out nothing.

Then she spotted something one day. She was sitting in

the office checking through reviews on her PC, which she did every now and again to make sure her company was performing well in the eyes of the public.

Today, though, there was something different. Something very unsettling. 'Martin!' she called. 'Come and have a look at this.'

Martin walked over to her desk, and she pointed to the recent reviews they had received. They were mainly negative and had reduced the overall review average for Babette from 4.8 to 4.5.

She looked up at him, noticing the stress lines that criss-crossed his forehead. 'It's him, isn't it?' she asked.

Martin shrugged. 'It might be, but it might be just a coincidence.'

'It's a bit much of a coincidence if you ask me. We've never had so many negative reviews as we have in the past few weeks; four of them have come in this week alone. And look at the words: "poor quality", "late deliveries", "incompetent staff". They've been mentioned in more than one of these reviews. It's obvious they've come from the same source.'

'Relax,' said Martin, '4.5 is still pretty impressive, y'know. And don't forget, we've already got plenty of customers. They're not going to walk away just because of somebody else's opinion when they know what we're really like. And not all the new customers come from online searches. Some of them come from recommendations.'

'But I'm worried, Martin. We can't afford for this to get much worse.'

'Just keep your eye on it for now and we'll see how it goes. If it's just a coincidence it might pick up again.'

Beth nodded. 'OK.' But even though she'd gone along with Martin, she wasn't as sure as *he* seemed.

An hour later Martin left the office, telling Beth that he needed to pay a visit to one of the wholesalers that supplied his bars. It was a false pretext. He was really going to visit his contact, Chris Bloxham. The computer hacker.

Martin knew as well as Beth did that Brady was most likely behind the negative reviews. But he hadn't wanted to worry her, which was why he'd played it down. He had a feeling though that if he didn't do something about it, the negative reviews would carry on coming in and they'd probably end up losing business because of it. He wasn't prepared to take that chance because of a little shit like Brady Harris. But before he took any action, he wanted to make sure that Brady was behind the reviews.

Martin met Chris Bloxham in the same bar as he had done previously and like last time Chris was looking dishevelled. In fact, he was wearing the same trousers, and Martin wouldn't have been surprised if they hadn't been washed since. But he ignored his thoughts as he greeted Chris's arrival and offered to get him a drink.

Once they were both seated with a drink in front of them, Martin spoke. 'I couldn't say too much on the phone as I was in the office and didn't want anyone to overhear. Are you any good with review sites?'

'What? Hacking into them, you mean?'

'Yeah, I need to know who's posting reviews, which account they're coming from.'

'Sure, no problem, as long as you make it worth my while.'

They agreed a price and Martin fetched up the review site details on his phone and showed them to Chris. 'How long will it take to get me a name?'

'Dunno, depends. Maybe a week. Maybe more.'

'OK, let me have it as soon as possible. I'll give you a third of the money now and the rest when you've finished the job.'

'Will do,' said Chris, dashing from the bar in search of his next hit as he had done last time.

Martin knew he wouldn't let him down though. For one thing he'd want the rest of the money. He also loved a challenge. And aside from all that, despite being a druggy, he was basically a decent guy.

58

Chris Bloxham had kept to his word and within a week he had come back to Martin with the information he needed. One of the reviews had come from Brady's laptop as Martin had suspected, and Chris had also furnished Martin with details of Brady's latest address in Fallowfield, which matched the address Brady had used for the job application.

The other reviews had all come from different devices belonging to other people, but Martin was nevertheless convinced that Brady was behind most of them. Since he'd found out his address, he had staked out Brady's movements for days and had eventually been rewarded with the sight of him handing cash to a youth in a café in Levenshulme. Unfortunately, just as the youth stepped back out of the café, Martin was called back to the office on urgent business.

Martin had been searching for the youth ever since. At least the café wasn't based in Manchester city centre, which made things easier, as Levenshulme was more residential. If it had been in the city centre, then the youth could have come from anywhere in Manchester.

The difficulty for Martin had been in getting time away from Beth when he could go in search of the youth. She'd been on edge since the bogus interview in case Brady reacted with aggression, but as that hadn't happened, she'd become a little more relaxed.

Martin had drawn on his own misspent youth in deciding on the type of places the lad might hang out. Somewhere he could lark about with mates either drinking illicitly or trying to obtain drink, as he didn't look quite old enough to frequent pubs. Martin decided it would be either local off-licenses or isolated woodland areas with plenty of hidden copses. But Levenshulme didn't have much of the latter, so the obvious choice was the local shops.

Tonight, he had told Beth he needed to deal with a staffing matter and that there was no point in her coming with him as he wouldn't be long. After spending a few minutes driving up and down the main road in the centre of Levenshulme, Martin spotted the lad. Despite the rainy weather, the lad was hanging about with a group of other youths outside a late-night kebab house. Martin's assumption had been almost correct, he supposed. Now the only problem was how to get the lad alone.

Martin was currently sitting inside his car across from the kebab house, pretending to be on his phone while taking surreptitious glances in the direction of the group of youths. The lad he was after was easy to pick out from the crowd as he was gangly with a spotty face and only a smattering of dark, greasy hair on top of his head, as the sides were shaved.

Martin figured he might be in for a long wait and was thinking of knocking it on the head as he didn't want to leave Beth alone for too long. He knew she'd be worried, despite her protestations; it was the first time she'd been home on her own since the mock interview.

But to his surprise, he hadn't been waiting long when he noticed some form of disagreement amongst the group. The lad he was pursuing was exchanging something with one of the others. Martin took it to be money for drugs, certainly something small enough to be passed from hand to hand, but he couldn't pick out the detail from where he was situated.

Whatever it was, the lad wasn't happy. He examined what was in his hand then seemed to be arguing about it. The other lad retaliated verbally before Martin's target put whatever it was inside his pocket then walked away.

The other lad stood and laughed but he didn't follow Martin's target. He obviously knew he'd got the better part of the deal. Martin's eyes switched to his target, who had distanced himself from the group of youths. It wasn't long before he turned into a side street, so Martin got out of his car and followed him on foot.

Martin pursued him through a maze of tiny streets, taking care to stay in the shadows. He didn't want to alert the lad too soon. When the lad reached the end of a row of terraced houses, Martin noticed there was nothing around but a scrap of derelict land opposite with no houses immediately overlooking it. He seized his chance.

He soon caught up with the lad and tapped him on the shoulder. The lad swung round, alert and ready for a confrontation.

'Who the fuck are you?' he demanded.

'Never mind who I am,' snarled Martin, grabbing the front of the lad's sweatshirt then scrunching it up till his fist was pressed tight against the kid's windpipe.

The lad tried to tough it out, pulling back and trying to

slap Martin's hand away while yelling, 'What the fuck do you want?'

Martin tightened his grip. 'Just a little word.'

The youth stared back but didn't say anything, merely shaking his head in confusion. Martin could see panic in the kid's eyes and felt bad as he was only young. But he didn't intend to hurt him, he was just putting the frighteners on till he got answers.

'Tell me about Brady Harris!' ordered Martin.

'Brady Harris? Who the fuck's he? I don't know no Brady Harris.'

Martin tightened his grasp further still. 'Oh, I think you do. The guy who's been paying you for a little job. Remember?'

'Nah, mate. I think you've got the wrong person.'

He made to walk away but Martin kept a strong hold on him. 'No, I've definitely got the right person. I saw him pay you. The question is, what exactly did he pay you for? Now, you're only a kid and I don't really want to hurt you, but if I have to, I will. So do me a favour and make it easy for yourself. I'll even throw in a ton as a little thank you.'

Martin saw the lad's eyes light up despite his fear. The prospect of a hundred pounds was obviously a tempting one. 'You don't owe Brady Harris any favours,' said Martin. 'And I'll make sure this stays between me and you so nobody else needs to know you've dobbed him in.'

'OK, yeah, I do know him.'

'Right, and what was he paying you for?' He could still see hesitation in the lad's face, so he added, 'And don't try fuckin' lying to me. I've already got a good idea. I just want it confirmed.'

The lad sniffed. 'Reviews. He wanted me and my mates to post bad reviews about a business. Some beauty company or summat.'

'OK, how many reviews?'

'Twenty.'

'Twenty? How did you get that many mates to post reviews?' Martin asked out of curiosity.

'I put it on one of our group chats, told them the company had pissed me off 'cos they'd charged my sis a fortune for a bag of shite.'

Amused, Martin took a bunch of twenties out of his wallet and handed it to him. He watched him walk away. When the lad had made some distance, he turned around and shouted 'Tosser!' then dashed up the street.

Martin didn't bother running after him. He'd got what he wanted and already felt bad enough for threatening a young kid. But at least it had worked. He now knew for sure that Brady Harris was responsible for the negative reviews. And Martin also knew that Brady wouldn't stop until he'd had his revenge unless he did something about it.

Beth was still shaken by Brady's reaction at the fake interview but was trying not to let it take over her life. So when Martin told her that he needed to go out she had insisted she'd be fine even though she felt trepidatious.

Beth tried to reassure herself. Other than the negative reviews, Brady hadn't done anything to get at her. And he hadn't gone to the police about her either, so she no longer had that to worry about. Brady was a coward who was used to bullying those weaker than himself. With

Martin by her side, maybe Brady would be hesitant about hitting out despite his threats.

She had some work she wanted to finish so she was currently in her home office. Martin had suggested she should relax more and take time out in the evenings. But she couldn't help herself. The business was constantly on her mind and if an idea came to her, she found it difficult not to act on it straightaway.

She was wading through some figures on her laptop, comparing the sales revenue for various items when she heard a scuffling sound outside. At first she ignored it, thinking it was probably an animal of some sort. The office was situated at the side of the house and the faint sound seemed to be coming from the back.

When the noise persisted and seemed heavier than any sound a cat or bird would make, she grew concerned. Beth crossed the office and peered outside. The night was gloomy with the patter of rain on the window and a strong wind blowing. Between the shadows was a large tree, which overhung the narrow path that snaked round the side of the house. It was swaying in the wind and the movement of leaves along the path confirmed her assumption that the sounds were probably due to the storm.

But despite that assumption, her heart was pounding, and she couldn't settle into her work. She was beginning to wish that she had insisted on going out with Martin instead of staying home alone. What if someone was outside? What if Brady had found her?

Then she admonished herself for her vivid imagination. The storm had obviously freaked her out. She still couldn't concentrate so she decided to finish what she was doing then settle in front of the TV with a glass of wine. But then the noise intensified. There was definite movement coming from the back of the house and an inner instinct told her it was more than just animals.

She stepped out into the hall, wanting to investigate but overcome with dread. Telling herself not to be silly, she made a tentative step toward the kitchen. It would help to put her mind at ease, and once she had satisfied herself that nothing was amiss, she could grab that glass of wine she had been contemplating.

Beth pushed herself forward and had almost reached the opened kitchen door when she heard the sound of breaking glass. She stood rooted to the spot and gaped at the back of the house; her pupils dilated as the adrenalin coursed around her body.

She saw a hand appear through the broken glass pane of the back door and reach for the key that she had left in the lock. Looking up, she picked out the glazed outline of a man on the other side of the glass panel. Panic seized her and she sped across the kitchen, eager to grab the key before he could unlock the door.

But she was too late. By the time she got there, he had twisted the key and was pushing the door viciously towards her. Beth's breath caught in her throat. After only a moment's hesitation, she turned and fled.

59

Beth raced towards the bathroom because she knew it had a lock on the door. She took the stairs two at a time, aware of the man closing in. As she reached the top step, she felt his hand brush against the back of her jumper, trying to grab hold. Beth leapt inside the bathroom, slammed the door shut and shoved the bolt in place before he had a chance to stop her.

Once inside, she let out a breath and slumped on the floor with her back to the door. She felt it vibrate as the man banged his fist against the wood panelling and cursed, 'Fuckin' bitch!'

She recognised Brady's voice and her terror intensified. He hadn't gone to all this trouble for nothing. Beth knew the lock wasn't strong enough to keep him out for long, but she had acted out of panic.

Now she realised what a rash move it had been. Her phone was still downstairs so she couldn't even summon help. The terrifying realisation dawned on her that she was only safe for as long as the door held.

When she felt the thud of Brady slamming himself against the door, she shot up, searching the room desperately for something that might help. Her eyes settled on the window, but it was too high to crawl through. And there was nothing she could use to heave herself up. But she could still call for help.

Beth reached up and loosened the stay on the window until there was a six-inch gap. She could see the open slit if she strained her neck upwards, but she couldn't see outside. Undeterred, she yelled for help at the top of her voice, wishing she had the comfort of knowing whether anybody had heard her.

Her yelling diminished the sound of Brady's toxic stream of expletives and insults. Beth turned to the door, trembling each time she saw it vibrate from the force of Brady's weight against it. She scanned the room again. Looking for answers. Or for something that might help keep him out. But she drew a blank.

Beth was sweating now. Her mouth had gone dry. And her heart was beating so loudly she could almost hear it. She threw herself against the door, trying to counter Brady's battering. The door bashed against her torso, jolting her body while she tried to force it back. Then she noticed the door frame begin to splinter. And she knew she couldn't hold out much longer.

Brady's shoving became more forceful as though he had sensed victory. As he heaved, he continued to shout.

'I'll fuckin' teach you not to take the piss out of me. You'll find out what it's like to suffer. And don't think your thug of a boyfriend can protect you this time. I saw the twat go out over half an hour ago.

'He's probably in one of his bars now chatting up some slag while you're home alone. It didn't take him fuckin' long till the shine wore off, did it? You silly bitch! I've been tracking you for ages, just waiting till I can get you on your own and really make you suffer.'

Beth felt one last mighty shove and the door rammed against her. It was free of its casing now, and as she jumped back in alarm, the door swung open, hanging precariously from a single hinge.

And there was Brady, sneering at her. His pained features were so menacing he was almost unrecognisable from the man she once married. But before she had time to placate him, he was on her. It all happened so quickly. Beth felt the weight of his hands pushing against her. And then she was on the floor with Brady on top of her.

She tried to dodge his fists as they hammered her face and upper body repeatedly, filling her with intense, searing pain. His curses echoed the force of his blows. 'Fuckin' bitch! Whore! Lowlife scum!' Then his hands shifted. The left one pinning down her arms. The right scrabbling at her trousers.

She felt the button give way and heard it ping against the tiled floor. Then he was tearing at the waistband, tugging it down. A feeling of dread assailed her. She knew what he was about to do. To regain ultimate control. And make her suffer the worst in pain and degradation.

Blinded by tears she lashed out, her nails scoring angry lines down his face. But he continued to tug at her clothing. And she felt the bareness of her upper thighs as he yanked her trousers further down. Her mind flashed back to that day in the woods. She felt the same desperation as she had then. But this time there was no rock to hand.

Beth continued to fight despite feeling bruised and battered. But she knew she was losing as she felt him grab at her underwear. She couldn't let this happen. She wouldn't. But how could she stop him? She shut her eyes and prepared for the worst, trying to take her mind somewhere else.

Then she felt a release as the weight of Brady's body left her. Beth opened her eyes and looked up to see Martin, his face contorted with rage. He heaved Brady off her and hauled him out of the door, thrusting him to the ground and pounding at him until Brady slumped motionless on the landing.

Then Martin rushed to her side, cradling her in his manly arms. 'Jesus, Beth! Are you OK?' he asked, and through her tears she could see the sadness in his eyes. 'Did he…?'

'No. No, it's OK.'

'Christ! Look what he's done to your face. Your beautiful face. The bastard!'

Martin let her down gently. She could see he was torn between comforting her and punishing Brady. Finally, his decision made, he turned around, ready to finish what he had started.

'Fuckin' bastard!' he yelled, thumping what remained of the bathroom door.

Beth lifted her painful head to see what was happening. Then she realised what had intensified Martin's anger. Brady was no longer there. He had seized Martin's moment of weakness and made his escape.

60

Martin had thought long and hard since the mock interview with Brady weeks previously. He'd seen the guy's reaction and instinct told him that Brady would never leave Beth alone. It appeared he was right.

He had known some bad characters in his life, and as far as he was concerned, Brady was one of the worst: spiteful, vengeful and calculating. The Bradys of this world could dress it up in any way they liked with their fancy clothes, flash cars and business acumen but it didn't alter the facts. People like him were bad through and through, and nothing could change the way they were.

Even though Brady had left Beth alone for several weeks, Martin still hadn't been convinced that that was the end of it. He had therefore made sure that he hadn't stayed out for long, returning to check on Beth and make sure she was alright. Thank God his instincts hadn't failed him. He only wished he had returned earlier as the attack had obviously shaken Beth up.

Brady must have been watching her for weeks. Perhaps he had followed her home from work to find out where she lived and then waited for an opportunity to strike. And now that he had failed, Martin had a feeling that he would try to find another way to hit back.

In the days following the attack Martin had been seething with anger. Every time he looked at Beth's injuries and thought about what that man tried to do to her, his fury threatened to bubble over. But she had pleaded with him not to do anything rash, knowing that once he started on Brady, he might not be able to control himself. And she didn't want Martin getting into trouble.

Seeing her so upset, Martin had acceded to her wishes. His biggest concern then had been to comfort her. She had been so shaken by the attack that Martin knew she needed his support. It wasn't as if they could call on outside help; if they reported the attack to the police, there was every chance that Brady would tell them everything about Beth's past, knowing he had nothing to lose.

For a few weeks she hadn't left Martin's side and had even been nervous about visiting her parents alone. But eventually he'd managed to coax her into regaining some of her independence, and this evening she was late-night shopping with her friend Sally.

It was good to see her getting back to her old self, but for Martin, what Brady had done hadn't gone away. He was still furious and knew that he couldn't leave things, but he hoped that now that some time had elapsed, he could handle the matter more calmly than if he'd acted straightaway. He didn't want to do something that he would later regret; he was through with making life-changing mistakes.

Martin already had Brady's address and now it was time to pay him a visit. Brady needed to learn that his actions had consequences. And Martin knew it was the only way of getting him to back off.

Martin walked up the stairs to Brady's apartment, willing himself to stay calm. He didn't want to do anything rash. He was here to put the frighteners on the guy, nothing else. It wouldn't take much, just a few punches and threats. He knew Brady's type; when it came down to it, he was a total coward.

He kept his touch light as he knocked on the door; too heavy a hand would only arouse suspicion. When Brady first appeared at the door, he looked casual, relaxed. But his face soon dropped when he caught sight of Martin.

Martin didn't give him a chance to react further. He plunged himself at him, pushing him further down the hallway and only pausing to aim a reverse kick at the front door, satisfied when it slammed shut.

'Get out, get out of my apartment! You're trespassing. I'll have you arrested,' yelled Brady with a quiver in his voice. But he didn't get a chance to reach for his phone.

'Who else is here?' Martin demanded, grabbing hold of Brady's lapels and shoving his fists tight against his throat.

'No one,' Brady wheezed, his voice small and his lips trembling.

But Martin didn't believe a word the guy said. 'Show me.' He turned Brady around and forced him along, prodding him in the back as he repeated his words. 'Fuckin' show me!'

He continued marching Brady through the apartment while he scanned each room for signs of other occupants.

Finally, satisfied that they were alone, he stopped in the kitchen. He grabbed hold of Brady's lapels again, making sure he had his full attention as he explained the reason for his visit.

'I suppose you thought you'd got away with that attack on Beth, didn't you?'

Brady attempted a shrug; dissatisfied with his reaction, Martin rammed his fist into Brady's throat. 'I said, didn't you? Answer me, you fuckin' worm!'

'She deserved it,' said Brady, clutching his neck while trying to sound brave. 'What would you have done if she'd done that to you? She made me look like a fuckin' fool.'

'You fuckin' deserved it!' yelled Martin, emphasising his words by hitting Brady again.

Brady's face contorted with pain. Undeterred, Martin followed up by giving him the full force of his fists. As he pummelled Brady's face, he drew satisfaction at seeing him wince. Brady put up a poor defence and it wasn't long till his nose was busted and blood was oozing from his nostrils as well as his mouth.

It took a few minutes until Martin had vented his anger. But then he stopped himself, amazed at his own self-control. He didn't want to do anything else he would regret, and for a few seconds he stood regaining his breath and surveying the damage. Brady was sprawled across the kitchen floor, which was smeared with his blood. Martin noticed that one of Brady's teeth had come loose and his lips were cut and swollen.

'Let that be a lesson to you,' he said. 'Don't you ever dare to lay a finger on Beth again. Because if you do, I'll come back and finish the fuckin' job off. You and her are even now. You took everything from her, don't forget. That's why she did the same to you. The buck stops here now. Unless you want me to go all the way.'

As he spoke, he aimed a sharp kick at Brady's torso. He heard a cry of alarm and taking that as a no, he turned to go. But in his eagerness to inflict minimal injuries, he had underestimated Brady's doggedness.

He was on his way out of the kitchen when he heard Brady getting up from the floor. The movement was swift and, surprised at Brady's resilience, Martin spun around. Brady was reaching for a kitchen knife. Before Martin had a chance to stop him, he was slashing it through the air.

'Put the fuckin' thing down!' warned Martin.

But Brady was determined. As Martin stepped towards him, arms out front, ready to wrestle him for the knife, he felt it cut into his flesh. Martin dodged the next blow, his hand lifting instinctively to cover the wound on his other arm. As he pulled it away, he felt the blood gush and noticed its crimson mass on his fingers.

Brady was intent on ignoring his warning and was still swishing the knife through the air. It gave Martin no choice but to retaliate. And he needed to act quickly. He wasn't going to let Brady carve him up till his life's blood oozed from him, leaving him weak and defenceless.

Martin charged, taking Brady by surprise. He knocked him to the floor and landed on top of him. But Brady had already managed to cut him again, leaving another gash on Martin's forearm, this one much longer and deeper.

With the force of the impact, the knife flew from Brady's hand. As Martin pinned him down, Brady reached out for it. But it was too far away. And his fingers scrabbled desperately.

Ignoring the pain in his arm, Martin wrapped his fingers around Brady's throat. Then, sliding to the side of him, he grabbed the knife with his free hand. He couldn't afford to issue another warning. Blood was gushing from the wounds on his arm, and he was already becoming weak, his fingers starting to loosen their hold around Brady's throat.

Martin daren't waste time grappling with him. So he did what he felt was the only thing left to do. While Brady continued to struggle, Martin took the knife and sliced it across his throat. Then the struggling stopped.

61

'Hi love, I'm back,' shouted Beth as she walked into the hallway, her arms laden with shopping bags. Juggling the bags, she locked the door then added, 'Sorry, I'm a bit late, I nipped into Sally's for a cuppa and a chat.'

She hung up her keys and carried the bags through to the living room, surprised to find Martin wasn't there. But she was sure he was home. She could sense his presence. So she went through to the kitchen calling, 'Martin? Where are you?'

Having searched the downstairs rooms, she carried on upstairs and found him in the bathroom. Beth could see him from behind, stripped down to his boxers and standing at the sink. He seemed to be washing his hands. Then she saw a pile of his clothing on the floor. Her hand shot to her mouth when she noticed that it was bloodstained.

Releasing her hand, she yelled, 'Oh my God, Martin!'

He swung around and the first thing she spotted was his arm. He had fashioned a tourniquet from strips of material, but it was drenched with blood. In his hand was a nailbrush and she could see that it was also stained pink with blood. 'Oh my God!' she said. 'What's happened?'

He stepped towards her, holding out his hands in a

placatory gesture. Then he took hold of her arms. 'It's OK, it's alright. Don't worry.'

But Beth was already showing the first signs of shock, her face pale and her body shaking. 'We need to get you to hospital. That's bad,' she said, staring at the blood-soaked material covering his arm.

'No, I can't do that. But don't worry. I've got a friend coming. He's a medic. He'll stitch the wounds up for me, no questions asked.'

'Oh my God! What is it? What've you done?'

'It's Brady,' he said but he didn't finish the sentence.

'Oh my God!' she repeated. 'You've not killed him, have you?'

She stepped away from Martin. She wanted to scream. To run. But the shock rendered her immobile and speechless for a moment.

'I didn't have a choice,' said Martin. 'It was him or me.'

Martin had expected Beth to be shocked when she found out what had happened. But from her reaction he knew that she was about to become hysterical. He had to calm her down. He couldn't risk her doing anything stupid.

'Beth, Beth listen to me, please,' he pleaded. 'I didn't mean to do it. I went round to see him, to have a word. I knew we'd never hear the end of things with him and that he'd be plotting other ways to get back at you.'

'But you don't know that!' she screeched.

'Believe me, Beth. I know. You'd have had no peace from Brady; he was like a man possessed. And it was because you took away the only things he truly loved: money and power.

Some people are born bad and there's only one way to deal with them. The hard way.'

'No!' she cried, but Martin could already see that his words were bringing her round to his point of view. 'I'm sorry, love. I did what I had to do. He came at me with a bloody knife. He was like a maniac. I had to stop him before he sliced me up good and proper.'

Martin saw Beth stifle a shudder. Then he noticed the shadow that fell across her features. She was reliving her own experiences, which made him feel bad. But he'd had to do it. He needed to make her understand why he'd killed Brady.

He stepped forward again and took hold of her, feeling her crumble in his arms. Martin stroked her hair and reassured her that everything would be OK. 'Shush, it's over now. He can't harm you anymore.'

For a few moments she sobbed, but then she raised her head and, looking into his eyes, asked, 'What about the police?'

'Don't worry. It'll all be taken care of, and I'll make sure no one can trace his death back to us.'

'But what will you do about your arm?'

'It's fine. My mate will be here any minute to stitch it up.'

'No, I mean, won't it be suspicious?'

'Fortunately I can wear something to cover it up, so nobody needs to know. I'm getting rid of the knife too. Believe me, Beth, no one will know a thing.'

He could tell that she was reluctantly beginning to accept what he had done, and his reasons for doing it. But he was still worried that she might hold it against him. 'Beth,' he said. 'I'm so sorry this had to happen but sometimes in life we're forced to do things we don't really want to. We don't always have a choice.'

He could tell from her face that his words had hit home. As far as she was concerned, they were both equal. They'd both killed a man under extreme circumstances. And he knew now that she wouldn't hold it against him when she had committed the same sin.

Martin had already decided not to tell her about the other men he had killed. The past needed to stay firmly in the past and he couldn't see any advantage in dredging it up now. He wanted to move on with his life, and with Brady out of the way perhaps he finally could.

She nodded imperceptibly. 'I understand. You did it for *me*.'

'I did it for *us*, Beth. I want us to put all this behind us.'

Before she could respond to his words, there was a knock at the door, and she jumped. He grabbed hold of her arm again to steady her.

'Don't worry. It'll be my mate. Do you want to stay upstairs?'

Beth nodded again and as he began to walk away, she whispered his name. He turned to see her mouth, 'I love you.'

It was all the acknowledgement he needed. Martin knew now that she was on his side. They would get through this together, and he was determined that they would come out of it even stronger.

Epilogue

Two Years Later

Beth looked around the dining room at all the happy faces. Her parents were there, Sally, other friends of hers, a couple of Martin's friends and some of the staff from Babette and Martin's bars. They were all inside the home that she shared with Martin, and the room was festooned with balloons and a banner on the wall.

'Is it time to get him yet?' asked Martin.

She looked at her watch and said, 'Yeah. Ideally, I'd leave it a bit longer but some of the guests are getting restless.'

'He'll be fine,' said Martin.

She dashed upstairs to the nursery where she found their son, Owen. He was already awake from his afternoon nap and standing up in his cot with a gleeful expression on his face.

Beth smiled, amused. He was such an alert little thing. 'Hello, sweetheart,' she said, tickling him under the chin. 'Did the noise wake you up?'

Owen chuckled, displaying his dimples. She picked him

up out of his cot and set him down while she searched for his changing mat. Before she had a chance to put him on it, Owen was already toddling towards the door.

'You don't want to miss anything, do you? Come on cheeky, let's get you changed.'

It wasn't long before she had Owen dressed and wearing a clean nappy. Beth was now feeling the excitement herself, wondering what her son's reaction would be to all these people in the house.

Martin met her in the hall. 'Great,' he said. 'I'll call the children in from the garden.'

As Beth stepped inside the dining room, her guests began making a fuss of Owen. She crossed the room with him in her arms then settled him into his highchair. Owen began struggling to get out until Beth put a plate of food in front of him.

The children rushed indoors, full of excitement. They were the sons and daughters of some of their staff and relatives who were thrilled to be helping Owen celebrate his first birthday. The food was soon demolished by the children while the adults picked at a buffet laid out in a separate area.

Then it was time to sing 'Happy Birthday'. The children all joined in enthusiastically while Owen gurgled, his face a picture of confusion. Beth's eyes met Martin's and they laughed.

It was such a happy occasion. She had finally got the child she desired for years, and who better to share parenthood with than her loyal, loving and fiercely protective husband, Martin?

Acknowledgements

As always, I would like to thank my publishers, Head of Zeus, for all your support over the years. As well as the people who I regularly come into contact with, there are many staff working behind the scenes, and I had the pleasure of meeting some of them in London over the summer.

Particular thanks go to Laura Palmer, my editor, Martina Arzu, for your suggestions, and Peyton Stableford for all your support and for making me so welcome when I met you at Harrogate this year. Thanks also to Lottie Hayes-Clemens for a superb job on the copy edits.

Thanks to my agent, Jo Bell, for all your support and thanks to all the staff at Bell Lomax Moreton for your help including John Baker, Sarah McDonnell, and Lorna Hemingway.

I would also like to thank my publicist, Sophie Ransom, who has worked tirelessly to spread the word about my books. I fully appreciate all your support and it was a pleasure meeting you at Harrogate.

Thank you to the wider crime reading community including book bloggers, reviewers and all the people who give up their free time to run social media groups where crime readers and authors can connect and share their enthusiasm and recommendations for crime novels.

Particular thanks go to the UK Crime Book Club, Book Mark and Gangland Governor, three excellent Facebook groups, which are very supportive to authors. Thanks also to Terry Melia.

I had two great trips over the summer to Harrogate Literary Festival and to the Head of Zeus ten-year celebration party in London where I met many fellow authors, bloggers and readers. It was lovely connecting with you all.

Lastly, I would like to thank my family and friends for their continuing support and for always being there for me.

About the Author

HEATHER BURNSIDE started her writing career more than twenty years ago when she worked as a freelance writer while studying for a writing diploma. As part of her studies Heather wrote the first chapters of her debut novel, *Slur*, but she didn't complete the novel till many years later. *Slur* became the first book in The Riverhill Trilogy, which was followed by The Manchester Trilogy then her bestselling series, The Working Girls.

You can find out more about the author by signing up to the Heather Burnside mailing list for the latest updates including details of new releases and book bargains, or by following her on any of the links below.

Facebook: www.facebook.com/HeatherBurnsideAuthor
Twitter: www.twitter.com/heatherbwriter
Website: www.heatherburnside.com